THE MURDER OF
ELLIOT CROW

A.R. Shanks

Cover designed by A.R. Shanks and Kimberly Shanks

This book is a work of fiction. Names, characters, places, and incidents either are products of the author's imagination or are used fictitiously. Any resemblance to actual persons, living or dead, events, or locales is entirely coincidental.
Printed in the U.S.

ISBN-13: 978-1-9809-5935-9

To my Family
Because you can't write about a quirky family without having one of your own
To Mrs. Hamilton
The first to read my stories

I've never stopped believing in magic.
What else can we call life but magical?
There have, however,
been moments in time where I have stopped
believing in myself.
Most people have at some point.
Some people have never believed in themselves at all!
Believing in one's self is a skill.
Like most skills it can be honed and practiced.
I'm proud to say that I'm still learning,
And I never plan to stop.

~A.R. Shanks

CONTENTS

CHAPTER ONE

The Death of Elliot Crow

There is a world that runs on belief.
Where stars fill the sky with silver fire,
Where the sun is born every morning,
And the moon born every night.
Where all dreams come true,
Stored in the pages of colorful books,
Where spiders weave their webs into every reflection,
Where anything is possible,
But only if,
You believe in yourself.

The sound of buzzing woke up the fifteen-year-old in the 'early' hour of ten o'clock in the morning. The sun was filtering in through the window, causing his fluttering brown eyes to snap shut tight with a grimace and moan of reluctance.

Slowly, he reached over to his bedside and picked up his vibrating cell phone. Taking one glance at the screen, he scrunched his nose and came to a quick decision. He forced himself to pick up the phone.

"What?" he breathed irritably.

"Elliot?" the voice coming through the other side was most definitely familiar.

"Sam, it's too early for this." He groaned, head hitting the pillow once again, "What do you want?"

"It's ten in the morning." Sam said with a voice of disbelief.

"We aren't all early risers like you." Elliot bit out, "Last time you called this early you were begging me to help cover your arse."

"It's Mel's birthday tomorrow." Sam said quickly, realizing that Eliot was going to hang up if he didn't get straight to the point.

"She's your girlfriend." Elliot pointed out, "Why do you need my help?"

There was a long pause before Sam spoke again,

"You know why."

Elliot could feel himself growing more and more irritated.

"Fine." He said, in the manner of someone who was about to do something against their will.

"Thanks, El." The relief was obvious in Sam's voice, "Meet you at the Cat's Eye."

Elliot huffed with indignation, then hug up the phone, hoping his disapproval had made its way across. Elliot grimaced again at the open curtains of his bedroom window and got up, only to close them and return his room to it's state of blissful darkness.

He turned on his bedside lamp and moved over to the drawer of clothing, picking out a pair of jeans and a blue t-shirt. As he made his way down the hall, he paused in front of the mirror near the stairs and ran a hand through his black hair to tame the nest on his head.

When he decided that he'd done the best he could and anything more would be a futile effort, he made his way down the stairs to the main floor. His father was in the living room reading the newspaper, and his mother was painting her nails black.

"You going out?" she asked, looking up from her nails with a raised eyebrow.

"I'm meeting Sam at the mall." Elliot clarified.

A smile played on her lips and her green eyes sparkled with mischief,

"Don't get into too much trouble." Elliot rolled his eyes, then made his way to the front door and slipped on his shoes. His mother was goth, had been since her years in junior high. His father was almost too normal looking in contrast. With messy, curly black hair and large round glasses that looked almost a little bit too large for his nose. He smiled, his usual goofy grin when he caught sight of his son.

"Oh, Elliot," His father stopped him from leaving, "Have you seen the envelope I left here on the table?"

"Envelope?" Elliot repeated, "I saw something like that...two days ago maybe. Why?"

His father frowned, his brow furrowed in a troubled sort of way,

"There was money in it for the fundraiser."

"Were we robbed again?" Elliot asked him, not particularly worried (it wasn't his money, after all), but something about the information set him on edge.

His father shook his head, he offered Elliot a smile, a dimple forming at the corner of his mouth,

"I probably just misplaced it, you know how clumsy I can be sometimes."

It was true, his father could be rather clumsy, almost comically so. He'd seen him walk into the lamp post on the corner more than once. It was one of his more embarrassing traits. His mother, on the other hand was the epitome of 'in-control' and calm. She often said she found her husband's clumsiness endearing. Elliot never brought it up, of course. Bringing it up meant they might start kissing and Elliot was quite sure no one wanted to see that.

His mother, with the black hair, dyed from it's original dirty blond. With eyes that were a rare shade of dark green. His mother, with a face so pale she might have been a vampire. With lips that were either painted a ruby red or a jet black just like her clothing. His mother, who purposefully went out of her way to be different and embrace the macabre. He didn't understand her. He didn't understand why she couldn't at least pretend to be normal. He'd lost a lot of friends over the years either because their parents didn't approve, or because they thought she was secretly a witch or something.

Elliot liked to think he wasn't like either of his parents. He wasn't particularly bookish, nor was he a goth. He was just Elliot.

His older brother Casper followed the same philosophy, despite their usually not getting along. Casper was only about a year older than him, but he already seemed so much farther ahead than Elliot. He spent his time out of the house, skateboarding with his friends at the park or driving off to his part-time job.

Elliot hadn't gotten his learners yet, though he knew he could. He'd worked a part-time job briefly, but he'd resigned only a few months in, earning very little money. He spent most of his days hanging out with his friends at the mall, playing video games, or studying. He had few other interests that he wished to pursue.

Elliot walked down the steps to their house and towards the train station. It was only a five-minute walk away.

The town was a small one. Most people took the bus or biked to the places they needed to go. The train had been built fifteen, maybe twenty years back. The mayor always said that they'd expand, but that didn't seem to be happening any time soon.

Still, it was used for those odd people who needed to travel those odd distances.

As they approached the mall, Elliot couldn't help but want to return home. He brushed the feeling off as having been forced down there to help Sam out and being dragged out of bed too soon. But still, even that didn't quite explain the sense of foreboding in the air.

He got off at his stop then walked across a sort of bridge-like runway that led directly into the mall. He was only half-surprised once he reached the Cat's Eye that Sam was already sitting there waiting for him. A mango smoothie positioned in front of him on the table.

"Yo!" Sam said, holding up his hand in a wave, a friendly grin on his face.

"Hey." Elliot said with a slight smile playing on his lips.

He looked around and found the place to be rather...desolate. The mall was usually at least a little bit busy during the weekend. It was one of the few teenage hotspots in their little town of Blackstone, Alberta. The only other person there was an unfamiliar man with an dark orangey hat that barely covered the sandy blond hair on his head.

"So," Sam said, interrupting Elliot's musings, "What are we going to get Mel?"

Elliot shrugged,

"I don't know. She's your girlfriend."

Sam frowned,

"You know what I mean." Elliot rolled his eyes. For as long as he could remember, Sam seemed to be under the impression that he was some sort of psychic. He called it 'perfect gift sense' or something. And considering the fact that they'd known each other since they'd been in diapers, that was a long time. His mother, and Sam's had met before the two of them had even been born in a gothic bookstore. Thus, their bizarre names. Though Elliot had to admit that he gotten the better deal. At least his name sounded normal. Pour Sam absolutely hated being called by his full name, Salem, and threatened whoever called him that with a good kick to the shin of an elbow to the ribs.

"I don't know..." Elliot trailed off, "Maybe a nice book or something? Melisa loves music too, but she bought a gift card or whatever a few days ago and girls like it when you give them more personalized gifts."

"Why a book?" Sam wondered, scrunching his brow in concentration.

Elliot just gave him a helpless shrug,

"She doesn't wear a lot of jewelry, and she seems kind of bookish anyways."

Sam nodded absently, seemingly coming to the conclusion that his reasoning made sense,

"Yeah...she really likes fantasy novels."

The decision was made and the two boys left the café. Sam was still holding onto his smoothie as they headed down to the bookstore.

The mall was host to a small store, no bigger than Elliot's living room at home that sold new and used books. They were hoping to expand sometime this year. Already there was a knocked down wall to the far end with a temporary wall in place to make the store still look presentable.

Elliot brushed his hands over the books apathetically. Sam and Elliot stood in the pathetic looking fantasy section which consisted of a single book case.

"Think she'd like this?" Sam asked, at least trying to make an effort, though it was clear he had absolutely no idea what he was doing.

Elliot took one look at the cover and quirked an eyebrow,

"Sure." He said, just wanting to go back home already.

Sam deflated,

"Come on man, you aren't even trying." He whined.

Elliot let out a sigh, then ran his fingers along the book case. He picked out a book and looked at the title, *Savior from Beyond the Veil.* Something about it chilled him to the bone. His eyes lingered on it a moment longer before he said,

"I think she'd like this one."

Sam took the book from his friend's hands. His gaze traveled between Elliot and the book. He turned it over and read the back. He cringed, brow furrowed in confusion,

"You sure Mel will like this?"

"No." Elliot said, rolling his eyes, "I told you, I'm not psychic or whatever. I just thought it looked sort of cool is all."

Sam frowned, then shrugged his shoulders,

"If you say so."

To Elliot's fascination, and mild annoyance, Sam went up to the counter and paid for the book without further questions.

Elliot shivered as Sam returned.

"Something wrong?" his long-time friend asked.

Elliot shook his head,

"Just a chill."

Elliot didn't get chills often, though when he did Sam always seemed to worry about them.

"We should leave." Sam decided.

"Sam, I'm fine." Elliot insisted.

"I have to do something at home anyways." Sam said dismissively, causing Elliot to grow even more annoyed.

"You're the one who forced me out here." Elliot pointed out.

"And I'm deeply sorry for dragging you away from your bed." Sam said in an almost sarcastic sort of way, though Elliot could sense some real worry behind his teasing and usually friendly demeanor.

"Sam..."

"Just go." Same said, "I'll take the train with you."

"Your house is in the opposite direction." Elliot said.

"I need to stop by the market."

Elliot's lips twitched downwards, realizing that there was nothing he could do or say to get Sam off his case.

"Let's just stop by the washroom first." Sam said, "I need to use the washroom."

Elliot snorted, but followed him over to the restroom anyways. Sam walked in, but the moment he was alone, Elliot took off.

He made his way up the stairs and towards the bridge to the train station. The train was already there, as though it had been informed of his arrival. He got on and took a seat just as the bell rang to indicate the train's leaving.

Part of him felt somewhat guilty at leaving Sam on his own when he probably only had the best intentions. But Elliot was rather frustrated with his constant insistence and over-protectiveness that came with him 'being psychic.'

Elliot shivered again. The sense of foreboding he'd felt before had grown. His eyes traveled away from his reflection in the glass of the train window and he felt his breath catch in his throat.

A man sat in the far end of the train. He wore an orange hat, he had sandy hair, his face was slightly shielded by a newspaper.

He'd seen the man at the café. And now...well, it was a small town, he tried to convince himself. Besides, he'd practically run to the train and away from Sam. The man had probably arrived before him. His shoulders didn't relax though as he forced himself to look away, back at his own reflection and the passing scenery.

As the train came to a stop he felt even more uneasy when the man got off at the same time he did. There was only a slight bit of hesitation before the man got up from his seat. A slight bit that made Elliot all the more suspicious that this man had been waiting for him. It made him want to stay on the train longer...though he mentally beat himself for being so paranoid.

As soon as he was away from the cameras at the train station, he knew he was in trouble. There was the sound of the footsteps from behind him speeding up.

He put up a fight. At least he liked to think he did. Somehow, he had managed to face his attacker. Adrenaline pumped through his system and the world around him seemed to slow down.

The man ...or maybe it was best to call him a boy. He was far younger than Elliot had earlier estimated, in fact, he might have guessed they were about the same age. He had unusually high cheekbones and his eyes looked widely spaced apart, giving him an almost bug-eyed appearance.

There wasn't any pain. Not at first anyways, but he knew something was wrong right away. He looked down to see the blood covered knife sunk into his stomach. With shaky hands, and a morbid sense of fascination, he touched the hilt and allowed his fingers to become coated in red. He tasted the tang of iron in his mouth and felt either blood or saliva trickle down his chin.

And then the boy smiled.

"Goodbye, Casper Crow." His voice was a harsh whisper, but the significance of the words hadn't been lost on Elliot, despite the millions of thoughts that swirled around in his head at that moment. This person, whoever he was, had gone after the wrong brother.

Then finally, the overruling thought was that he didn't want to die.

The sadist twisted the blade into his gut and his whole body exploded with pain until that was his entire world. For one strange moment, all the colors of all the surrounding world appeared far more vivid than he could ever remember them being. As though his life until that point had been ventured through while he was half-asleep.

He fell to the ground and didn't even hear the man walk away. His body went cold, and then, as he watched his own blood creep across the concrete, the chill of dying faded and he began to feel pleasantly warm.

CHAPTER TWO

Time is No One's Friend

He didn't expect to wake again. Elliot could recall his mother talking about the 'eternal sleep'. She'd even discussed it at large during dinner at times, when all Eliot wanted to do was hide away in his room and forget ever having had the conversation. It was those times that he realized his father wasn't normal, because no normal father would speak of such things so casually during a meal with his wife.

They'd touched on many theories. Reincarnation, heaven, hell, purgatory, the universe ending, the next level...well, the two of them together could write a book or, perhaps a whole chronology of books on the topic. Never had Elliot wanted to remember every word more. He'd rarely paid attention to his mother's morbid musings, but as he woke up on the cold floor to the sound of ticking and whining gears, he really wished he knew what theory would coincide with...wherever he had found himself now.

His eyes blinked open with the odd realization that he couldn't feel the knife wound anymore. Slowly, as though testing out his body, er, soul? He made his way into a crouching position. His hands were red and sticky with drying blood. His shirt clung to him with the same wetness as before.

He stood up slowly, not feeling anything wrong whatsoever save the fact that...

"I'm not breathing." He realized.

He lifted his shirt and pressed his hands over his abdomen where he knew the knife had impaled him. There was no wound. Although, with the amount of blood covering his body, he couldn't be sure he hadn't just missed it.

Deciding to check it later after he'd found a place to wash up...if there was a place to wash up, he lowered his shirt.

He was in some sort of chamber on a wooden bridge that creaked with every step he took. He half-expected to fall right through the boards upon realizing that they looked to be half rotted. Either he had somehow become completely weightless, or the boards were being held up, suspended through magic. There was no way, under ordinary circumstances that they would be able to support him, or anyone for that matter.

The chamber was large and could have likely encompassed his house two or three times over. The whirring, creaking and ticking came from the gears and gizmos that made up the walls of the room. The noise set him on edge, even more so than his precarious walk.

Elliot felt that what featured most prominently was the man that sat on a throne in the very heart of the room made of rusted metal. He leaned over a table of coppery material. At least he assumed it was a man. His back was to Elliot and the black cloak that covered his figure made it difficult to discern.

Well, Elliot thought, I certainly won't be getting any answers if I just stand here all day.

"Excuse me!" he called out, and he was absolutely fascinated to hear his voice echo around the entire chamber. He had the strangest sense that it was traveling up to the ceiling he couldn't see. The wall of gadgetry seemed to go on to infinity.

The head of the cloaked figure lifted up. Then slowly, the person, and Elliot found that he was correct, in that it was a man, turned around.

Elliot froze where he stood. The man's face was pale, even more so than his mother's who powdered her face to be chalk white.

Before he could blink, the man's nose was inches away from his own. How had he traveled so fast? There had to have been at least a thirty, maybe forty-foot distance between them originally.

The man's eyes were the palest shade of blue that Elliot had ever seen, veins traveled beneath his skin and he wondered if he had ever once seen the sun.

"Who are you?" the man demanded in a strange raspy, echo of a voice that was deep and resonated with power.

Another chill traveled through Elliot and he knew this man was dangerous.

"E-Elliot." Elliot stuttered, "I...I'm Elliot Crow."

"Elliot...Crow." The man repeated as though he had never heard another person's name being said before.

"Yes?" Elliot wondered fearfully.

He took a step back, trying to distance himself from this strange and dangerous man. He couldn't bring himself to do anything more than that.

"Why are you here?" the man rasped again and Elliot immediately felt another chill pass through him.

"I..." he swallowed, "Honestly, sir, I-I was hoping you could tell me that."

The man's face was blank, though Elliot got the sense that he was shocked by his answer. Elliot wondered if this man might be death himself, or some sort of reaper. He looked a bit like some of the depictions of death that his mother had shown him from some of her occult books. The silence stretched out long enough that Elliot supposed the man was expecting him to say something more.

"I...I was stabbed to death." Elliot said, not sure what it was he was supposed to add. He supposed being berated for stating the obvious was better than this torturous quiet.

"You are dead?" the man questioned, eyes traveling down to the blood which covered his shirt and jeans.

Elliot shifted in his spot, but nodded his head mutely, wondering what was going to happen now. A part of him realized that it was rather odd that Death would be so surprised that he was dead. Unless he was wrong and this wasn't Death.

"How did you get here?" the man asked almost accusingly.

Elliot was feeling just a little bewildered at this point,

"I...I died." He repeated dumbly, "I was stabbed. Then I woke up here and...and I saw you."

The man grunted, eyes moving away from the blood on his shirt and pants and up towards Elliot's face. Elliot couldn't help but shiver again as their eyes met. Pale blue eyes, staring into dark brown.

"You shouldn't be here." The man said, "I don't know how you got here, but you shouldn't be here."

Elliot shrugged his shoulders again, the ability to speak seemed to leave him as he wondered what he was supposed to do about that. He couldn't see any doors to leave by, come to think of it.

"Um...okay." He settled on saying, feeling dumber and more out of depth than he had before if that was possible.

"Are you...are you Death?" he felt a bit silly asking, but he wasn't about to learn anything if he didn't ask questions.

"I am Time." The man stated in a perfect monotone, "And this is my domain."

In a flourish of his cloak, he spun around and glided around Elliot in a circle, if possible terrifying him further. Elliot was vaguely aware that the man, Time was gliding far over the edge of the platform he was standing on at some points.

"Tell me, child...have you anything unresolved in your life? Anything left undone?"

Elliot turned as Time vanished in front of him, reappearing in a hazy black mist behind him. The man, Time, looked to be almost intrigued if Elliot was reading his expression right. And it was rather difficult to pick up anything from his body language or face what with his large cloak being in the way and his emotionless voice.

His killer's face flashed in his head. The man with the scar on his forehead with the sandy-blond hair. He was angry. Then the anger that this man had killed him quickly faded to sadness at the thought that he had died and that he'd never see his family again. His mother. No matter how strange she might be with her bizarre ideas of how the world worked. That there were spirits that made up everything and invisible creatures everywhere. In a way, she had been right, Elliot thought, since he had become some sort of ghost.

His father, the quiet man with a calm smile who seemed to have set himself the impossible goal of reading every book the world had to offer. His brother...

"Casper!" Elliot exclaimed, looking at Time with alarm. All his fear seemed to vanish in an instant as urgency overwhelmed him, "Casper is in danger!" He then sobered, realizing that any effort he might make would be futile, "But...I'm dead."

All the ticking that had moments ago made up the chamber stopped as silence fell around them.

"Drat!" Time huffed, then made his way back over to his table in the center of the room. He sat down at his desk and Elliot watched with curiosity as he started working on a pile of pocket watches.

They were all gold, and they were all broken, all sporting various degrees of wear and all stopped at different points.

Time stopped a moment, looking back over his shoulder at Elliot,

"I certainly can't have you stand there." He stated causing Elliot to shift.

Just what did the man want? What was he going to do?

"Come over here, child." Time motioned.

His feet seemed to move of their own accord, despite Elliot's fears. He felt shaky. Worried for his fate, and for the drop into the bottomless chasm below his feet. He forced himself not to look down as he crossed over the bridge towards the center platform.

With dead, pale blue eyes, Time bore his gaze into the dead boy. Elliot made no move, too terrified. But despite his fears of what might happen to himself, he couldn't move his mind away from Casper.

It wasn't like they had the best relationship. They were brothers after all, it was their job to annoy the heck out of each other. But he was still Elliot's brother, his stupid, older brother who had gotten himself involved in something that had gotten Elliot killed.

Time's eyes didn't move away from Elliot once. He didn't so much as blink.

"There might be a way." Time said.

Elliot took a moment to process his words,

"W-what?"

"There might be a way…" Time repeated, "To save your brother." "How?" Elliot blurted, no longer caring for the consequences, he was already dead anyways. "I'll do anything."

"There are several ways to communicate with the living." Time stated, "I am no expert in these matters. I am Time. I make the earth move, I make the grass grow. All must come to me in the end." He paused, as though allowing Elliot to absorb all this and let the information sink in.

And sink in it did.

"You mean," Elliot said slowly, "you're time, like…the time on a clock or…or the passage of time?" a bit of disbelief entered his voice, but Time didn't appear to be fazed by it.

"Of course, child." Time said impatiently.

For a man who must have all the time in the world, he wasn't particularly patient.

"That is what I just said."

"How do I communicate with the living? How can I get a message to my family?" Elliot asked, deciding not to bother saying anything more on the matter of Time being…time. It would only get confusing and the only man who seemed to have information appeared to be growing bored with him.

"I am Time." The powerful being decreed once again, growing annoyed, "I do not care for such matters."

In other words, Elliot thought, quite capable of reading between the lines, he didn't know.

"Have you a proposal?" Elliot decided to ask, recalling one of those strange gothic Victorian dramas his mother watched. They had asked something along those lines when they wished for someone to speak their mind. He had a feeling it would be a phrase Time was familiar with.

"I have an acquaintance whom I cannot reach on my own." Time stated clearly and unconcerned, "I ask that you deliver a package to him for me."

"Why can't you leave?" Elliot inquired curiously.

"Those with Responsibilities cannot leave their domain."

"And what's in it for me?" Elliot asked slowly, he didn't want to anger the man. Being. Time. Whatever he was, but he at least wanted to know why he was doing this.

"If he is not aware of a method of communication you may use, someone he knows will." Time said and now Elliot was certain he was growing irritable.

"Thank you." Elliot's response was quick, not wanting to test Time's temper further when he was helping him, "I'll do it." He added if this wasn't clear, "How do I find your…acquaintance?" Elliot noticed that Time had avoided the use of the term 'friend.' He vaguely wondered if he had any friends. Time didn't seem particularly interested in being friendly and even though they had just met, he seemed to give off an air of reclusiveness.

'Time is not our friend' he had heard the phrase several times on several different occasions. He was beginning to wonder if there might by chance be some other hidden meaning behind that statement.

In a wisp of black smoke, a brown box appeared at the table Time had been working at. The sudden appearance nearly made Elliot jump.

Time turned around as though the sudden manifestation were the most natural occurrence in the world.

"I cannot send you there directly." Time explained dully, "To the city. Greythorn, Ontario. I can drop you off there. You'll have to find that man on you own." He growled out the words 'that man' as though his name were some sort of sin.

"Who? I mean, what's your fr-acquaintance's name." Elliot corrected himself hastily.

"Trinket Deadlock." Time said, his voice returning to it's once before dull monotonous drawl as he picked the package off his table and placed it in Elliot's hands.

It looked about the size of those boxes his father used for storing his magazines, though a bit deeper than that. It was surprisingly light; much lighter than the ones his father would fill up at least.

"How do I find him?" Elliot inquired, wondering how someone got 'acquainted' with Time anyways. Whoever this 'Trinket Deadlock' was, he doubted he was anyone normal. Even his name sounded strange.

"Ask one of the cats." Time said, "They always seem to know where he is, even when he moves his house they always know."

"Cats?" Elliot repeated.

It seemed, however that Time didn't want to waste anymore of...er, himself? Time? on Elliot as the room around him vanished, simply blinking out of existence.

Was it perhaps a bit odd that the first thing Elliot processed was that his feet weren't touching the ground?

He realized the fact that he had to be at least a thousand feet up in the sky moments later and did the only logical thing. He screamed bloody murder.

Could someone die twice? Elliot wondered in a strange passing moment. Was there an after-afterlife?

He knew that he should probably feel more afraid, but his fear was strangely forced. His heart wasn't pounding in his chest and thus he had zero adrenaline pumping through his system. He couldn't breathe either. But he was still afraid. Perhaps it was all an echo of the survival instincts he had had when he was still alive. Or maybe not, considering the measures he'd taken to prevent his death had been lacking at best.

He also found himself wondering if Time would be upset if whatever was in the package was broken. Then, he figured that he didn't really care all that much considering where he had been dropped off.

'Wham!'

He had definitely hit the ground. Yet he hadn't felt any pain from his interaction with the concrete pavement.

Oh, here was most certainly blood, and a lot of it too. At least he thought it was blood. It didn't exactly look like blood, what with it not being red at all, but an inky sort of black. It didn't seem to have the same sticky quality blood had either. But it was seeping from his head and torso.

Was he in shock? He wondered.

He'd heard that when people go into shock that they couldn't always feel their pain. Elliot felt nothing though. In fact, he was pretty sure he could move...

Pathetically, he crawled across the pavement, feeling his body stitching its self back together.

He wanted to throw up, but found he wasn't capable.

"Of course." Elliot mumbled, then let out something like a laugh. Had anyone been nearby they might have mistaken him for being insane. Elliot was beginning to wonder if he even *was* sane anymore.

He looked up at the sky with a glare,

"This is why people don't want to be your friend!" he shouted, wondering if Time could even hear him.

He let out a sigh, looking down at himself. His wounds were already nearly healed. The black ink which had once painted the ground had retreated back inside him, or had simply vanished as though it had never been there to begin with.

Still feeling nauseous, he flexed his arm experimentally.

"The package!" he remembered and immediately looked around in hopes of finding the missing brown box.

It was over by a tree which had been planted in the middle of a circle of concrete in the middle of a park of sorts.

There were people nearby, but had they been able to see him, Elliot doubted they would have ignored a boy who had suddenly fallen from the sky and somehow survived.

He had to try anyways. He picked up the package in his arm and wandered over to a woman who looked to be in her late twenties. She was watching a child in the park, probably her kid.

"Excuse me, ma'am?" Elliot asked her and was disappointed when she didn't react. He probably shouldn't have gotten his hopes up.

He tried some of the children. One of them actually ran straight through him! He shivered, realizing, at last that this method wasn't going to get him anywhere.

He moved over to one of the benches and sat down, still shaken by his fall. Had he been alive still his heart would be pounding and his breathing would be rapid...had he been alive he probably would have died...again.

"Alright." He whispered to himself, realizing he was going to have to move at some point.

He was here to find Time's 'acquaintance' so that he could find a way to save Casper. He repeated this over and over in his head. The fall had deterred him only a little. And only because it had made him examine his impossible situation. Even now he wondered whether he was being silly in even trying to continue on. How could someone like him, someone so ordinary hope to navigate such an impossible new world?

But he had set his mind on saving his older brother from whatever he'd gotten himself involved in. After meeting Time and falling from the sky, he would *have* to continue.

He had to save his brother, he repeated to himself again. Then slowly, he got up off the bench and started wandering off in a random direction.

He didn't know where he was going and he already felt lost.

Time had said to ask a cat. Could cats even see him? He could vaguely recall his mother once saying that cats were said to possess supernatural powers, and were revered in some cultures as being able to see the dead. Elliot didn't have any other information to go on and even something unconfirmed was at least something.

It was all so very strange to Elliot. He could recall arguing with his mother many times over her obsession with the supernatural and her goth dress. He wondered if he'd ever be able to apologize to her, to tell her he had been wrong.

Elliot had always wanted to be normal, especially after having grown up in a very abnormal family. Now he found himself longing to hear his mother talk to him about one of her strange occult books. About vampires and werewolves, about the possibilities behind the veil of darkness. About her job and her friends. It couldn't have been more than a half an hour since his death and he already missed them.

It was so peculiar, he mused, how a person could spend a whole day away from the people they care for without giving it a second thought. Yet, when they were gone permanently, every aching moment became a longing to see them once more. Or maybe, it was simply knowing that they never would see each other again that made those moments so terrible.

CHAPTER THREE

Trinket and Gear

Elliot found himself in a neighbourhood full of blooming white flowers that decorated the boulevard. Mayday trees, he recalled his mother once telling him. He couldn't remember if there was any significant meaning behind the tree or flowers which was usually the only reason his mother knew about trees or flowers to begin with.

He realized, with a heavy heart that that had been one of the many times he'd tuned her out.

He was jerked out of his self-pity at the sound of a soft mewl. Definitely a cat, Elliot decided, looking around and trying to find the source.

His neighbourhood had been full of cats, but this particular road was surprisingly lacking. Or maybe it was because he was looking for a cat that it was lacking in cats. He didn't ponder on this thought as he was well engrossed in his search.

He heard another 'meow' and he was now certain there was a cat close by.

It took him a moment to comprehend that the sound was coming from above.

"Of course, it can't be that simple." Elliot sighed with exasperation. There was always a catch. The only cat he had found in the past three hours just so happened to be caught in a tree.

This wasn't a mayday tree, Elliot observed, it was some sort of pine. It was growing in one of the yards and he hesitated briefly before walking onto the grass. He knew walking onto someone else's property wasn't, well...you weren't supposed to do it. But then he remembered that he couldn't actually be seen and decided it didn't really matter anyways.

Surely, he could be forgiven for a bit of trespassing when someone's life was at stake?

He set down the package he was meant to deliver a little off to the side so that, if he did fall, he wouldn't hit it. Then again, the package had already withstood the abuse it took to plummet out of the sky about a thousand feet in the air. He doubted he could do any damage to it if it could withstand that sort of abuse.

The tree's branches weren't particularly low, but if he climbed up onto the fence it was easy enough to jump from there and onto one of the lower branches.

He awkwardly swung his legs up and tilted his body over, lifting himself on top of the branch. He moved over to the trunk and shimmied up the side towards a somewhat small, orange tabby cat with the brightest green eyes he had ever seen.

He grabbed onto the next branch and slowly made his way over to it.

"Here kitty kitty." He said, well aware of how far up he was. He carefully moved towards the cat which didn't really look too concerned at it's situation.

"Come on." Elliot whispered, "I'm gonna get you down."

The cat moved towards him, much to Elliot's relief. There was no way the branch would be able to hold him if he moved any closer to it. His previous theory of weightlessness already forgotten.

He scooped up the cat in his one hand and moved down the tree at a slower pace than he had moving up it.

"Almost there." He murmured when he reached the lowest branch.

He grimaced when he realized he probably wasn't going to be able to swing over to the fence again. But the ground wasn't too far away. The cat wouldn't be harmed if he dropped from here. He moved the creature into a more comfortable position, cradling her carefully.

He let go of the branch then slid off the edge, landing on the ground. The cat let out a sudden hiss of dislike and scratched him on the hand.

"Sorry." Elliot huffed, leaning down and letting the cat go.

It started running off and he realized his mistake,

"Wait!" he called after it, and of course it didn't stop.

He quickly scooped up his package and ran after it,

"I need you to take me to Trinket Deadlock!" he blurted.

Much to Elliot's fascination, the cat froze on the spot, then slowly turned around to look at him. It gave a slight head bob, as though to say, 'I'll take you, then. But no more jumping out of trees.'

Elliot watched in startled bewilderment as it completely changed course, running back towards him and down the neighbourhood of white flowers. He quickly picked up his package and took chase.

The cat was pretty fast, and the fact that it often jumped up and over fences didn't help. After about the second intrusion on private property, Elliot didn't hesitate to hop over whatever fence the cat did.

What surprised him the most was when they stopped at a bus stop. From the odd behaviour the cat seemed to be exhibiting, Elliot couldn't help but conclude that it must understand him to some degree. Were all cats this intelligent, or was it just this one?

Perhaps it was a Cheshire cat, he mused. He wasn't entirely certain how he felt about being Alice though. Didn't Alice follow a rabbit?

The bus arrived no more than five minutes after they had. The cat walked onto the bus and Elliot quickly followed. He instinctively reached into his pocket to pull out some money before realizing that the bus driver couldn't see him, nor did any of the other passengers.

"Right, dead." Elliot shook his head, "I forgot."

The cat shot him an amused look and Elliot rolled his eyes,

"I know it's silly." He said, "But I only died a few minutes ago, really."

The cat nodded in understanding and Elliot was sure it understood him perfectly well. He looked around and realized something,

"Oh right," he said, "normal people walk through me." He said, "But...but I picked you up before to get you out of that tree. Are you a spirit too?"

As though to answer his question, and really, it probably was to answer his question, the cat moved over to an old woman who had been siting by the window and jumped up onto her lap.

"Oh my!" she exclaimed, "Goodness dear, who do you belong to?"

"Alright, not a spirit or ghost." Elliot decided, sitting down in the seat beside the old woman who was now fully engrossed in petting the creature behind the ears.

"My mother always said cats had a supernatural sense or something...but you seem far more intelligent than a normal cat."

The cat puffed out it's chest proudly and Elliot couldn't help but laugh. It he wasn't careful he might end up inflating the creature's ego.

The day was beginning to die as the sun bleached the sky a blood red.

The bus came to it's final stop at a shady looking part of town. The cat jumped off the seat. The old lady had gotten off long ago and there was only one other person still onboard besides the driver, Elliot and the cat still on the bus. A punkish looking man with a Mohawk, ear gages and several facial piercings.

It looked as though he was getting off as well.

Elliot followed the ginger tabby off, thanking the driver, despite the fact that he couldn't hear or see him.

"Where to now, cat?" Elliot asked just as the tabby took off down into a darker alley.

He wondered just how long this would end up taking. The cat seemed to know all the shortcuts, the only problem being that these particular shortcuts weren't really meant for people.

Elliot found himself squeezing in between two buildings, then jumping up onto a fence and over onto a shed of sorts and up again onto some sort of ledge. He jumped down onto another fence and into another divot between another two buildings.

He had no idea how long he'd been running, though he was rather glad no one could actually see him. It would be embarrassing to be seen following a cat like this.

As he passed through into an open area, Elliot realized that the sun wasn't setting anymore, but rather, it was high up in the sky.

He looked back over his shoulder and saw a sort of crack in the middle of nowhere. He was standing on a hill of very green grass. Elliot had never before seen grass that was so green.

He turned back to see the cat looking back at him. It made a small gesture with it's head as though to say, 'well, come on, we haven't got all day.'

It took off again, not bothering to look back to make sure Elliot was following.

Once they had reached the bottom of the hill they passed over a bridge which crossed over some of the clearest water Elliot had ever seen. It was a small stream. If Elliot were to make an estimate he'd say it was about fifteen feet across. He could see fish swimming about, though they were no fish that he had ever seen. They all looked to be a bit like carp, save for the fact that they were all vivid colors, none being the same color as the other.

His attention snapped back to the cat which had gotten a bit ahead of Elliot at this point, walking onto a cobblestone road on the other side of the bridge and beneath an old stone archway. He ran after it, passing beneath the arch. The road rounded into a circle where stood in the center a statue of what looked to be a tin soldier painted a vivid red and gold.

There were surrounding buildings, but only one appeared to have a door. The cat stood beside the lone entrance, tail curled around it's feet. It started licking its front paw. Obviously, it had decided that after such a run it deserved a good grooming.

Elliot slowly approached the door, but paused before looking back down at the cat,

"So...this is it then?" he asked it awkwardly.

The cat seemed to roll its eyes as though to say, 'Well what do you think? Silly boy.'

"Thank you." Elliot said politely.

He hardly had any allies and he wasn't so sure he could count Time as one. It wouldn't kill him to be polite to the few that did help.

Gaining a bit of courage, he gave a knock. There was a bit of green paint that had pealing off the old wood. It fell to the ground, unable to withstand the attention.

Elliot jumped at the sound of something crashing inside.

"One moment, one moment!" a man's voice called from inside, "Gear! Gear, get the door!"

"I'm busy!" A female voice shouted viciously.

There was a scream from the man and Elliot was beginning to wonder if he ought to leave. He looked back down at the cat nervously,

"Is this...normal?" he asked it.

The cat only meowed in response, though it sounded suspiciously like confirmation.

"Be there in a second!" the man's voice came again followed by the sound of a loud 'bang!' causing Elliot to jump. His eyes traveled back to the cat which seemed to be quite unconcerned with the whole thing. Although, Elliot supposed cats were normally unconcerned by most things.

The door swung open, revealing a man in a wrinkled black suit and a top hat which covered his rusty red hair. His eyes appeared to be in a permanent squint and his face was a tad longer than average, giving him a shifty look about him.

"Um, hello." Elliot greeted hesitantly.

"Hello." The man said his eyes widened in alarm when he noticed the blood stains on his shirt, "Oh my gosh! What happened?" he exclaimed, "Come in, come in." he ushered him inside his house while Elliot felt a strange sense of daze at the suddenness of it all.

"Gear! Gear come here! There's a boy here and he's covered in blood!" the man shouted.

"It's fine!" Elliot protested though any further words seemed to die as he caught sight of the house's interior. He wasn't quite sure it could even really be called a house.

The floor was plain concrete and it was far bigger on the inside than its exterior façade. Inside was a giant ship, almost like a metal boat only Elliot wasn't so sure one was allowed to stand on the top deck. It didn't look as though it were designed to allow people outside while it was in motion. No railings or safety features to be seen, despite there being an upper platform that one could, hypothetically stand on.

Still, it was huge! Big enough to swallow up his school at least ten times over.

There was a girl. She looked like she might be about Elliot's age. Her skin was darker, probably of Indian descent with wild frizzy hair kept back from her face by large green lensed goggles. She was held up by three different ropes and a harness, a wrench in hand that she appeared to be using on one of the windows. She turned around and the strap from her baggy overalls slid down the side of her arm.

"What do you mean 'he's covered in blood!?'" she shouted, then paled when her eyes fell on Elliot. She let out a string of colorful language that Elliot didn't recognise (and that was an accomplishment as Sam had quite a vocabulary as well).

She grabbed one of the ropes with her gloved hand and with the other hand tested out a gear feature and started fiddling with it,

"Darn thing always sticks!" she hissed.

Finally, it released and she propelled herself down, landing with both feet. She quickly unlocked her harness and came running over to the two of them.

"Where's the wound?" she asked looking Elliot over and snapping him out of his stupor.

"There isn't one." Elliot said quickly, "And even if there was it wouldn't matter." Elliot stumbled forward when he was met with a sudden force over the back of his head. It took him a moment to realize, since there was no pain, that Gear had slapped him.

"What the ** are you saying! You *** masochist! You wanna die or something!?"

Elliot just stared at her dumbly until his brain started working again,

"Well, it's a little difficult to die twice." Elliot replied slowly.

This gave the duo pause.

"You're dead?" the man asked looking him over disbelievingly.

"I'm pretty sure I am." Elliot confirmed, "I was stabbed in the gut. Next thing I know I'm waking up and a man called 'Time' is telling me I shouldn't be there."

The man tilted his head to the side, his eyes sparkling,

"That certainly doesn't sound right..."

"I don't have a pulse." Elliot added in helpfully, "I was dropped from over a thousand feet and just...got up and walked away. I bleed black blood. But I know I was human before."

Was being human optional? Elliot pondered. He figured it best to cover all bases anyways. Optional or not.

The man hummed thoughtfully, still looking Elliot over and causing him to shift uncomfortably.

"You're not covered in black blood now." He pointed out.

Elliot looked down at himself, surely enough, his clothing was clean, well, minus the red blood from the stab wound that had killed him. His hand trailed over where the wound had been as he shifted the package to one arm. It hadn't dried. It was still a perfect red color, almost like he was still bleeding even though he knew he wasn't.

"Ghosts are usually white and many, many shades of grey." The man explained, "Can other people see you?"

Elliot shook his head,

"No. I tried approaching a few people. I only died a few hours ago." He admitted, "My murderer wasn't after me though, he mistook me for my brother which is why I need to find a way to communicate with the living somehow." He blabbered out, his mind had been running on auto piolet up until then and all his worries seemed to come pouring out all in a few short sentences.

"And why come here?" the man asked him curiously, "I'll help you, of course." He added in, "But who sent you?"

"Time did." Elliot said, suddenly remembering why he had sent him. He held out the box he'd kept clutched against his chest, "He wanted me to deliver this to a man called Trinket Deadlock."

"Ah…" the man's eyes shone with realization, "Well, I just so happen to be Trinket Deadlock." He said, taking the package from his hands, "I'm rather surprised Time would send you to me. It makes sense in a way though, I suppose. Those with Responsibilities aren't allowed to leave their respective domains. Time cannot leave the domain of time, thus, whenever available, he'll send a messenger." He paused looking at the box warily, "I do so hope this isn't a bomb. That would be inconvenient."

Elliot wondered if perhaps this man had a screw loose. There weren't many people out there who would consider a bomb as an 'inconvenience.'

"You can't just go collecting every stray you come across." The girl huffed.

But Trinket laughed merrily,

"This lovely ball of joy here is Gear." Trinket introduced the girl, "She is my apprentice." He added in helpfully.

Elliot nodded cautiously. There was something about Trinket he didn't entirely trust. Maybe it was his face, the squinted eyes and constant smile. It made him think of a predator.

"What is it you do, Mister Deadlock?" he asked politely.

If he was willing to help, not matter his reasons, Elliot was hard pressed to turn him down.

"I am a wizard." Trinket's smile widened further, "And an inventor."

Gear scowled, muttering something under her breath much to Trinket's amusement.

"Something on your mind, Gear, dear?"

His nonchalant attitude seemed to make her even more mad.

"Of course, I *** have a problem, you *** ****." She hissed.

"My, my, language, dear." Trinket looked like he was nearly laughing and Elliot concluded that he was enjoying this far too much.

So, wizards were real too? Elliot wondered looking at the two of them with amazement.

"We were supposed to go to Paris next." Gear huffed, "You promised!"

"Gear, dear, we have plenty of time!" Trinket said.

"Yes, because you *** him off!" Gear said kicking him in the shin.

Trinket grabbed his shin, obviously in pain. Yet, he still smiled. Weird, Elliot thought. His father had friends over for poker every now and then. He had explained to Elliot that everyone had tells but it took a true master to hide those tells. The term 'poker face' had come up a few times and suddenly Elliot realized why he was so uneasy.

This man had no tells. The smile was a part of the façade. It hid his true feelings and emotions, and when people hid every aspect of their thought, the people around them tended to grow unnerved. Elliot had felt a very similar feeling sitting in at one of his father's games and watching the players. There had been one man in particular who's mask was still firmly implanted in Elliot's memory, Harrison Noire. He always had droopy eyes, making him look like he was at a crossroads between boredom and not getting enough sleep the night before.

He gave off the same chilling feeling Trinket did. The only difference was that Trinket's smile was more unnerving due to the lack of humour behind it.

A smile without humour, no matter how long it lasted always made people at least a little distrustful.

"You don't have to go out of your way or anything." Elliot said quickly, although he really did need the help, "I just need information." He said, "If I don't do something my brother will die. Just please tell me if you know of a way for me to contact the living."

Trinket hummed in thought,

"We of the spirit world don't generally contact those of the living world, or material world that is." He crossed his arms over his chest.

Elliot felt his heart break at the news before Trinket added in,

"There are ways though."

Elliot looked up sharply as Trinket's smile grew wider,

"Several ways in fact, but each come with a price, see."

"A price?" Elliot repeated cautiously.

"As you are now," Trinket began, "Some of those options might not work for you. The first option is to travel to the realm of reflection or the 'mirror world,' as it's sometimes called."

Elliot was caught off guard when the smile fell from Trinket's face and even Gear seemed to stiffen.

"The realm of reflection is a dangerous place, especially for those who don't trust themselves. For you, this option is out."

Elliot once again found himself feeling like he was being scanned over, like Trinket might be looking directly into his soul.

"I don't trust myself?" he repeated.

Trinket shook his head,

"You've some good instincts, but you don't trust them. In fact, I'd say you don't trust anyone much."

"What do you mean?" Elliot challenged.

Did he trust anyone? He trusted Sam, right? They were best friends after all. He found himself thinking back to the day of his death. Sam had warned him against leaving without him. He'd brushed off his fears as being based on superstition, his own superstitions to add to that.

"You know I'm right." The smile returned to Trinket's face, "It's quite simple, I should think. You don't believe in yourself, nor in other people."

Elliot felt the need to take a step back, like he'd done something wrong, but he stubbornly stood his ground causing the smile on Trinket's face to twitch. It was like he had passed an unspoken test.

"Ah, I'm quite good at...I suppose you might call it fortune telling." Trinket said airily, "I get a certain feel from people."

Elliot noticed Gear roll her eyes at the assertion, but she didn't protest it making Elliot think that there must be at least some truth behind it. Trinket was supposedly, a wizard, after all. Maybe it was some sort of magic.

"That's why it is impossible for you, as you are now, to enter the realm of reflection and get out unharmed. Even if you are already dead."

Elliot nodded. He didn't like it, but he didn't know how this world worked and Trinket, though he wasn't sure he liked the man all that much, seemed to know what he was doing.

"The next option is to travel to the realm of waiting souls." Trinket said, "But I wouldn't put much stock in that either. It's a boring place where boring dead people go, hoping that their loved ones might one day call upon them for a séance."

"My mother mentioned a séance once." Elliot admitted, "She used to have them every now and then to call on her mother. It never did work."

Trinket nodded wisely,

"It wouldn't if she had left this world without any regrets, and it's pointless to have more than one séance for a dead person unless it's already worked once before. And let's not forget to mention that you're trying to warn your family of danger. No, it would be far faster to communicate some other way." He decided, "Although, the fact that you mother believes in the occult could definitely be used to your advantage." He looked thoughtful, "Perhaps...maybe..." he mumbled to himself softly until Gear slapped him over the back of the head, just as she had done to Elliot,

"We can't read your mind, you idiot! Tell us already." She demanded.

"Alright, alright." He said trying to calm her, though that seemed to be having the exact opposite effect, "It's just a rumor, mind you." He said thoughtfully, "But I do believe that the king of dreams is looking for an apprentice."

"The king of dreams." Gear repeated incredulously, "That ****!? What the *** is your problem!? You wanna scar the kid!?"

"What? Who's the king of dreams?" Elliot interrupted her rant, causing Gear to huff with indignation.

"Trust me," Gear said, "You don't want to meet him. I met him once and I still have a headache. He's absolutely barmy. Bonkers. Mad!"

"Now Gear, dear." Trinket said in a faux soothing tone that Elliot might have called condescending.

"The king of dreams isn't mad. He's just a bit eccentric."

"He's mad." Gear stated bluntly then looked over at Elliot critically, "Just go home, kid. Pass on, rest in peace. Have a good afterlife. You'll meet your brother and it will all be fine. Dead or alive, it's not like it particularly matters."

"It does matter!" Elliot shouted, then realized he'd yelled. His voice echoed around the entire garage.

Both Trinket and Gear had gone silent.

"It matters." Elliot repeated, faltering a bit at Gears words.

"You don't seem so sure." Trinket pointed out, catching the uncertainty in his voice.

Elliot steeled himself and tried again,

"It matters." He stated a bit softer, but he believed himself this time, "I will meet them again." He agreed, "But I don't want to meet them soon. Not like this. I don't think...I never really got to live." He didn't know where that had come from, but the pain in his gut told him it was the truth.

"I was so obsessed with being normal and separating myself from my parents' strangeness that I never realized how amazing they are. Not until I died. I'm terrified." He admitted, "I can't imagine what would happen if Casper died, because he still has so much to live for, and I know that he separated himself just like I did. Maybe not in the same way, but he did. If he dies too, my mom and dad will spend the rest of their lives grieving for the both of us. I could never live with myself if I could do something about that and didn't. And I know this might sound strange to you, but I want to believe, even though I'm dead, and I know I'll meet them someday again in the future. I want to believe that their lives matter, that everything they did had some sort of meaning! So, I'll save them." His whole body shook and his jaw clenched. He wasn't going to back down, even if he had to beg. He had met Time himself. He had fallen over a thousand feet; he had followed a freaking cat! He was not going to back down now.

Yet something in the back of his mind was nagging at him, warning him that he wasn't even at the half-way point of his journey. So yes, he certainly was terrified about what he might have to do in the future, and whatever horrors he might be about to face.

He was fifteen and he hadn't done much with his life other than fading into the background and doing his best to stay out of the spotlight. He had wanted to be normal. But now, he was starting to come to the realization that normal would do nothing to save his brother's life.

His thoughts were broken by the sound of someone clapping.

"Bravo!" Trinket said, his smile wider than ever, his hands applauding, "Well said. I think we can most certainly do something for you, Mister..."

It was then Elliot realized he hadn't even introduced himself.

"Elliot." He said, "Elliot Crow."

"Eliot Crow." Trinket said, as though tasting the name, "A good name." he decided, "Come then, Elliot Crow." Trinket waved his hands about dramatically, "Let us discuss this aboard the Youfoe!"

"Youfoe?" Elliot wondered.

"It's what the flesh bags call our ship whenever we accidentally flicker into visibility." Gear explained reluctantly.

Youfoe? Elliot thought to himself, rolling the word around in his head a couple of times.

"You mean, UFO?" he guessed.

Trinket allowed a bit of confusion to show on his face.

"Unidentified Flying Object." Elliot said slowly, "Or UFO. It's usually used to describe an alien space ship."

"Oh." Trinket looked a bit disappointed, "I thought they'd given us a good name too."

Gear just rolled her eyes,

"We'll have to come up with another name then." She said decidedly, leaving no room for any argument.

"Come on." Trinket said, suddenly bouncing back from his momentarily sadness over their name not being particularly 'unique.'

He grabbed Elliot's arm and dragged him along until he was certain the boy was following behind him.

A staircase unfolded from a large metal hatch door on the side of the ship and Trinket practically skipped his way up in his own sort of merry way.

Gear scowled, disapproving of his behaviour as she climbed the steps after the two of them. Elliot tried to ignore her, though not to the extent where if she spoke he wouldn't respond. But commenting on her behaviour would likely get him slapped over the head again. Not to mention, he wasn't entirely certain that assault was prohibited in this...spirit realm or whatever strange parallel world he'd landed himself in.

Gear let out a small shriek as she nearly tripped over the orange tabby cat which quickly slithered its way around her feet and over to Elliot who had just entered the vessel.

"Oh, it's you." Elliot said, recognising his guide from only a few short minutes ago, "What are you doing here?"

The cat shot him a raised eyebrow sort of look, '*helping you, dummy.*' It seemed to say.'

"Thanks." Elliot said oddly. Even though he'd only known the cat for a few hours, he'd grown a bit attached to it, and if he wasn't mistaken, the cat had grown attached to him too.

"That your familiar, ***?" Gear asked casually.

"Er, no." Elliot said, "We just met. She seems to want to help me though." Gear raised a skeptical eyebrow,

"You do that again, cat, and I'll ***** your ears then **** your *** tail and ***."

"There's no need to be cruel." Elliot defended, feeling strangely protective of the small creature.

The cat didn't seem to be particularly affected by Gear's threats however. Gear rolled her eyes and increased her pace until she was right by Elliot. She closed the door and spun the round metal wheel until it was locked tight.

"This way." Gear gestured for him to follow, "You already lost sight of Trinket, right?"

Elliot looked back over his shoulder down the hall and realized she was right. He followed along behind her, a bit embarrassed at having not paid any attention to his surroundings.

It was a straight, narrow hallway, but not so narrow that two people couldn't walk side by side, albeit awkwardly in that those two, hypothetical people would probably be touching elbows as they moved along. Elliot was quite content walking behind her though, not really wanting to engage in a conversation with Gear at all.

They entered into a large and rather luxurious looking living room, at least it looked like it was a living room to Elliot. Had he not known he was actually on some sort of bizarre giant ship, and a flying one, according Trinket and Gear, then he might have assumed it was a normal house if not belonging to someone more well off than his family.

Trinket wasn't there, but Gear gestured for him to sit down on the large, antique, green couch. She, herself took a seat in the cream-colored chair to his side.

"Trinket probably went off to fetch us some tea." Gear said unconcernedly, "He'll be back in a moment."

"Tea?" Elliot wondered. Why tea?

"Right, you're a newbie at the whole 'dead' thing." Gear snorted as though there were some sort of joke in there that Elliot didn't understand. For all he knew, there was.

"Ghosts can't eat." Gear elaborated, "They can drink tea though. I suggest you get used to the taste of boiled grass, kid. It's the only thing you'll be able to taste for a *long* time."

From the smirk on her face, Elliot had no doubt she was telling the truth. Come to think of it, the thought of food did seem rather off putting. Like he'd just had a big meal and the thought of even a single bite might make him sick.

"Now, now," a familiar voice said.

Trinket stood by the door, a tray of tea in his hands,

"You didn't have to say it like that, Gear, dear. It's true though." Trinket added with a look that Elliot guessed was supposed to be apologetic. It would have worked a lot better had he not still been smiling.

"Tea is good for the soul." Trinket said, "And it's not just all one flavour. There are plenty of different varieties out there. This is my own little blend. I apologise if it tastes too bitter. I prefer strong tea and most people aren't a fan of that."

"That's fine. Thank you." Elliot said, trying to hide the fact that he wasn't really a tea fan anyways.

Trinket set out the mugs and Elliot noted that there wasn't any cream or sugar. He didn't bother asking for any either. His mother had told him before that some teas weren't supposed to be drunk with anything added and that in some cultures it could be considered an insult.

He didn't know whether that was true in this case or not, but even if he did feel uneasy around Trinket, he was still helping Elliot, or at least willing to help Elliot.

He picked up the mug and took a small experimental sip. It was still hot, but he did get a bit of flavour. It was an odd blend of what tasted strangely like cinnamon and peppermint. It didn't taste bad, or at least it didn't taste like boiled grass.

He could live with it.

"It's quite tasty." He complimented absently.

"Why thank you." Trinket beamed, "Now then." He crossed his legs, and leaned back. His smile hadn't fallen, but the air had turned serious.

"My recommendation is to go to the king of the dream kingdom and asking him for an apprenticeship."

He spoke as though this king was someone Elliot ought to know, and he supposed he ought to if the man was a king. But he still had to be honest,

"I'm sorry," he apologised, "I don't know who the king of the dream kingdom is." He admitted.

Trinket raised an eyebrow,

"You said you died recently...If you don't know who the king of dreams is, then I suppose you don't know much, if anything of the spirit world." He looked thoughtful as he leaned back in his chair, "Perhaps I ought to explain from the beginning then?"

"If you would." Elliot said politely, hoping to learn as much as possible.

Trinket gave a nod of acknowledgement but his eyes had moved to the side, as though in deep thought,

"As you've probably already learned, the spirit world is one that operates on a separate plane from the material world. Spirits can affect the physical world to an extent. The usual moving around inanimate objects and so forth. As you've already apparently discovered, some animals can interact with spirits. The most powerful tend to be cats, foxes, wolves, coyotes, dolphins, snakes, most reptiles and turtles." He added in helpfully just as the ginger tabby from before leaped up onto Elliot's lap surprising him.

Trinket grinned as though having already seen the cat coming.

"That one seems to have taken quite a liking to you...Ghosts and spirits are two separate things that exist on the same plane. The most blatant difference is that ghosts are dead, spirits are not. You are a ghost, but for some reason you're colorful. Ghosts are not colorful." His eyes twinkled, looking Elliot over once more with fascination as though he were some sort of prized science experiment.

"So...I'm not a ghost then?" Elliot wondered.

Trinket shrugged his shoulders,

"I honestly have no idea what you are." He admitted, "You're obviously dead. Spirits like Gear and me have a pulse, our blood is red. Yet, you say you do not have a pulse, and you don't appear to be breathing either." He added in thoughtfully, "You bleed black. Ectoplasm is black, see. Kind of inky, not sticky like blood." Elliot nodded immediately,

"That sounds like my blood." He agreed.

"Not blood." Trinket corrected, "Ectoplasm. Only ghosts have ectoplasm."

"So, he's a ghost." Gear said, obviously growing tired of the circular conversation.

"If he was a ghost," Trinket said slowly, "He wouldn't be able to touch that cat there." He pointed to the cat curled up on Elliot's lap. Gear straightened, seeing the obvious problem,

"Then which is it?" she wondered, growing more confused the more this particular conversation went on.

Trinket shrugged,

"Not a clue." He admitted once again. Then, seeing Elliot's confused expression decided to elaborate a bit, "Spirits are the only ones capable of interacting with the physical world to a degree. Ghosts can't interact at all."

"Oh." Elliot said simply, remembering how Trinket and Gear had freaked out when he had arrived covered in his own blood. It explained a lot.

"Ghost often stay behind because they have unfinished business from when they were alive." Trinket continued, "They all eventually fade away though, once their business is either taken care of, or their friends and family have moved on...or until it doesn't matter anymore."

Elliot shivered at that last one.

"You seem to have some unfinished business." Trinket decided, "But that doesn't explain why you seem to be some sort of hybridization of a spirit and ghost."

"Nothing seems to explain that." Elliot mumbled, and he doubted he'd be getting any answers any time soon.

"Spirits are everywhere." Trinket added, "You've got your spirits, your wizards, your witches, those are humans who have achieved spirithood." He added in helpfully, "Then you have your elementals, rain spirits, water spirits, most of those guys, if not all of them are servants of a spirit referred to as 'those with responsibilities.' You already met one." He hinted.

"Time." Elliot answered automatically.

"Those are the most powerful spirits out there." Trinket agreed, "Time is arguably the strongest, or one of the strongest at least. But he's hugely reclusive."

"I got that impression." Elliot said dryly.

Trinket chuckled at this,

"Indeed...To humans they would be the equivalent of deities or 'gods' as you might say."

Elliot had to stop his eyes from widening. He had sort of suspected something along those lines after meeting Time, but to have it confirmed was still a bit...shocking.

"Often times there's a hierarchy of sorts." Trinket added in, "Time, for example, would be above Death and Life. Not only for his age, but Death and Life can't operate without him. Death gathers the souls of those that have died, he gives them to Time who then fixes them and gives them new time, then hands them back to life who puts the souls into new bodies. Once their time is up, death collects them and hands them back to Time and so on and so forth." Trinket explained with a lazy hand gesture, "Now, the king of the dream kingdom is a whole other can of worms. Mainly because he doesn't reside in any hierarchy."

"What about sleep?" Elliot interrupted, "Wouldn't he be above the king of the dream kingdom?"

Trinket smiled, as though a bit amused at the question, there was a hint of encouragement behind his smile however,

"I can see how you might draw that conclusion. But no. Dreams are an entirely different realm." He furrowed his brow as though trying to come up with a way to explain something, "This world...I suppose you could say it's real. The solid world has much realness, the spirit world has a little less, and the dream world nearly has realness, but doesn't. It's difficult to explain, really. Dreams are beautiful and dangerous creations, and they are creations." He added in helpfully, "They can be manipulated, caught, turned around, and destroyed. It is a fantasy in some ways. But sleep has no control over dreams. No, no." He shook his head, "Sleep weakens the veil between fantasy and reality, and that is why it's possible."

"Possible?" Elliot repeated in but a mere whisper.

"Oh yes," Trinket agreed, "The dream king can enter dreams, see. He creates and weaves them like a spider's web. But because the dream realm is another world, it is possible to enter it."

"Enter a dream?" Elliot parroted with visible disbelief.

"It's not safe." Gear suddenly interrupted, much to Elliot's surprise. She didn't seem to be the sort of character who would be concerned for safety. But the look she shot Elliot spoke more than words ever could.

"It's not." Trinket agreed, Elliot quickly turned his head over to him, "Not even for you, Elliot Crow. Not even for the deceased." He let out a sigh, "Every world will have its dangers. In any of them, the most dangerous thing to do, is to not believe in yourself. And dreams...dreams are all about belief."

CHAPTER FOUR

In Which a Decision is Made

Trinket insisted that Elliot stay the night in the Youfoe even though he didn't feel particularly tired. The copper haired, wrinkled suit wearing man had quickly won the argument as Elliot didn't actually have any place to go anyways, and Trinket said they'd be heading in the direction of the Kingdom of Dreams and would be glad to drop him off. Gear had grumbled a half-hearted protest, but was, in the end, ignored.

Elliot didn't have any dreams that night. He never met the veil of sleep that weakened the line between this world and fantasy. Instead he stayed up reading in Trinket's library. His father would have been proud.

Trinket didn't have a TV, and the computer was used strictly for work. The library really was the only option.

The ginger tabby cat from before slept beside him on the couch for a portion of the night, but woke up sometime around one a.m. and began running about the ship. She somehow managed to get her paws on some string and Elliot spent some time playing with her before growing bored again and going back to his reading.

It was so strange, not growing tired. He didn't so much as yawn as night turned into morning.

Trinket made his way down to the library at about seven in the morning, not looking tired in the least. He had come to tell Elliot that he and Gear were about to have some breakfast. Elliot couldn't actually eat, as he still found the thought of food to be repulsive. But Trinket had made some tea, something different this time.

As Elliot made his way to the kitchen he noticed that Gear was there pouring herself some coffee, and obviously still half-asleep.

"Good morning my beautiful, dearest, Gear!" Trinket chirped.

Gear shot him a sleepy glare,

"I *** hate you." She grumbled.

With such clashing personalities, Elliot had to wonder how the two of them hadn't already driven each other insane. He looked between them uncertainly. Maybe he was reading the whole dynamic wrong and they actually already *had* driven each other to insanity. It would explain a lot.

Trinket set out a pot of tea and two mugs out on the table. One for Elliot, and one for himself.

Elliot poured himself a cup and took a sip. It was different from the tea he'd been served the day before. There was a definite lemony flavour to it. He still wasn't a huge fan of tea though. He drank it slow.

He jumped a bit when the ginger cat hopped up onto his lap.

"She seems to like you." Trinket observed, "Perhaps you should keep her. She'd make a good familiar."

"You mean," Elliot scrunched his face, "Like an animal witches used to control?" he vaguely recalled his mother talking about familiars, not to mention they were a popular topic in fantasy novels. But he could honestly admit that he knew nothing about them. He felt a pang go through his heart when he realized familiars were a conversation topic his mother and father had used several times in the past.

Why hadn't he paid more attention? He asked himself once again. It seemed to be a popular question as of late.

"Is that what the humans believe?" Trinket hummed, "Yes, I suppose that's somewhat accurate. Spirits with a high level of intelligence can have a familiar, a creature they bond to in order to aid them in their interactions with the material world. They also can aid in the use of magic."

"My mom always said 'there's magic everywhere.'" Elliot recalled absently, not having realized at the time just how true that statement had been.

Trinket nodded his head, his expression softened,

"She sounds like a wise woman."

"I was an awful son." Elliot admitted.

"Most teens are." Trinket chuckled in an attempt to comfort him, it wasn't really working.

"I said some awful things to her." Elliot admitted, "My mom's a goth. I was teased a lot in elementary school because she 'looked like a vampire.' After that, I guess I felt ashamed of her. I wanted to be normal."

"You won't get anywhere being normal." Gear interrupted, it looked like she had woken up. Her eyes were more alert, she looked a bit bored with the conversation topic though, her chin was resting against one hand while the other held onto her cup of coffee.

"Well, at least nowhere fun." Gear added, "I feel a bit sorry for her. I was human once too, you know?"

This surprised Elliot, but he didn't say anything. His expression must have said enough because Gear smirked,

"All wizards were once human." She said smugly, "One thing I learned from human school, the weird kids are always picked on. But they generally tend to go the farthest, know why?"

"Why?" Elliot asked her, feeling a bit foolish.

"Because," Gear said in a factual sort of voice, as though the answer were obvious, "they know themselves best and the friends they have, though few, will always be true. I feel sorry for her, because she's probably used to that sort of behaviour. After a while, that stuff just doesn't affect you so much, but when it's spouted out by someone you love..."

"That's enough, Gear." Trinket interrupted, seeing Elliot's face.

"It hurts worse than ***." She finished, looking at Trinket smugly.

Was that really true? Elliot wondered, thinking back to all the arguments they had ever had, the disappointed looks he had given her, and the heartbroken ones she had tried to hide.

If he hadn't felt like an insensitive jerk before, he sure did now.

Trinket cleared his throat, drawing Elliot's attention back over to him. He looked a tad embarrassed,

"Anyways," he began, "We'll be taking off soon. We just have to do one final check."

"Leaving?" Elliot murmured.

"To the Kingdom of Dreams, of course!" Trinket's smile re-emerged, "I did say it was on the way, no?"

Elliot nodded, recalling Trinket saying something along those lines the day before.

"Now, we won't be able to take you all the way there." Trinket warned, "The only way to get to the Kingdome of Dreams is to take the train."

"The train?" Elliot repeated slowly. Of all things to use to get to a magical kingdom, he was taking the train?

"The train is free." Trinket added in, as though believing that was what Elliot was worried about. His smile widened, "But there's a catch." He said teasingly, "The train doesn't stop anywhere. It's very easy to leave the kingdom, see, but it's very difficult to enter. The train only goes one way and there are no points where you can get on."

"Then how am I going to board it?" Elliot asked, growing more confused by the moment, "And why build a train with no stops?"

"Ah," Trinket said with understanding, "See, every realm has to have a method, or mode of transportation that other people can use to enter it. Of course, there's no clause that says Those with Responsibilities have to make it easy to board. It's a loophole, see."

Elliot frowned, wondering if he even wanted to meet this king at all if he was going to be difficult. But a brief vision of his brother laying in a pool of his own blood hardened his resolve.

"Alright, fine then. So, all I have to do is board a moving train. I can do that." He didn't feel so sure, but after all the madness he had gone through, he didn't *think* it was impossible, "I'm guessing the King of Dreams doesn't like a lot of visitors."

"Oh no." Trinket shook his head, "On the contrary, he loves visitors. He just enjoys the entertainment of people trying to get to his kingdom more."

"Oh." Elliot said dumbly, his opinion of the man was falling the more he heard about him.

"Like I said before." Gear grumbled, taking a bite of her toast, "He's a jerk."

"He's not a jerk exactly..." Trinket defended.

Gear just snorted, but didn't say anything more on the matter.

"Anyways," Trinket said shooting Gear a look before quickly turning back to Elliot, "You're only going to have one shot at this. The train only travels to the kingdom of dreams once ever five months."

"When is the train leaving?" Elliot asked.

Trinket's grin threatened to split his face,

"Tonight. But don't worry. If we leave at about nine we should be able to make it in time. We're giving ourselves an hour to run the standard checks on the ship, and really, it shouldn't take that long anyways, then we'll be off. Make sure you don't leave anything behind."

Elliot wanted to say that he didn't really have anything he *could* leave behind, but kept silent, deciding the comment was aimed more at Gear anyways.

The ginger tabby cat rubbed up against him once again, jumping back onto his lap and purring delightedly when Elliot rubbed her head.

"You going to take her with you?" Trinket asked, eyes trailing on the cat.

"She's probably someone else's." Elliot shook his head causing the cat to mewl in protest.

Trinket chuckled at this,

"It seems she's already made up her mind on that front. Take her with you. I think she'd make a great familiar."

"You keep saying that." Elliot said, a confused look on his face, he still wasn't entirely certain what a familiar did.

"Like I said before," Trinket explained patiently, "Familiars can aid a spirit with interactions in the material world. They also aid in magic."

"Magic?" Elliot repeated.

"Most ghosts can't use magic." Trinket said with a soft hum, "But I think you could. Your cat thinks you can, otherwise she wouldn't want to be your familiar in the first place." He leaned forwards in his chair, spreading marmalade on the remainder of his toast, "Familiars gain more intelligence when they find a spirit they're compatible with. The spirit then seals the bond by giving their familiar a name."

Elliot looked down at the cat curiously,

"You want me to name you?"

The cat nuzzled up against him playfully, as though that was all she wanted.

"Don't name it something stupid like 'red' or 'sandy.'" Gear scowled, "And I know you're dumb enough to do that too."

Elliot rolled his eyes, already growing used to Gear's constant jabs.

"You don't want your familiar being unhappy with her own name." Gear continued, "Makes things more difficult. Ask her before naming her."

Elliot had to think a bit. He'd always wanted a pet, but his father was allergic to animal hair. He knew that they had had a dog named 'Cujo' when he was a baby, but he had been hit by a car just before Elliot had turned two years old.

His mother would have loved to have a cat, she loved dogs, but cats had been her favourite. She probably would have named it a gothic name like,

"Do you like the name Rosary?" he asked the cat.

The ginger kit hissed and Elliot took this as a no. Elliot nodded, he wasn't entirely certain he liked the name either.

His brother might have named her something plain, but with a skater theme or something.

"Ace?" he questioned.

The cat didn't particularly approve of this name either, but Elliot felt he was getting closer. Ace wasn't really a good name for a girl cat anyways.

His father traveled a lot to different places in the world. He would want to name the cat a more unique, maybe foreign name.

"China?" it was the name of a country, but it sounded pretty, like a porcelain doll.

The cat looked away as though to say, 'are you really making an effort here?'

Elliot thought a bit more on this. What would *he* want to name her? Oftentimes he just went with the flow, he stayed in the background, not wanting to stand out. But 'normal' just wouldn't do anymore. If he wanted to save his family, he'd have to be better than that. He'd have to give up on normal, especially in a world where being abnormal seemed to be 'normal' anyways.

He could remember his mother and father talking about Egyptian gods, something that, they had said had first drawn themselves to each other. He didn't think he could call the cat 'Egypt' though. But the country did come to mind when looking at her sandy colored fur.

"How about Cairo?" Elliot said in a voice that hinted more at realization than a simple question.

The cat's head snapped up to look at Elliot and he knew, and the cat knew that from then on, Cairo would be her name.

CHAPTER FIVE

Nineties Rock and Lightning Storms

The thing about anxiety is that when one is anxious about something, one finds it nearly impossible to focus on any task other than thinking about what they are anxious about. At least, that's what it was like for Elliot who had tried picking up a book, only to set it down after realizing he'd been reading the same sentence over and over again before staring at the thing blankly.

Gear and Trinket had finished with their checks and as soon as they did, the ship had started to life. Humming and vibrating beneath his feet with the power one might expect from a hand-made sophisticated machine.

The piloting section of the ship was made of glass, even the ceiling, allowing Elliot to watch as the roof of the building they'd just been in was pulled away.

They rose up into the semi-cloudy sky. Elliot felt his stomach drop in a similar way he experienced going up in an elevator.

"Okay…" Trinket pressed a button on the side panel. It was a large, red, very noticeable button. The change after was quite noticeable with the outside shell of the ship going completely see-through. Invisible, Elliot corrected with awe.

When they were well in the air, he found himself watching the clouds drifting by with something akin to curiosity. He soon found himself twitchy and went back to trying to read the book he'd borrowed from the library, only to find himself once again in a battle of futility.

"How about some music?" Trinket suggested, though whether it was because he was aware of Elliot's nerves, or if he just wanted to listen to music, Elliot didn't know. He did suspect it might be the former though.

The music came on, blaring through the speakers that Elliot couldn't see or find. It was some sort of bizarre pop tune that appeared to be in a completely different language.

"Oh no," Gear said dangerously, "We are not listening to more of your J-pop ***!"

"But Gear..." Trinket whined like a child.

Gear clicked her tongue and switched it over so that they were now listening to what sounded like some sort of nineties or eighties band.

"Nineties rock, kid." Gear smirked over at Elliot, "It's the ***."

Elliot assumed she meant it was the 'best' and once again found himself wondering why she kept trying to find excuses to swear. It was certainly better than whatever it was Trinket had been trying to get them to listen to. Actually, he found himself enjoying it quite a bit. It was...different but in a good way. He hadn't been around in the nineties and he'd never really been exposed to a lot of music from that particular time period.

It was a bit different from what he was used to, but it wasn't bad. Sometimes he would recognise a song that played every now and then, but those were rare. Trinket would switch it over to his weird music once in a while, humming along to the song.

"What language is that?" Elliot finally asked. He'd been wondering for a while now...

"Japanese." Trinket said happily, at least Elliot though he was happy. It was hard to tell from anything other than his voice.

Gear scowled, obviously not a fan of the music in the least. Trinket's smile appeared to widen,

"You see, Elliot," he began, turning to him and Elliot really wondered if he ought to be keeping his eyes on the sky, "Music is different wherever you go. Sure, you'll find North American pop influences in every country, but people see the world different. Japanese, for example uses a lot of imagery, I find."

Elliot had difficulty believing that the high, almost squeaky voices of the Japanese singers could describe anything particularly 'in-depth' let alone something particularly poetic. Soon, Gear had once again wrestled away the dials that controlled the music and had switched it over to her more relatable nineties rock music.

As the ride went on, the sky grew darker as black clouds covered up the sun. The first drops of rain began to fall on the glass of the front window. Then, as though a switch had been flipped, it started to pour.

"Oh dear." Trinket said, not at all looking worried, "It seems we're going to have a bit of tricky weather."

"Trinket." Gear said warningly, "This could be bad. We're heading into a lightning storm."

Trinket hummed in agreement.

"We could go around the storm." Gear tried to reason with him.

"The train will be heading in our direction." Trinket said, "It will be right in the heart of it. No, my dear Gear, if we have any hope of catching the train to the Kingdom of Dreams, we'll have to ride it out."

Gear's lips thinned, not at all liking the idea of 'riding it out.' Elliot barely noticed the music being turned off as veins of light crackled in the sky right in front of them, barely missing the ship.

"Come with me, Crowfood, 'less you wanna die." Gear gestured to him.

Elliot looked back at Trinket whose eyes looked uncharacteristically focused on the sky, not even noticing Elliot's gaze. He quickly turned back to Gear who had turned around and was now walking out the door at top speed. Elliot broke into a brief jog, following after her as they made their way down the narrow corridors.

Gear opened up a small, dark room that Elliot hadn't seen before. He entered after her, then, upon Gear's gesture, closed the door behind him.

There was nothing inside, save for what looked like some sort of hatch on the floor. Gear started turning the handle, a sort of wheel thing, like one might see in the movies. The door popped open and Gear quickly pulled it all the way.

She looked up at Elliot again,

"Come on. We're almost there."

Elliot nearly fell over as the ship teetered dangerously. Gear let out a curse,

"*** weather. Just what we *** need. Come on, Crowfood."

Was that his new nickname? Elliot wondered to himself as Gear made her way down a ladder. Elliot followed down behind her. The room bellow was some sort of engine room and from the way smoke seemed to be leaking from the pipes, and from the dangerous moaning and clicking, Elliot got the sense that it was straining to keep up with the demand of it's pilot.

"We should be alright for now." Gear murmured, eyes traveling over to one of the pipes. A moment of uncertainty crossed her face, before her eyes hardened and she gave a nod, as though reassuring herself that she was right in her assessment.

She made her way over to what looked like a set of school lockers, green with peeling paint. She hit one of the doors with her fist and the door swung open. She reached inside, pulling out rope and leavers.

"Here." She threw something that looked a bit like a harness over to Elliot, "Put that on."

"What? Why?" Elliot asked, looking from the harness and up at her.

"Because I'm going to lower you onto the train." Gear said simply as though it were the most ordinary thing in the world and not at all something he ought to be concerned over.

"What!?" he yelped, wondering how in the world that might possibly be considered a good idea.

Gear rolled her eyes,

"It's no big deal. I lower Trinket all the time when we need work done."

"During a lightning storm?" Elliot asked her skeptically, "Onto a train?"

"Shut your *** mouth, Crowfood! We're *** doing this for you. And it's not like you'll die again. Why are you scared?"

Elliot hesitated, not really sure why he was scared. It wasn't like anything could really hurt him anymore, could it? Besides, wasn't this his only shot at saving Casper? Making up his mind, he stepped into the harness, tightening the belts where he needed too. Gear made her way over to him, looking over the straps and tightening the one around his hips a bit more.

"Now, this is important, Crowfood, so listen up." Gear said impatiently, "This clip here at the side –"

"The red one?" Elliot interrupted, having found it odd that there would be only one red clip when the rest were a neutral gold color.

"Yes, the red one. You might not be able to see it in the dark though, so remember where it is." She warned him, "When you're down there, when you're over the train, you're going to pull this clip and the harness will basically unclip its self. You'll need to grab onto something real quick, got it? You only have one shot." She warned him.

Elliot nodded his head quickly, realizing this was it. He was really going to do this.

Gear clipped the rope onto the harness and gave it a quick tug to make sure it stayed. She moved over to another hatch buried under papers and tools of all sorts. She brushed them all back so that they were out of the way.

Snap! Fssss....

Gear cursed as one of the pipes came loose, blowing smoke everywhere. She clicked her tongue,

"Get over here, Crowfood. The train's approaching."

Elliot came over, staring down through the hatch. The wind beneath them blew up his hair, though it didn't look nearly as crazy as Gears which was already wild to begin with.

She looped the rope from Elliot's harness through a bar attached to the wall and grabbed the other end.

"You ready?" Gear's voice seemed to lose it's usual mocking quality and took on an intense air that Elliot had only heard her use once before so far.

Elliot looked down through the open hatch. He couldn't see the ground, just blackness. He licked his lips, for the first time in a while, he thought he could feel his heart pounding. He knew it was impossible, but that was what he felt. Maybe it was something like a phantom limb...He shook his head, eyes not leaving the black hole into the abyss of the night.

"I doubt I'll ever be ready." He admitted to Gear, "But I'm going."

He got down onto his hands and knees, slipping down through the hole. He grasped the edge of the floor. His eyes widened with panic as he realized he was hanging in mid-air. The wind buffeted his body and he could feel his fingers slipping, until he finally let go.

His harness caught him after a short drop of about a meter. He breathed in and out over and over.

"Come on, Elliot!" he scolded himself, "You can do this...you can do this..." his eyes were shut tight, but he felt himself being lowered, for the life of him he couldn't figure out how fast he was going though.

He clutched the rope of his harness in his hands, then opened his eyes when he heard a very close boom of thunder. He looked up and felt his hands shake with anticipation and fear.

His head swerved at the sound of something below, a whistle...

"The train!" He exclaimed.

He could see the lights slithering across the ground like a serpent on a mission, it wouldn't be long before the train was where he needed it to be. Elliot estimated that he was at about fifty feet above it now and despite the horrible weather, he was beginning to see the outline of trees and other features when the sky lit up.

The rain poured over him and by now, it felt like he'd just submerged himself in water. The train was closer, so much closer and now Elliot was about thirty feet above it.

"I'm not gonna make it." He whispered to himself.

Boom!

Elliot looked up to see sparks of electricity running over the Youfoe, but what really caught his eye was the bright red and yellow glow that appeared to be coming from the engine room he was being lowered out of.

"Gear!" He shouted, "Get out of there!" It was useless. He knew she couldn't hear him, not from that distance, and certainly not over the howl of the wind and crackling thunder.

His eyes widened with horror as he saw fire crawling across the rope. The rain appeared to be putting it out before it could reach the outside, but the part that was in the engine room was not going to last long.

He looked down. He was so close. The train was now below him. He wasn't going to make it in time!

Elliot only thought about his options for a moment.

He could let go of the harness now and maybe make it onto the train. Or he could wait another five months for the next time.

He wouldn't die, he was already dead. Gear though...Gear was still alive. If he let go of his harness, she'd know and she'd leave. In the end, it was obvious what his choice was. He pulled the red strap of his harness and immediately felt its release.

He let out a small scream as he fell for a short fifteen feet onto the slippery roof of the train. He didn't really account for the water making his landing slippery. He probably should have.

He tried to find something to grasp, anything at all, but he fell over anyways.

"No!" he cried out as he fell over the edge. He quickly pushed himself off the grass and tried to grab onto something again. His eyes widened as his fingers grasped something wet, yet still graspable. He felt his shoulder pop out of place, but swung his other arm around, grabbing the metal bar and lifting off. He pushed himself towards the small nook, knowing he wasn't quite safe yet. He very carefully found a platform with his feet.

He'd done it.

Elliot felt laughter bubble up from deep in his chest, then soon, he was on his knees in the small shelter between the train cars, laughing and crying like a mad man.

"I did it." He whispered to himself, then looked up at the sky.

The air ship was still afloat and Elliot prayed that Trinket and Gear were alright. He took a breath, knowing he couldn't do anything about that right now. He wanted to go to them...somehow, but he had no way of communicating.

He felt his previous resolve set firmly in his mind. He was going to save Casper. He was going to save his brother and it would do him no good now to get up and go to them.

He shakily got to his feet again, then opened the door to the car in front of him. It was warm inside with several empty seats meant to carry a large amount of people. Yet, Elliot thought to himself, he had his doubts as to whether it carried all that many people ever.

Trinket had said that the King of Dreams enjoyed watching people try to reach his kingdom. That thought worried him a bit. He looked around, though he didn't know what it was he expected to find. Was the King of the Dream Kingdom watching him now?

He swallowed hard, then moved towards one of the seats to sit down. Just how long would it take for him to get there anyways?

Elliot closed his eyes, his body still shook and it definitely was not from the cold.

His eyes opened again when he felt a sudden weight on his lap. He nearly jumped up, only to find that the weight was a very familiar looking sandy-colored cat.

"Cairo?" he wondered, looking at the small creature with disbelief, "How?"

The cat purred, then moved off his lap to the seat beside him. She didn't like being wet, Elliot thought to himself absently.

But how *had* Cairo gotten there? Elliot wondered to himself. Gear and Trinket hadn't mentioned a means of bringing her down with him and Elliot had just assumed that after his visit, he'd meet up with them later somehow.

Maybe it was magic?

He didn't really know much of anything about magic, but he did know that wizards could use magic, and Trinket was a wizard. But if Trinket and Gear had a way of teleporting them then why use it only on Cairo? Elliot furrowed his brow, recalling just how little he knew about this strange new world.

Elliot leaned back in his chair, really wishing he had some dry clothes right about then. He looked around. He was alone...

He took his shirt off and shook it out, trying to get rid of all the water. When he put it back on though, he didn't feel any better off.

He let out a breath, then looked out the window. Out at the blackness only briefly illuminated by the veins of electricity that pulsed across the sky.

As time passed, the rain started to lessen as morning spread out over the earth's edge where the cloud line was thinnest. By then, Elliot could see the world rather clearly and he was quite sure that the grass was not supposed to be silver.

When had that changed? Elliot wondered to himself.

His clothes were not damp and even dry in places, leaving him semi-comfortable. Cairo had found his lap quite satisfactory enough that she had moved from her spot beside him and back up onto it as though to demand his attention. She'd look up at him almost disapprovingly when he stopped petting her. But now, Elliot's attention was focused outside the window.

There were trees outside, which was ordinary, and even a few buildings, or perhaps they were houses. They were smaller than most. But what really caught his attention were the shelves full of books, all stacked neatly and evenly.

As the train moved on, it became apparent that the number of shelves were increasing. The decorations on the shelves were becoming more elaborate, like some sort of foreshadowing for what was to come.

Elliot noted one shelf in particular that reminded him vaguely of those marble ancient Greek designs with golden leaves popping out of it in a curious show of texture. But it had passed so fast that Elliot felt he hadn't been given the proper amount of time to admire it.

Finally, the train began to slow until it had completely stopped. Elliot got up from his seat and Cairo jumped down off his lap. He looked down at his companion.

"I guess this is it." He said nervously, knowing all the while that he was, in fact, talking to a cat.

Somewhere in his mind he felt rather certain that she understood him quite well, however...or maybe he was just going crazy.

Elliot decided not to think about that any further. He was in the Kingdom of Dreams. He might be about to meet the king. How was one supposed to greet a king anyways?

He once recalled his father scolding him and his brother for eating too quickly, saying something along the lines of "is that how you would eat in front of the queen?" Thankfully, he wouldn't have to eat in front of the king, what with being dead and all. Elliot wasn't entirely sure that his good manners were even good enough to be displayed in the presence of royalty.

Cairo rubbed up against his leg comfortingly.

"Let's go." Elliot told her, starting his walk off to where he'd first entered.

CHAPTER SIX

The King of Dreams

He opened the door of the car, then closed it behind him after Cairo had trotted out onto the grass.

"Welcome!"

Streamers burst out from Elliot's left and his right. A strange man with dark skin and crazy frizzy hair that went off in every which direction had been the one to speak. The only thing that kept his hair down was the golden crown on top of his head. His legs were abnormally long and the strange pastel blue dress suit made him look even stranger. He wore a tie-dye dress shirt beneath his jacket with a loose, red tie around his neck.

He hadn't seen him when he'd exited the train cart, yet, there he was. His words seemingly having brought him into existence the moment he'd turned to close the door.

"Welcome, traveler, to the Kingdom of Dreams!" the man burst out into obnoxious laughter that set Elliot on edge.

A strange looking man dressed up in a black suit wearing dark sunglasses unrolled a scroll. His hair was grey as slate and his face was abnormally pale. Though not as pale as Time, Elliot recalled absently.

He cleared his throat, then he coughed, and then, he made a sort of short choking noise. Elliot wondered if he was really alright. After nearly a minute of coughing and grunting, he finally spoke.

"Now announcing, his royal highness. Ruler of the Kingdome of Dreams. King Slomoe the first!" he quickly dropped the scroll and applauded.

"Thank you! Thank you. Please...hold your applause." The Dream king raised a hand for silence.

The man stopped clapping and bowed off to the side. Elliot wondered if he ought to have clapped as well, though he was a little too...shocked to really do much of anything.

"I am King Slomoe." The man, Slomoe introduced.

"Uh, it's very nice to meet you...your highness." Elliot added the last part quickly, recalling that that was what people said when addressing royalty, "My name is Elliot Crow."

"Elliot Crow." Slomoe repeated as though testing the name and judging whether it was even worthy to be spoken out loud. He gave a nod, though Elliot had no clue what he was nodding about.

"It has been...Green, how long has it been?" Slomoe looked at the man who had announced him.

"One year and eight months, your majesty." The older man bowed.

"Yes, of course it was, Green." Slomoe dismissed, as though having known that all along, "It's been one year and eight months since the last time I've had a visitor. I do wish people would come more often." He sighed, before brightening again and looking at Elliot, "And what brings you, young Mister Crow to my domain?"

"I..." Elliot looked down at Cairo, as though wondering for a moment if she knew what was going on. He looked back up at Slomoe immediately, "I was told by Trinket...Trinket Deadlock that you might be able to help me."

"Go on." He waved his hand, as though motioning for Elliot to continue.

Elliot reached back inside himself for his resolve. His eyes found Slomoe's and he spoke slowly,

"Someone is trying to kill my brother, my older brother, Casper. I died, but he's still alive and I need to warn him. Please take me as your apprentice so that I can save him." Not really knowing what else to do, he bowed, right from the waist as he'd seen the announcer man, Green do only moments before.

He closed his eyes, praying that Slomoe would say yes. He heard the king hum to himself, mulling the proposition over.

"No."

Elliot tensed up, eyes opening wide with disbelief. This was his only chance. His mind wandered back to Trinket's and Gear's air ship, his fears about whether they were alright or not, his brother...He straightened.

"Please?" he tried again, "Please."

Slomoe shook his head,

"Dreams are a dangerous place, and I don't take on apprentices who cannot believe in themselves."

There it was again, what Trinket had told him before about believing in himself. He couldn't give up though. He'd gotten this far already and there was no way he could possibly go back.

"Is there anything I can do to change your mind? I'll do anything."

Slomoe stroked his chin thoughtfully,

"Anything, you say?"

He was undeterred by the spark in the king's eyes that promised something unpleasant. He needed to trust himself, right? So why not trust himself to complete whatever task the king gave him? Whatever it was, he could do it. *I can do it.* He repeated it in his head over and over again.

"Alright, then." Slomoe nodded, "I will give you a test. If you pass, then I'll take you on as my apprentice. If you fail..."

"I won't fail." Elliot's eyes sparked with a fire.

His mind went over what he'd been through in only the past day alone. He'd managed to find Trinket, he'd been propelled out of an airship during a lightning storm in order to board a moving train. If he could do all that, then he could do this. He could believe in himself.

Slomoe raised an amused eyebrow,

"That's the spirit! Well then, let's see..." he snapped his fingers, as though the idea had just occurred to him, "You shall retrieve for me a crystal heart from within the realm of reflections."

Elliot felt his stomach sink.

"The realm of reflection is a dangerous place, especially for those who don't trust themselves. For you, this option is out." He recalled Trinket telling him.

If being lowered onto the back of a moving train during a lightning storm was a safer option, then would he really be okay? He looked back up at Slomoe. If he didn't go, then he wouldn't be able to get the apprenticeship. If he didn't get the apprenticeship, he couldn't communicate with his family.

"Okay." Elliot said, "How do I get there?"

A dark look passed over Slomoe's face, but it was gone so quick that Elliot wondered if he'd only imagined it.

"Through a mirror, of course." The king grinned widely, "But for now you can rest, perhaps have a cup of tea? You did just arrive here, after all and it has been so long since I've had any visitors."

Elliot nodded his head hesitantly. He really wanted to get on with his journey. He needed to keep going or he'd never get to warn his family about the man that had killed him.

"Green." The king clapped his hands, "Go tell Orange to organize some tea for the two of us, some good tea, if you please."

"Yes your majesty!" Green straightened, then with a surprising amount of energy for his age, took off down the grass and into the maze of books.

Was everyone here named after a color? Elliot mused to himself.

"This way, Elliot Crow." Slomoe pointed in the exact opposite direction in which Green had scampered off to, then started walking on a path to the right, a completely different direction in which he'd pointed and nowhere near close to the direction Green had run off.

Elliot was momentarily stumped on which way the strange king wished for him to go until he said, "Follow me!"

He quickly walked after him and Cairo padded by his side.

"Is that your familiar?" Slomoe looked down at the cat curiously.

"Yes, she is." Elliot nodded, "Her name's Cairo."

"Cairo..." Slomoe tested, "A decent name. I would have gone with something more along the lines of 'Anialialia.'"

Cairo looked rather put out by the strange sounding name, but Elliot didn't say anything, worried he might insult him.

"But Cairo's good." The king finished, "Do you like sweets?"

A little startled at the sudden change in topic, Elliot nodded,

"I guess, I can't really eat them now though."

Slomoe nodded in agreement,

"Right, you *said* you were dead. Did you know you're covered in blood?" His voice, at least in the first sentence was rather doubtful, but amused at the same time, as though knowing something Elliot didn't.

Despite knowing, Elliot looked down anyways. Even though the blood seemed to have dried and was now a brownish color, it was still, quite obviously, blood.

"Y-yeah. I'm aware." Elliot grimaced, wondering if he was going to have to find some clothes. He'd already spent a night in the ones he was wearing and he was feeling gross and uncomfortable. Slomoe seemed to have given up his attempts at a conversation in favour of humming a strangely off-beat tune that poked and prodded at the back of his brain with familiarity.

He shouldn't know that song, Elliot couldn't help but think to himself, even though he couldn't pick out exactly what the tune was himself.

They walked through a small entry between five very wide and tall book shelves set up in the shape of a pentagon. In the center was a long, wooden table that stretched out for nearly twenty feet and lined with mismatched chairs of all colors, sizes and shapes.

Slomoe took a seat at the very end of the table, then gave a gesture,

"Please, sit, sit." He indicated the seat next to him, yet Elliot got the sense that that wasn't at all where he actually wanted him to sit.

He moved towards the indicated chair, only for the feeling to nag at him just a little more. With a flash back to his death and Trinket's words of "*trust yourself!*" echoing through his mind, he opted to sit in the spot he felt would likely be the most comfortable.

Slomoe raised an eyebrow but didn't at all appear to be insulted by his choice.

"Perhaps I misjudged you, Elliot Crow." He hummed thoughtfully, breaking the tune he'd been using previously, "Perhaps you do have potential to trust yourself."

Slomoe poured himself some tea from a steaming pot by his right, filling up a white china tea cup. One that looked exactly the sort that one might use for important guests or on special occasions. Or maybe one that his mother and her friends would use no matter the occasion.

It suddenly clicked in Elliot's head where he had heard that tune before. It was something his father used to sing. He'd probably written it for his mother back in their high school days in an attempt to impress her. He'd written several poems and songs trying to gain her attention.

Underneath a bloody moon,
The spider lilies bloom.
As the months of Autumn come to lie,
The banks of grief from mid-July.
It's time to watch the summer die,
It's time to watch the summer die.
Now, the cursed flowers bloom.
Until the frosted reaper come,
And in gloomy sheaves of grey,
Shall claim the cursed blossoms slain.
Goodbye again.
Just you and me,
Trapped inside lost memories.
Then meet again someday.
Someday...

Elliot had heard his father sing the song enough times that the words had been burned into his soul. His father had always claimed that it was by far his worst work. Perhaps not the words, but the rhythm of the song its self was simply too out of beat and awkward when paired with the words that it gave the poem a peculiar sort of sound. But it was his mother's favourite.

He'd never heard mention of spider lilies outside of his father's song, so he'd looked it up long ago, bewildered by the flower and why his mother seemed to find them so romantic.

Of course, spider lilies turned out to be a symbol of death and hell. A blood red flower famous for blooming in graveyards.

Spider lilies haunt my dreams.

"Where did you hear that song?" Elliot finally asked Slomoe, "The one you were humming?"

Slomoe appeared amused at the question, setting down the tea he'd been slurping.

"Where do you think? Elliot Crow, Elliot Crow, there are many Elliot Crows out there. But I know which one is which." Slomoe tapped his head, a smirk playing on his lips that reminded Elliot of Sam when he was about to try something that might impress either him or Melisa.

"I am the King of Dreams!" He spread his arms out wide, "Of course I would know! It is the one song that was written for you, ya know?"

Elliot furrowed his brow,

"My dad wrote that song for my mother."

"No, no, no." Slomoe shook his head, "Are you the King of Dreams? No? I am, you say? Well then, I certainly know what I'm talking about. Your father dreamed that song just before you were born. He wrote lots of poems and songs for your mum, but that song in particular was meant for you." He pointed at Elliot who was thrown for a loop momentarily.

His father had written that song for him?

"Wanted te write a song about new beginnings. He thought ye'd be a bit like your mum. A bit uncertain, at first before you grew out of it and figured out who you were. It was a nice dream, of course."

Elliot tried not to feel insulted, but it felt like he was being told that he hadn't lived up to those expectations. He wanted to lash out, before a sense of gloom fell over him. Maybe he really hadn't lived up to his father's dream. He wasn't sure of himself. Most people weren't of course, but he was starting to realize that he really didn't know who he was.

He'd gone most of his life so focused on trying to be normal that he hadn't really contemplated his own identity. Now, in a world where it seemed quite normal to be at least a little bit eccentric, Elliot found himself with time aplenty for such ponderings.

He looked down at his empty tea cup. He hadn't poured anything for himself, but he found himself craving something to sip on.

"Might I have some tea?" Elliot looked up at the king who smiled in an amused way. Though Slomoe seemed to be amused with everything anyways.

"Of course. Catch!"

Elliot barely had time to think before the tea pot was slid across the table towards him. He quickly grabbed the handle.

"Good, good. Excellent reflexes." Slomoe nodded approvingly.

Elliot poured himself some tea to drink, before sliding it down the table back to Slomoe who refilled his own cup. Elliot took a sip. It was a sweeter concoction and he actually found that he enjoyed Trinket's blend better.

Only two days and I'm already acquiring a taste for tea, Elliot thought to himself.

"Before you go to the realm of reflections," Trinket interrupted himself, "Let me give you a bit of advice." He leaned forward onto the table, staring at his cup and swirling the tea around in a luxurious sort of way. He looked back over at Elliot, "Always believe in yourself. You won't survive long if you don't."

"Trinket told me the same thing." Elliot said in an unusually quiet voice.

Slomoe hummed,

"Trinket Deadlock was always very adept at advice giving." He seemed to agree, "What he might not have told you, is that there are two steps to believing in yourself. The first step is to trust your instincts. The second is to believe you can do something, no matter how impossible it might seem to others and no matter what you're told. You're a bit odd, you know? It seems you did the second step before the first!"

"I did?" Elliot wondered.

"Of course, you did!" Slomoe exclaimed, looking surprised as though Elliot really ought to know this already, "You *believe* that you can save your brother. You *believe* that you can contact your loved ones and warn them of the danger no matter what other people throw at you. But, you still have a very bad habit of not trusting your own instincts, and they're very good instincts too." He looked Elliot up and down appraisingly.

A bad habit, Elliot thought, thinking that was a rather peculiar way to describe it. He did find himself agreeing though. It had been his own fault that he had died, having gone off when his instincts had warned him not to, even when his friend had warned him not to.

"Once you start a habit," Slomoe said a little calmer than before and far soberer than Elliot had heard him speak so far, "good or bad, it becomes very difficult to break. I stand by what I said before. I will only take you as my apprentice if you can retrieve a crystal heart from the realm of reflections."

"I'll do it." The words were out of Elliot's mouth before he could stop them.

No, Elliot thought to himself, he didn't have room for doubt now. He couldn't doubt himself. He needed to save Casper and if he had any hope of accomplishing that, he needed to enter the realm of reflections.

Slomoe had told him that there were two steps to believing in ones' self, which meant he needed to focus on those. Whether he was psychic like Sam claimed (and he was starting to think that maybe that was an actual possibility), or whether it was just a very good intuition, it didn't matter anymore.

Cairo jumped up onto his lap and looked up at him with her wide, green eyes. Elliot got a strange feeling that she wanted to help him. He looked up at Slomoe,

"Do you mind if I take Cairo with me?"

Slomoe raised an eyebrow,

"Far be it from me to separate a wizard from his familiar. Do as you please, ya know?"

A wizard? Elliot wondered to himself. He decided he'd ask Slomoe what he meant when he got back. It was something he did often when he wanted to give himself incentive to see someone again, to leave a question hanging. Maybe it was a form of stubbornness, or maybe it was just a personality quirk.

Elliot finished up his tea,

"Thank you, your majesty, the tea was very delicious." He complimented.

"Of course, of course." Slomoe waved casually, then got up, a single eyebrow raised in an inquisitive manner, "I assume you wish to go now, then?"

"If I may?" Elliot agreed.

Slomoe gave him another look of amusement,

"You're unusually polite, ya know?"

Was he? Elliot wondered a bit to himself.

"Especially for a teenager." Slomoe shook his head, "But, then again, the last teenager I met enjoyed adding in curses to every second word."

"Gear?" Elliot guessed, unable to think of anyone else who had a mouth like hers.

"Yeah, that one." Slomoe agreed, "You'd look very good in a hat, ya know?" Elliot paused again, once again a little bit startled by the sudden change in topic. It seemed that Slomoe got bored when they stayed on one subject for too long.

"Maybe not one of them knit hats that the teens wear, but a top hat." Elliot had no plans on wearing a top hat but decided it best to nod along politely anyways.

"I...hadn't considered that." He said honestly.

"You don't consider much."

Was that a jab? Elliot wondered.

"Oh, where is Blue?" Slomoe frowned, "Blue? BLUE!"

After a long silence that seemed to stretch out over nearly five minutes, a man came running into the clearing. His face was pale and sweat appeared to be forming on his brow.

"Where is my mirror? I need the mirror. Elliot Crow is going to enter the realm of reflections now."

Now? Elliot knew he was ready...sort of. But what was with the sudden transition? The man, Blue, bowed at the waist then ran off back into the maze of book shelves. Slomoe clucked his tongue,

"Really, you'd think he'd already know what I wanted. Blue doesn't speak, ya know?"

Elliot nodded, not really knowing what to say.

"He's mute. Had his voice stolen by the witch of the masquerade. Well, no real loss, ya know?"

Slomoe seemed to say 'ya know' a lot, Elliot thought absently. It made him want to nod along, even though he got the sense that he wasn't asking for any sort of confirmation. He did have a question though,

"Who's the witch of the masquerade?" Elliot asked him curiously.

A smile formed on Slomoe's face. It appeared slowly, as though the corners of his mouth were crawling up towards his cheeks.

"The witch of the masquerade, she steals voices, ya know? Collects them. Of course, she can only take your voice if you show her any sort of emotion. Trinket was the only person ever known to have outwitted her. 'Course now she's obsessed with him, wants his voice for her collection. That's why he's one of the most famous wizards out there, ya know?"

Elliot actually hadn't known that. Trinket was famous? Then again, Time had known him, and so had Slomoe. That was two people who were considered gods in their own right who knew Trinket by name.

Blue came back, carrying a large mirror decorated in a golden frame. He set it down in front of Elliot. A voice rang through Elliot's head warning him that there was something wrong with the mirror.

"This isn't a normal mirror." Elliot said uncertainly.

Slomoe hummed, approaching Elliot from behind, and then, caught off guard, he gave Elliot a mighty push, sending him into the glass.

CHAPTER SEVEN

Tapping on Glass

It felt like he was falling into water. The world cracked around him as the mirror swallowed him up. It looked a bit like the world had been covered in a spider's web. Although, it would certainly have to be a very large spider to spin a web like that.

Disoriented and momentarily unable to figure out down from up, Elliot fell forward, crashing to the ground.

He grimaced, noting a scrape on his hands that appeared to be oozing with black liquid. The wound knitted its self together quickly before Elliot pushed himself off the ground, slowly getting to his feet. He felt the need to be cautious.

The grass was green, he observed. Not silver like in the kingdom of dreams. In fact, Elliot found himself in a field that appeared rather similar to the park back home.

It was the park back home! Elliot realized.

"Mroaw."

Elliot looked down to find Cairo looking right up at him, warning him.

"Okay," Elliot spoke out loud, "This must be the realm of reflections." He guessed, knowing that Cairo wouldn't be talking back to him, but finding his talking to her helped to sort his thoughts, "But why does it look like Blackstone?" he wondered, "You'd think it would look like a reverse kingdom of dreams or something. We did just enter a mirror."

Cairo let out another meow, but Elliot felt words enter his head, like a voice that Elliot might imagine Cairo would sound like if she was human.

Those with responsibilities cannot intrude on another person's realm.

"I see." Elliot said, not at all deterred by the fact that he was hearing voices, "So then...this is a reflection of the real world...then there must be someone here with responsibilities." He realized the last part rather suddenly.

Of course, there is.

Elliot gave a nod,

"Alright. All I have to do is find a crystal heart then go back." Although he had no idea how he was going to get back.

There was no copy of the mirror he'd come through, which meant he'd have to find another way back to the Kingdome of Dreams.

He really hoped he wouldn't have to jump onto a moving train again. Deciding it would do him no good to simply sit around, he picked a direction to walk in.

"I wonder," Elliot thought out loud once again, "what do you think they did with my room? Do you think the realm of reflection would show that?"

Cairo sent him a wary look.

"Come on, just one look." Elliot promised, "I just...want to see my home." He started walking before Cairo could even protest. There was no one around. In fact, the whole place looked like a ghost town. Sometimes he'd see objects being moved, as though lifted by invisible people. Elliot paused, staring in the glass of a window. They were downtown, where a lot of people hung out on their days off. In the glass, he could see crowds of people moving about. Yet, there were none in the world that Elliot saw.

"So then," Elliot spoke, "That's the real world."

There were no people in the world of mirrors, only a reflection. An illusion even. Hadn't his mother said something about mirrors? Legends or something? He couldn't really remember. It was starting to frustrate him just how little he'd paid attention to her.

When he got close to the glass, he could hear them. It was a little bit muted, but Elliot figured it had something to do with his looking at the ghostly reflection of something that wasn't necessarily meant to reflect as a mirror was.

So then, Elliot thought to himself, maybe he could contact his parents if he saw them in a mirror!

With a new determination, he continued his walk towards his house. He was a bit far away, but that didn't deter him any.

On a whim, he went down to the train station, deciding that since there were cars moving about with invisible drivers, that the train was likely running too.

Surely enough, after a wait of six minutes exactly, the train arrived at the station. Only one door opened and Elliot got on.

The train didn't often have many passengers and he realized, when he did get off at the stop by his house, that he was very lucky to have had someone on board open the door to allow him off.

It almost seemed surreal as he traveled off into the alley, everything was reversed, mirrored and it left him somewhat disoriented. But he found his way home again after accidentally taking a wrong turn. He opened the door, wondering at the strange ability of his to affect this mirror world and wondering if the real world was reflected just as the mirror world was.

He didn't bother taking off his shoes, looking about to try and find a mirror, something he could use to communicate.

The hallway mirror! He thought to himself, running off up the stairs. He couldn't see anyone in the reflection. He sat down on the steps, waiting for someone to get close, to find any indication that they were there, that he wasn't just waiting in vain.

He stubbornly sat there until his legs started to fall asleep and his butt started to grow numb. It must have been an hour, Elliot estimated. Nearly an hour before he heard the door opening behind him. In the reflection of the mirror he saw someone come out of his room.

It was his father. Damien Crow always worked from home. It was where he was most comfortable. If Elliot was going to come across anyone while he was home, it was going to be him. He was looking worried about something. Concerned, even.

"Dad!" Elliot called.

His father didn't seem to hear him, walking towards the stairs. Elliot banged his fists against the glass,

"Dad! Come on! You need to listen! Casper's in danger! You need to listen!" His father looked up momentarily, then seemed to double-take. He could see him, Elliot realized with relief. His father could see him.

"Elliot?" Damien Crow gapped. He looked around, trying to find his son in the hallway. But he wasn't there.

"You need to listen!" Elliot shouted at him, "Casper's in danger!"

"What?" his father's voice came desperately, "Elliot, I can't hear you!" Elliot stepped back, realizing he wasn't going to be able to get anywhere if no one could hear him. What could he do?

His mouth formed a grim line. Maybe if he mouthed the words?

"Casper!" He said, "Cas-per!" he repeated slower.

"Casper?" his father tried, "What about Casper?"

"Danger!" Elliot shouted.

His father looked confused, so Elliot tried again.

"Danger!" Elliot said, "Da-n-ger." He made certain to exaggerate each sound.

"Danger?" his father repeated.

Elliot nodded his head.

"Casper's in danger?"

"Yes!" Elliot nodded quickly. Glad that he'd finally gotten his message across.

"What danger?" His father asked him, "Why's Casper in danger? Is it the person that hurt you? Is he going to come after Casper?"

Elliot nodded again. He'd never really been good at charades, but he was starting to wish that had been a talent of his. Wait...there was something wrong.

He couldn't quite pick it out, but it was something to do with what his father had said. Something that seemed...off.

Cairo let out a hiss and Elliot turned around suddenly. Black shadows were crawling towards him. Like the tendrils of some creature Elliot had never seen before creeping up the stairs. His instincts screamed at him to run.

He took one last look at his father, before he took off.

"Elliot!" He heard his father's voice behind him as he rounded the corner into his room.

Cairo was behind him. Elliot closed the door, then looked around wildly, trying to find an exit. The window! He opened it up and started working at the screen. He gave it a kick and it partially gave in. The darkness was slowly making its way through the crack beneath his door. He gave the screen another kick, then started tearing the screen apart by hand, ripping it off. He grabbed Cairo who shot him a dark look.

You promised there would be no more jumping!

"I promised there would be no more jumping from trees." Elliot argued, "There's a difference. And it's not like we have much of a choice now."

Cairo seemed to agree reluctantly as Elliot picked her up in his arm. With his free hand, he hoisted himself onto the ledge and jumped.

He awkwardly landed on the roof of the shed, sliding down but managing to get a foothold at the last moment in the small divot where the roofing ended.

"We need to find that crystal heart." Elliot said.

He let Cairo go, allowing her to hop up onto the fence. She gave a small gesture with her head, as thought to say,

Follow me.

Elliot didn't hesitate, following after the ginger tabby, balancing on the top of the fence. He looked over his shoulder, noting the tendrils of black were crawling down the side of the house.

Cairo started running, and Elliot ran after her in an amazing show of balance that even he hadn't known he possessed.

He hopped down after Cairo, rushing after her and turning down the back alley. What was a crystal heart anyways? He probably should have asked that before accepting the task, Elliot mused to himself.

It's a dangerous world if you don't believe in yourself.

CHAPTER EIGHT

A Game of Words

By the time Elliot felt safe, he had already run all the way across town, but Cairo hadn't stopped. A crystal heart was what he needed. A crystal heart…and he still didn't know what one of those looked like.

Cairo started to slow down and Elliot slowed with her. He could sense it too, that something was wrong. There was a pressure in the air that added more weight to Elliot's shoulders. It wasn't necessarily bad, but it wasn't particularly good either.

"Cairo." Elliot warned.

The cat seemed to understand his unspoken words and got a little closer to him. He turned around suddenly, just in time to see the shadows again. He cursed under his breath, then he and Cairo took off running.

How was he supposed to find a crystal heart (whatever that was) if he was spending all his time running from the shadows?

"You're not very good at this, are you?"

Elliot turned suddenly, his head snapping to the side. A boy who had not been there before was running beside him. He looked younger than him. He was obviously of Asian descent, and a lot younger than Elliot, maybe ten or eleven. He was dressed in shorts and a white t-shirt, rather plain but comfortable for the coming hot summer weather.

"How about a game?"

"Where did you come from?" Elliot's eyes widened with panic. He certainly couldn't take care of himself, Cairo and another person. Not when he was already struggling with the first two.

It took him about a second to realize just how ridiculous that thought was. The kid must know where he was, inside the mirror. So, he must also know the danger he was in.

"Come on, already, let's play a game of words."

Elliot knew that if he looked over his shoulder he'd be doomed, so he kept running, trying to ignore the shadows behind him.

"The game is simple." The boy said, either oblivious to the fact that he was being ignored, or simply not caring, "I pick a category. The category is 'animals.' Now, say an animal. Come on, hurry, before we're caught!"

"Animals?" Elliot finally picked up on what he was saying. How on earth was that supposed to help!? He saw a shadow creeping along the edge of the street.

Pick an animal already! He heard someone scream.

"Bat!" Elliot shouted.

The shadow to his right was stopped suddenly, as though having hit a wall.

"Good." The boy breathed a sigh or relief, "Now I say the name of an animal that begins with the letter yours ended with. Bat...that's a 'T'..."

Elliot had to jump when he felt something nip at his right heel.

"Tarantula!" the boy exclaimed happily.

Elliot risked a glance over his shoulder. The shadows had been blocked, they'd even slowed down a little bit. Elliot faced forward again, wracking his brain.

"Alligator." Elliot said quickly. The two of them turned a corner.

"That's an 'R,' right?" The boy pondered, scrunching his brow, "Rat."

"Tiger." Elliot responded almost immediately this time.

The boy started to slow and Elliot found himself slowing as well, as did Cairo. The small cat was panting and Elliot wondered if she could even go on much longer. He looked back up at the boy that had apparently saved him,

"Um, thanks for saving me back there." Elliot said uncertainly.

"No problem." The boy waved away, "But why are you here? You do know that the mirror world is dangerous, right?"

"I know." Elliot said quickly, "But I need to find a crystal heart." Maybe he'd be able to help him.

"A crystal heart?" The boy shook his head, "That's impossible." He finally said, "You should just go back."

"I can't." Elliot said, "I need one to save my brother. I can't go back yet." The boy crossed his arms, looking Elliot over appraisingly.

"Well, you did help me defeat the shadows...But the only place I can think of where you might be able to find a crystal heart is in the Kingdom of Mirrors. You don't want to go there, trust me."

"Why not?" Elliot asked him, "Why don't I want to go to the Kingdom of Mirrors?" he was starting to grow sick of all these new problems that kept coming up. He just wanted to save his brother.

"Because the ruler, she takes people's souls. The shadows, they're controlled by her." The boy shifted, "She's not someone that a wizard with no training can get past. You should just leave, before she catches you."

"I need to save my brother." Elliot said again, his voice was firm and unwavering. He couldn't leave until he did what he needed to do, and he wasn't going to leave until he found a crystal heart.

He couldn't just let his brother die, not when he could do something about it, and he would do something about it. Casper could be the most annoying person in the world, but he did care for him, even though he'd never actually admit it out loud.

"I'm Toshi." The boy introduced, he looked at Elliot with a certain wariness not found on the faces of most children.

Appearances are deceiving.

"I'm Elliot." Elliot introduced himself. He looked at Toshi again, trying to figure out what about him was setting him on edge. It wasn't that he didn't think Toshi could be trusted. Actually, he got the sense that he *could* be trusted, and Elliot rarely trusted people right off the bat like that.

Appearances are deceiving, Elliot repeated in his head, deciding it was some sort of hint.

"It's nice to meet you." Toshi said, giving a slight dip of his chin, "If you ever need to ward away shadows, you can play that game again, the game of words. It's stronger if it's played with more than one person, but it will still work if it's just you."

That was good to know, Elliot thought, realizing just how close he'd come to being captured earlier. Having some sort of defense against those things would certainly be helpful in the future if Toshi wasn't around.

"Words are powerful." Toshi told him, "So...you want to get to the Kingdom of Mirrors?"

"Yes." Elliot said, "Can you tell me where it is?"

"I'll tell you how to get there." Toshi decided, "But, in return, could you do me a favour?"

"A favour?" Elliot repeated, feeling his unease climbing. Why did people keep asking him for favours, anyways?

But, looking around at the desolate ghost town that was the reflection of Blackstone, Elliot knew that he wouldn't have much of a choice in the matter. There was no one else around he could ask directions from. No one else to tell him where he ought to go, or how to defend against the woman who ruled over the Kingdom of Mirrors.

"Alright." Elliot decided, "What's the favour?"

Toshi seemed to brighten, relief painted his features, making Elliot question whether he had ever thought he'd accept.

"The Witch who controls this world stole something important from me." Toshi explained, "It's a mirror. But the glass is black. Miranda, the witch, she has a special office at the top of the tower. Um, it's the east tower. When you face the door, it will be the one that's forward and to the right. At the very top of the tower is the office. I have no doubt that she keeps crystal hearts there too." He sounded a bit bitter as he spoke the last part.

"I understand." Elliot nodded, "I'll do it. If it's on the way anyways, I suppose I might as well..."

Toshi nodded, but there was a look of worry in his eyes,

"I can't enter, so you'll have to go yourself." He reached into his back pocket and took out a single key made entirely out of glass. He thrust it forward and Elliot held out his hand quickly in response, taking the strange object.

"Turn it twice around in any lock, then open the door and you'll find yourself in the Kingdom of Mirrors. It works both ways. Whatever you do, don't lose that." Toshi warned him.

"I won't." Elliot promised. He was a little worried that it might break due to how delicate it appeared to be.

He looked around, noticing several houses nearby all of which, obviously having front doors and locks to put a key in. He took a step towards the nearest house. He paused a moment, then looked back over at Toshi.

"I'll be back." He said, though more for himself than for the strange boy that had saved his life. For some reason, making a promise out loud made him feel like it would be easier to fulfil, that he was far more likely to return if he made the promise to return to someone, especially now that he was more aware of the dangers he'd be facing. Or maybe less aware.

The more he found out about this strange world the less he felt he knew.

He turned around, forcing himself not to look back as he made his way up the walkway to one of the houses. He stopped at the door, taking out the glass key. It fit inside the lock perfectly, even though it looked like it probably shouldn't have. He turned the key twice around. The door gave a soft 'click' swinging open of its own accord.

The inside was certainly not a house, but some sort of open space. He withdrew the key from the lock, putting it in his back pocket. Cairo paused, looking down at the cut off line between the ghost-town version of Blackstone and the path in front of her made of white glass.

It was Elliot who took the first step. As soon as his foot touched the ground, he felt something like an electric shock. Undeterred, he took another step forward. Now both his feet were on the glass walkway. Cairo walked out in front of him, staring over at a large castle which appeared to be made out of white marble. It looked a lot like those old, ancient Greek buildings that Elliot had only seen in picture. He jumped a little bit when the door behind them closed. The path appeared to be floating in the middle of nowhere with nothing to support it, as did the castle which sat on a round ground of white glass.

"No going back now." Elliot whispered, not until he had done what he'd set out to do. He turned back to the castle, there was something deeply unsettling about it. Like it wasn't quite right. If Elliot were to try and put it into words, he would say that the building looked sick. Though of course that was a bit ridiculous, considering that inanimate objects most certainly did not catch illnesses. Or maybe they did. Elliot had seen so many out of the way things as of late that he wasn't entirely sure what could be considered ridiculous and what might be considered reasonable.

Elliot opted to stand still, staring at the enormous castle for just a little while longer, before Cairo seemed to get bored and started walking ahead. Elliot took this as his cue to follow behind the cat.

They both stopped when they heard something. A deep rumble coming from beneath their feet. Black shadows jutted up from the sides of the path.

Elliot's mind went blank a moment before he broke into a run, Cairo following by his side.

"Game of words." Elliot recalled, "Animals...um, uh, cat!" he said quickly.

The shadows that had been reaching for him and Cairo were repelled backwards, as though bouncing off a trampoline.

"Tortoise!" Elliot tried, thankful the shadows were growing rather sluggish now, and only after two words!

"E...elephant!"

That had been a close one. He wasn't in the clear yet. The walkway was strangely not slippery, and one would think it would be, considering what he thought the material was made of.

"Tiger." Elliot said, using the word he'd used in his previous game with Toshi, "Uh, racoon. Nymph. Hippopotamus! S...S...What starts with an 'S'?" try as he might, he was stuck.

They were so close to the door of the castle. Should they even enter through the front door? They were technically breaking and entering, after all.

He tried the door, only to realize it was locked. He probably should have expected that. His eyes widened as he turned around.

"Snake!"

The shadow was repelled backwards again and Elliot let out a sigh of relief. He could have sworn Cairo was glaring at him,

Seriously? It took you that long to come up with 'snake'?

Elliot shrugged his shoulders weakly, not sure what he was supposed to say to her.

"Eel." Elliot said again, knowing he'd have to keep this up, "Come on, Cairo, let's go around and try to find a window."

The two of them veered off to the right as Elliot tried to keep up the game of words.

"Lama. Aardvark. Kangaroo. Ostrich."

He'd never been particularly fond of word games, and Elliot was rather sure he'd run out of words soon. He found a window, several of them by the side, but none of them could be opened. He slammed his elbow up against one, but couldn't quite break the glass.

"Hamster." Elliot said quickly when one of the shadows was approaching.

He picked up a white stone that looked like it was made out of the same material as the glass-like path and slammed it up against the window as hard as he could. It was useless though.

"Rat." Elliot said absently when he noticed another shadow getting too close.

Cairo looked up at Elliot with a hint of exasperation.

"Okay..." Elliot thought out loud, "I'm guessing...either the glass is special, or...maybe there's some sort of spell on it? Turtle." Another shadow was repelled backwards.

Think, Elliot! Elliot scrunched his face, trying to find a solution. He jumped out of the way of another attack.

"Elk!" Elliot shouted. The shadow was driven into the stone wall of the castle. Elliot raised an eyebrow as he noted a large chunk of stone had fallen off the wall.

Maybe, Elliot thought, moving in front of the window.

"Come and get me!" he shouted, daring them to attack. His hands twitched and his legs felt shaky, ready to move at a moment's notice.

The shadows didn't seem all that intelligent, so maybe he could trick them into breaking the glass for him. Once the barrier around Elliot had worn off from his game of words, they struck. Elliot dove to the left at the very last second.

"Koala!" he shouted, nearly overriding the sound of breaking glass.

He got up to his feet quickly. Cairo was giving him an impressed look.

"No need to look so surprised." Elliot felt a little bit proud that his plan had actually worked, "Come on, I'll help you in first." He paused, noting that the shadows appeared to be retreating.

"That can't be good." He murmured.

He shook himself from his stupor and helped Cairo in through the window, then climbed into the castle himself. He cut himself several times on the broken shards of glass, but didn't really feel it as he swung his legs over and jumped down to the ground. Cairo was waiting for him.

Elliot walked through the room slowly, the glass beneath his feet crackled and crunched like autumn leaves. He was in some sort of dining room. In his mind, he knew they couldn't be that far from the east tower. But he also got the sense that the witch that lived in the castle would likely be aware of the intruders in her domain.

The room seemed to lack color. Elliot looked around, noting the whites and blacks and greys that decorated the room. What little color there was seemed to have been washed out.

Elliot didn't want to be in the castle longer than he needed to, something about the place didn't sit well with him at all. Especially the mirror hanging off the wall perpendicular to the window he and Cairo had just come through. He walked by the table and around the edges of the room towards the door.

He turned the doorknob and pushed it open cautiously, looking both ways in case the owner might be on her way. Cairo trotted out first, completely fearless. Elliot walked out behind her, his muscles tense. He didn't really know what he would do if he actually was confronted by the witch. He didn't really know any spells. His only means of defense was the game of words and he had no clue if that would even work against an actual person.

With every step, Elliot could feel himself growing more and more uneased. The feeling of something being wrong was becoming more present. It took him a while before he started to notice that he must have been walking for nearly ten minutes without coming across any sort of room at all.

"Cairo, let's stop a moment." Elliot told the ginger tabby who was looking up at him curiously, "There's something not right." Elliot said, "Shouldn't we have come across more rooms by now? There were lots of windows outside, but there aren't any here, and no doors that seem to lead to rooms that have them." He crossed his arms, his face taking on a contemplative expression, "Do you think we might be traveling in circles?"

It was a peculiar conclusion, mainly because Elliot was sure the two of them had been walking in a straight line. But with magic, anything could be possible, right?

This was a trap, then. He probably should have realized it wouldn't be that simple, that the witch would have traps set up. She had sent shadows after him, after all.

But how was he supposed to break the spell? He knew nothing of magic, despite Slomoe's claim of him being a wizard.

"Some wizard." Elliot muttered to himself bitterly, "I can't even cast one spell."

Cairo brushed up against his leg encouragingly. Elliot offered her a weak smile. If he kept walking, he wouldn't be going anywhere. So, he did the only thing that seemed logic at that moment. He sat down, back pressed against the wall.

He wasn't about to give up. He still had a brother to save. He still needed to find the mirror the witch had stolen from Toshi and give it back. He still needed to find a crystal heart.

He looked at the wall opposite to him. The dreaded, blank wall. He took in a breath and closed his eyes. He often did that when he needed to think. He'd been told over and over to trust his instincts, and he'd done his best to trust those voices he often heard. Those voices that seemed so adamant to give him advice. He'd done all he could to trust his feelings on certain matters since arriving in the realm of reflection. But right now, he was coming up blank. His 'instincts' were unusually silent.

He opened his eyes when he felt Cairo brush up against him. He looked down at her curiously.

"Familiars can aid a spirit with interactions in the material world. They also aid in magic."

Elliot jolted, he never had figured out what Trinket had meant by that.

"Cairo," he looked down at the cat. For the first time, he actually acknowledged that maybe...maybe she actually was as intelligent any other human, that maybe she knew more than he did about such things as magic.

"Could *you* tell me, how I might get out of here?"

Cairo gave him an odd sort of look.

"You're my familiar." Elliot said, "And Trinket said that familiars can help with magic." The more he spoke, the more he felt he was off in his assumptions. Trinket had been implying something else. Something about familiars that he was missing. Something he wouldn't be discovering now.

"Okay..." Elliot got up from his spot and started to pace back and forth in front of the cat that was watching him curiously, wondering what he might try to do next.

"Trinket and Slomoe said I had magic." Elliot said, "That I could use magic."

Of course, silly boy. That you can use the game of words is proof enough of that. That you have a familiar should also have clued you in.

Elliot nodded his head, knowing he was spot on. He was a wizard, which meant he *could* use magic. But he didn't *know* how to use magic. Not properly. He was starting to think in circles and his thought processes were becoming far too redundant for his liking.

"Let's walk back." Elliot decided.

CHAPTER NINE

Sword of the Worthy

He started walking back in the direction they'd come from. Fifteen minutes was nothing compared to all the running they'd been doing as of late. Halfway there, he decided to pick up Cairo who appeared to be growing tired. He sometimes forgot that Cairo was still among the living and in need of rest. The pour cat had been running about all day and he didn't want her to tire out if they needed to start running again.

She leaped out of his arms though when she spotted a mouse running through the halls. Jumping on it and quickly digging in. Elliot waited for her, figuring it wasn't as though they didn't have time.

After nearly fifteen minutes, Elliot found the dinning room he'd broken into.

"So, it *is* still here." Elliot thought out loud, "Which means..." he trailed off, not really sure what that meant. It was about the only room he and Cairo had come across so far. Elliot walked inside, hoping beyond hope that he'd find something useful.

There wasn't really anything there though, other than books on a shelf, about five of them. Broken glass on the floor, the long table decorated with empty plates, cutlery and a large mirror that hung off the wall.

Wait? A mirror? In the Kingdom of Mirrors? Despite the name, it was about the only mirror he had seen so far and Elliot found himself curious.

He approached it, looking over at the window and realizing the shadows were gathered outside. If he went out now, he'd be chased. That didn't mean he didn't have a way back. He absently felt the glass key in his back pocket before looking into the mirror.

He didn't know what he had expected to see, but he was disappointed when he only saw himself. He was just about to turn away when something caught his eyes. He turned back to see that his reflection wasn't copying his movements. Not completely.

His mirror twin shot him a grin, then pointed up. Elliot slowly looked upwards at what appeared to be backwards writing at the very top, and a lot of it too.

Of course, Elliot thought, this was a mirror, so it would have to be a reflection.

ruoY .retaw eht ni fael A .noisiv A .noisulli na tub ,uoy ton ma I

?yhtrow uoy era tuB .eb lliw syawla tahw ton tub ,eb dluoc tahw wohs I .lous rouY .fles
laedi ruoY .erutuf

Elliot really wished he had something to write what he saw down so that he could work it out. Instead, he opted to go for the next best thing and read it out loud. He had to remind himself that he had time.

"I...am...not you, but an...illusion. A vision. A leaf in te – *the* water. Your future. Your...ideal self. I show what...could be." Elliot paused, mirror reading was starting to get a bit easier, "But not what always will be. But are you...worthy?" he looked back at his reflection who looked rather smug. Smirking at him. Daring him to prove that he was worthy of...whatever it was the mirror wanted him to be worthy of.

Was it some sort of riddle? Elliot wondered. Would it help him?

"An illusion." Elliot repeated, "Mirrors don't show what's really there...or...or maybe they do?" Elliot thought out loud, thinking back to his father. How Elliot had tapped against the glass, trying to warn his father of his murderer, about who the real target had been.

It made his head hurt trying to think about it. He'd never been much of a philosophe, nor was he all that good at riddles.

"A person's reflection." Elliot thought out loud, "They aren't really there. Yet, there is a whole other world within the mirrors. The realm of reflection where people can enter."

His reflection was staring back at him calmly.

"If I am a reflection, if I'm in the realm of reflections," Elliot thought to himself, sudden understanding dawning on him, "I'm in the mirror. I'm the reflection. But you aren't me. You don't show the truth, I guess you never claimed to." He conceded, "But no matter who you are, or what it is you want, could you please help me so that I can save my brother?"

His twin looked a bit sad, then said something that Elliot couldn't quite pick out.

"I'm sorry." Elliot apologised, "I can't hear you."

The reflection looked thoughtful, before he pointed, then shook his head.

"You can't leave?" Elliot guessed.

The reflection nodded in confirmation. Elliot crossed his arms, looking thoughtful. He rather wanted to help this other person, no matter their identity. A strange thought occurred to him.

"Reach into your back pocket." Elliot told him.

The reflection raised an inquiring eyebrow, reaching into his back pocket just as Elliot said, then taking out a glass key. He looked rather surprised and Elliot took the key from his own back pocket out.

"There was this boy who saved me, in the realm of reflection." Elliot explained, "He gave this to me to get here. He said you need to turn it in the door two times and you'd be able to leave. I don't know if it will work, but it's worth a try, right?" The reflection looked excited, nodding his head, then pressing the key up against the mirror. The glass rippled. Through the spider's web woven through the glass came a long object. The glass of the mirror glowed with a light so strong that Elliot was forced to shield his eyes.

When he sensed the intensity lessen, Elliot lowered his arm he'd used to shield himself from the light to see a sword floating in front of the mirror. The glass now showed a completely different scene. His town, but it was upside down.

His eyes fell once again on the sword, still half-sunk inside the mirror. He grabbed the hilt wrapped in a blue cloth, then with a mighty tug, he drew the sword from the glass.

He looked at the blade with awe. It was completely white, not silver as most blades were.

Elliot looked around, wondering if it was really alright to take this.

Well, he thought to himself, *I can always return it later.*

Right now, he needed some way passed the walls, and the sword was just about the only seemingly useful thing he had found up until then.

He looked down at Cairo,

"Let's see if this will help. Maybe if I work at it, I can break down a wall or something." He didn't know if that was possible.

He hadn't even been able to break a window, so how was he to be expected to break a wall?

He felt the sword vibrate in his grasp, as though it were trying to reassure him of something. This was a magic sword, Elliot realized. So maybe...maybe he really could break down a wall.

He slowly walked out into the hall. His paranoia forced him to cautiously peek out before stepping out of the dinning room. Cairo, once again had no such qualms, walking on ahead of Elliot.

He followed after his familiar and took a look around, wondering if this might be another trap.

It's not.

He felt himself relax a bit as the voice of his 'instincts' seemed to return.

"Okay." Elliot said mostly to himself, lifting the sword with both hands, he swung the sword down on the wall across from the lone room he'd just exited.

He was surprised when the sword actually passed through the wall before Elliot had to pull it out. It cut with ease, the sort that could only be explained by magic.

Elliot gave the wall another cut, this time horizontal to the damage he'd previously done. A ripple passed through the hall and Elliot fell back, the sword still clutched in his hands.

Before his eyes, rooms began to appear along the hall. The illusion, or the loop, or whatever it was had been dropped.

"The tower should be down this way." Elliot said firmly, a feeling of elation filling him up as he realized he'd actually done it. He'd broken the spell. Somehow.

CHAPTER TEN

The Boy in the Mirror

Once upon a time, a long, long time ago when the earth was only just coming into existence, there lived a benevolent king. By some strange quirk of fate, the king gained favour from the moon and the water, and so, it was decided that he would be one of those with responsibilities. Kagami, the king became ruler of the realm of reflections and continued to rule peacefully and in harmony with those with responsibilities for centuries onward. He rarely, if ever made enemies, always opting to leave his world open for anyone who wished to come. A sanctuary for those that needed it. And people did come, many people. People of all sorts and from all over. Young, old, wearing robes of gold, wearing rags, long hair, short hair, he was always surprised and fascinated by the people who came to visit him.

King Kagami found humans to be exceptionally interesting, growing obsessed with humanity, and making up an entire study out of it, with pictures and charts of all sorts. Yet, despite all the many people he befriended and all the lovely acquaintanceships he attained, there was a void deep within his heart that longed for something more. Perhaps it was his longing that had attracted the young witch, Viola. An Italian girl who had set off from her small hometown to aid those with ailments of the heart.

Kagami turned out to be, perhaps her most curious patient so far. He was not really seeking the love of a significant other. What Kagami longed for with all of his heart was a child. Someone to love and nurture, to hold and to raise. So, Viola set out to grant this wish.

To make a body was an easy task, to create a soul was just a little bit trickier and required something a little bit more. Using a fragment of the magic the king had used to create the passageway between his world, she used it to make the child's soul. And thus, on January fifteenth of the year fifteen ninety, a baby came into existence.

She approached the king herself with the newborn wrapped up in a nice blanket. Bowing her head low, she gently placed him in his arms.

"I have cured your ailment of the heart." Viola said, "This child is yours through and through. His soul was created with your magic, his body created from your glass."

The king looked at the sleeping baby boy with awe. He had never before seen something so incredible. So, beautiful. There were no words to describe him. The king was left speechless, wondering how anything in the world could be so perfect.

"My son." Kagami choked out. Tears fell down his face as he gazed longingly at the small miracle in his arms, "Toshi." He decided, the name came to him immediately. He looked like a Toshi. Like a reflection.

As time passed, Toshi grew up. He was loved and doted on by the king. Kagami proved to be a very good father, teaching his son the good of the world and sometimes, when it couldn't be helped, the bad. He would spend time teaching Toshi about people and introduce him to his friends. Some of which had children around the same age as Toshi.

Toshi's existence had been met with much worry and even a bit of fear. No one with responsibilities had ever had a child before. Some kept their children away from him, while there were others that were a little more open minded.

Growing up, Toshi had not been blinded by the fact that his existence was peculiar. Sometimes he would often wonder if he ought to have even existed in the first place. But he never dared voice those thoughts to his father. He knew the strain that those whispers and malicious looks put on him. Yet, he was also aware that if given the chance, he would go back into the past and beg Viola to create him all over again. It was something he often said to Toshi when he sensed his son's troubled mood.

After twenty years, Kagami started teaching his son magic, something that Toshi proved to be very talented in. The only problem was that Toshi's magic was wild. It lacked a certain fineness that even those with very little skill seemed to possess, and often times it would lash out, especially when he got overly emotional.

"I do not understand." Toshi said one day, he was starting to grow afraid of his magic, of the damage that it could do to people. He was unsure of himself and growing fearful of his powers.

Kagami offered his son a patient smile,

"You are frightened?"

Toshi nodded hesitantly, not sure as to whether or not this was some sort of trick question.

"Do not fear, Toshi." He placed a hand on his son's shoulder, "It is alright to be uncertain every now and then. It's very natural. However, it is important to keep ones self grounded. To believe in yourself."

"Believe in myself?" Toshi whispered.

Kagami smiled.

"No matter where you are, no matter what you do, you will live a life of no regrets, but only if you believe in yourself."

Seeing his son's worry not receding as he had hoped, Kagami held out his hand. In a glow of white and golden light, a round mirror appeared. It was about eight inches across, perhaps the size of a soup plate, decorated in a frame of dark turquoise and golden flowers.

"This is my gift to you." Kagami handed the mirror to his son, "It will aid you in your magic. With it, you will be able to control your powers."

Toshi looked at the mirror with awe. He had never before seen a mirror that looked so beautiful. It was clearly one of his father's greatest designs. It was immediately, from that moment on, Toshi's most prized possession.

With the mirror, Toshi's magic started to improve. He never lost control since the day it had first been given to him. He loved magic. Whenever he did it, his father would look at him with such pride. It made him want to get better, to learn all he could about the mysteries that magic had to hide and uncover them, much like his father wished to do with humans.

It was sometime around Toshi's fifteenth birthday that the shadows came. They started to attack those that would enter the Kingdom of Mirrors. Soon, like a disease, the shadows started to spread and once again people began to whisper. To cast their suspicious glares at Toshi. His existence had put things out of balance. Those with responsibilities were not supposed to have children, after all.

It was not long after that a woman came to their castle. She was a beautiful woman with long black hair and dramatically painted, bright red lips. Her name was Miranda and she was a witch, introducing herself as Viola's cousin.

Kagami had welcomed her with open arms upon hearing Viola's name, the name of the woman that had created Toshi. Toshi however, had been wary of Miranda. Something about her had not sat well with him. But he'd brushed his concerns aside, deciding that if his father liked her, that he could come to like her too.

Miranda was a very skilled witch, and overall, a very intelligent woman. At gatherings, the men would flock to her, hanging off every word that came out of her pretty, red-painted lips. Even Kagami found himself intrigued by her, and ever so slowly, he was seduced.

By the time the year was over, Miranda was made Kagami's bride. Toshi knew he ought to have been happy, but as soon as they had wed, he felt himself slowly being pushed away from his father. At first, he thought the feeling to be illogical. But after two years, Toshi found that he'd barely seen his father for more than seven days despite living in the same castle.

On the day of the couple's seventh anniversary, Toshi woke to find that the mirror his father had gifted him, his prized possession, was missing. Finding this to be peculiar, he set out to look for it.

It was only just a few minutes into his search that he felt the world start to shake. The barriers of the realm of reflection began to tremble.

"Father!" Toshi gasped, knowing that he must be in danger.

Forgetting about the mirror, he ran down to his father's room, praying that he would find him there. He did find him there. Miranda was standing over the king's body, holding Toshi's prized mirror which had turned black with some sort of dark magic. Perhaps the darkest magic Toshi had ever seen.

Having studied magic for many years now, Toshi knew, or at least had an idea as to what Miranda had done. There were theories about magic being capable of taking away the responsibilities of those with responsibilities. To take it and gain control of their realm for themselves. It had been tried before, but never had anyone succeeded.

Yet, instead of feeling the responsibilities of the realm fall on the shoulders of Miranda, Toshi felt all of the realm and all of the magic of his father's world, all of the realm of reflection suddenly fall on him.

But Toshi did not want the responsibility. This was his father's realm, not his. He had no right to it. He couldn't even control his own magic without his mirror!

And of course, Miranda knew this all too well. She had integrated herself into both Kagami's and Toshi's lives. She knew all their strengths...and weaknesses.

It would not matter if Toshi managed to wrestle his mirror back or not. Because it was tainted by the horrible magic that had killed his father. It would take him a long time to actually fix the magical mess that Miranda had created.

Knowing she had more power over him, she attacked, hoping to imprison Toshi. To use him as her medium as she ruled the Kingdom of Mirrors. It was only by luck that Toshi managed to escape.

Miranda, however, never left him alone, and she never would. Not until she could claim the realm of reflection as her own.

So, on and on for century upon century, Toshi continued to run. Playing the game of words, just as he and his father used to when he had been afraid as a child. Just as they used to play when the demons came and the shadows scared away those inside their kingdom. They would play a game of words. And with each word they played, they would banish the demons farther and father away.

No one entered the realm of reflection anymore. There were no parties. No dances or guests dressed in colorful fabrics, laughing over lame jokes.

Toshi was all alone. All he could do now was help those that accidentally entered his realm get back home before the shadows caught them.

No one actually *wanted* to stay in the realm of reflections. At least, not until Elliot Crow.

CHAPTER ELEVEN

Miranda the Witch

To Elliot, it felt as though the stairs of the tower went on forever. The stone steps spiraled upwards towards the sky. Light filtered through the top window. He'd wondered for a while if maybe this was another trap like the hallway, but after a while Elliot was very sure that he was getting closer to the light. He passed by a window and stopped to look down momentarily, as though to make sure he really was getting higher and it wasn't just his mind playing tricks on him.

Surely enough, he was at least fifty feet up, yet still not even half way there.

He'd picked up Cairo long ago, knowing she wouldn't be able to make it otherwise. By the time, Elliot had reached the top of the tower, he felt a shiver run down his spine.

"A chill." He whispered.

The sort of chill he'd gotten the day he'd died. He stared at the heavy wooden door with trepidation. There was something behind that door that was dangerous. Dangerous even to the dead, to him who couldn't die again. He set Cairo down. The small cat stared at the door intensely, and Elliot got the sense that she was quite aware of the danger opening the door would entail. But both of them were willing to go through with it.

It was different, Elliot looked at the doorknob, it was far different from the time he had died. He hadn't trusted back then that he was in danger, now, he was aware that he was in danger, but he was heading towards it purposefully.

Maybe it was because he believed in himself. He clutched the sword from the mirror in his right hand. Then, with his other, free hand, he turned the doorknob and pushed the heavy door open.

He was in danger. Great danger. But this time he knew about the danger because he trusted himself, his instincts. He trusted Cairo whose eyes were alert and her muscles tense beneath her fur.

He also believed that no matter what the danger he was about to face, that he would be able to get out of it and make his way back to the Kingdom of Dreams.

The first thing he noticed when he saw the room was the woman inside it. He'd nearly mistaken her as some sort of doll for her stillness and posture. Her perfect, olive skin and teasing red-painted lips and long black hair that didn't have a single strand out of place. But she wasn't a doll, Elliot told himself, and he had a lot of trouble keeping his eyes off of her.

She might have been, perhaps, the most beautiful woman he had ever seen. Instead of relaxing his guard, Elliot found himself tensing.

She is unarmed, Elliot told himself, but his instincts told him another story.

"My, my," the woman spoke, eyes falling on the sword in his hand, "And where did a boy like you obtain such a dangerous thing?" her voice was slightly scolding, charming and melodic. Almost hypnotic.

Should he answer her? Elliot wondered, was there even anything to say? He kept his mouth shut, brown eyes unmoving from her face.

This was Miranda, the witch of the mirror.

Finally, Elliot's thoughts seemed to clear, moving away from her beauty and her taunting words and to the situation at hand.

"I'm sorry to intrude." He began slowly, "But there's something here that I need."

"I can't say I have ever come across a thief with manners before." Once again, her smile was teasing.

"Takes one to know one." Elliot said before he could even think about what he was saying.

In hindsight, it may not have been the best thing to say. Miranda's eyes narrowed dangerously, her eyes grew darker in a way in which no human eyes ever could.

Elliot felt another chill.

She isn't real!

Elliot jumped out of the way, just as a shadow came jutting up from the ground. Miranda's shadow had moved across the floor, stretching out and curling around. Elliot swung the sword down and was actually rather impressed to find that it was effective in stopping the shadows.

That was it, Elliot thought to himself with a sudden realization, that was the trick. This woman really wasn't real, so then...what was he fighting exactly?

He knew it was silly, but first he wanted to make sure.

"You aren't real." Elliot said with a certainty that he definitely didn't feel.

Miranda's lips moved up in an amused smile,

"I'm not real, you say?" it was a teasing sort of voice, the sort that Elliot figured might bring any man to his knees.

"No." Elliot was actually surprised at his own conviction this time. The more she spoke, the more certain Elliot grew, "You aren't real. Who are you? Or...what are you?" he didn't know what the proper question was to ask in this instant, so he simply went along with his instincts. It seemed he'd be hard pressed to find any instant in his life where his instincts had steered him wrong. So, for now, he would believe in himself, just as he'd promised himself he'd do since entering the realm of reflections.

One of the shadows leaped up from the ground in an attempt to stab him in the back, but Elliot turned around and cut through the dark tendril once more. His whole body shook, tingling with something like anticipation. That might have been the adrenaline, he acknowledged vaguely.

"No." He said out loud.

Miranda frowned, as though the word were a foreign concept to her.

No?" she repeated.

Elliot licked his lips, then, taking a deep breath, the shadows were apart of Miranda, so then, maybe the spell Toshi had taught him would have the same effect. He started sputtering off animal names as fast as his brain was able to come up with them. Surely enough, it appeared to be working, though he felt rather ridiculous screaming "Bunny!" at the top of his lungs.

Cairo let out a soft 'meow,' then jumped up onto the tall table pressed up against the wall. She batted the drawer underneath her with a single paw.

"What's that?" Elliot asked Cairo, "There's something in there? Yak!"

He opened the drawer quickly, but there was only a single object inside. A pocket watch which appeared to be made of glass. Elliot picked it up curiously, holding it up to the light of the window. No, this was crystal, not glass.

A crystal heart.

How was this the crystal heart? Elliot wondered. It certainly didn't look like a heart. Yet, he knew this was what Slomoe had sent him here to retrieve.

A crystal heart...much like, maybe, those pocket watches that Time would fiddle with. Elliot was starting to think that maybe Time had far more to do with his journey than he'd originally thought. Had he known? Elliot pondered to himself, his eyes traveled to a mirror with black glass that didn't appear to reflect a thing. It hung on the far wall opposite the door. He walked passed Miranda, giving a final cry of "Kangaroo!" noting that Miranda seemed to be having some difficulty moving, then took the mirror off the wall.

It was a lot of things to carry, Elliot grimaced, realizing he'd have to come up with a more convenient way to carry all these things. He put the crystal pocket watch around his neck, letting it rest over the center of his chest. He tucked the mirror under his left arm, then put his sword in his left hand. He took out the glass key Toshi had lent him, then put it in the lock of the tower door and turned it, before pushing it open. He allowed Cairo to exit the Kingdom of Mirrors first, propping the door open with his foot, then walking through himself and allowing the door to close behind him, disappearing, or rather, fading out of existence like some kind of phantom.

He was right by his house, a bit away from where Toshi had been, but, within only moments, the small boy came running towards Elliot, appearing from around a corner. He was looking at Elliot with amazement, and maybe a bit of disbelief.

"You...you defeated Miranda?" Toshi shook his head, mouth falling open, then closing again, "You must be a very powerful wizard to have gotten passed her." Elliot shook his head,

"I...don't know about that." He said uncertainly. All he had done was use the spell that Toshi had taught him, right?

"Is this your mirror?" Elliot asked Toshi, taking the mirror out from under his arm and handing it over. Toshi took the mirror from Elliot, not taking his eyes off of the black glass, as though it were the most precious treasure in all the world.

"Yes...yes, it is. Thank you." Tears formed in his eyes, falling down his face, then solidifying and dropping to the ground like small crystals.

"Please," Toshi said, "If there's anything, anything I can do at all..."

"Well," Elliot said, "There might be something." He admitted, "I want to try to communicate with my father again." He explained, "Or someone from my family. I need to warn them that my killer is going to come after my brother." Toshi looked at Elliot in confusion,

"Killer?"

Elliot nodded,

"I was stabbed." He put a hand on his stomach where his wound had once been, he felt a twinge of pain, before it vanished, "But the person who did it, he got the wrong brother, so I need to warn them."

"But you're not dead." Toshi shook his head, "Even I know that. Ghosts are grey, colorless entities. You have plenty of color. You're alive."

"But I don't breathe." Elliot reiterated, "I don't have a pulse –"

"That still doesn't mean you're dead." Toshi shook his head hesitantly, although Elliot noticed something rather peculiar about him, and for the very first time. He was uncertain of his answer, unlike Trinket and Gear. His demeanor was very different, very painful, like life had warn him down.

He didn't believe in himself, Elliot realized. A strange feeling twisted in his gut as he thought back to the peculiar events he'd been through, wondering all the while if there was something he was missing from this story. Something he wasn't quite getting.

Slomoe would know, Elliot thought to himself, or Trinket.

But as it was, Elliot couldn't believe he was a very powerful wizard, as Toshi seemed to think. He was just lucky. Elliot knew that he had far more to learn about this world if he ever wished to understand exactly what was happening in the realm of mirrors.

Elliot furrowed his brow, thinking over what Toshi had told him, and what Trinket had told him, and even Slomoe.

"You're dead?" Trinket asked looking him over disbelievingly.

"I'm pretty sure I am. I was stabbed in the gut. Next thing I know I'm waking up and a man called 'Time' is telling me I shouldn't be there."

Trinket tilted his head to the side, his eyes sparkling,

"That certainly doesn't sound right..."

"Right, you said you were dead." Trinket's amused, and firmly disbelieving voice recalled.

"What danger?" His father asked him, "Why's Casper in danger? Is it the person that hurt you? Is he going to come after Casper?"

It was the last one, what his father had said that had really made it click. He'd said 'hurt him,' not 'killed him.'

"I'm not dead." Elliot realized, his eyes widened at this new revelation and for a moment, he thought he caught a glimpse of something. A white room, and the sound of a repetitive beeping noise. He wasn't standing up, but rather, he was lying down.

A hospital bed? Elliot thought for a moment, his thoughts uncertain and fuzzier than before. Then the vision and feelings were gone and he was back in the realm of reflections. Toshi looked at Elliot curiously,

"You weren't there for a moment." Toshi told Elliot curiously, "It was like you flickered."

"That's because..." Elliot's voice grew silent.

Because he wasn't really there. He was still alive! He was in a hospital, but...then, was this all a dream? He wondered, then thought back to his father, how he'd desperately been tapping on the glass of the mirror. He heard his instincts, or what he was now calling his instincts, screaming at him that no, this wasn't a dream and that if he thought like that (even if there were similarities between the two), he would really die before the day was up.

Elliot quickly made a change of plans. If he was still alive, then it was possible for him to wake up, or return to his body, and the only people he knew of that might know how to help him were either Trinket or Slomoe.

"Toshi," he quickly turned to the boy, "Please, I need to get back to the Kingdom of Dreams." He said, "You can get me there, right?"

"Well, yes." Toshi agreed, "But, only if that was where you came from before coming here..."

"It was." Elliot nodded, "I need to get back right away. Please."

Toshi gave a nod, a look of determination crossed his face. He didn't know why this was so important to Elliot, but he knew that it was most certainly important.

"Alright, this way." He gestured.

Elliot followed him into his own home, Toshi opened the door, entering first with Elliot in close pursuit. They made their way up to the top of the stairs and to the full-length mirror. His father was no longer there, of course. Elliot couldn't help but feel a bit sad at that.

Toshi pressed the key into the mirror, in much the same way as Elliot had seen his reflection (or rather, the sword?) do before.

The glass rippled, it looked as though it were breaking into a web of cracks. But through the distortion, Elliot could see Slomoe sipping on tea, much as he had been doing when Elliot had left him.

"Thank you." Elliot told Toshi gratefully.

"No, thank you."

Elliot didn't turn around to acknowledge the thanks. He hadn't really done anything. Right now, all he could focus on were the swirling questions banging up against the walls of his mind. He wasn't going to get any answers or help in the realm of reflections.

So, staring at the glass a moment longer, Elliot backed up a couple of feet, then took off into a run, straight into the glass.

It was a bit like traveling through a kaleidoscope, yet, without the feeling of getting anywhere. There was something about traveling through mirrors that was almost dissatisfying. But Elliot didn't really ponder on those feelings for very long, especially when he landed back in the Kingdom of Dreams.

Slomoe...didn't seem all that surprised by Elliot's resurgence from the mirror he had pushed him through only a few hours ago. Had he really believed he would come through? Elliot wondered, or was it simply a happy surprise?

His eyes fell on the crystal heart around Elliot's neck, and then to the sword in Elliot's hand.

Cairo came padding through the glass only moments after, brushing up against Elliot's leg as though to reassure him that she was there.

"The crystal heart." He noted, "Well, well, ya came through after all, ya know?"

"I did." Elliot said carefully, "But, I want to know something, before I give you the crystal heart." It was a bit of a gamble, holding the thing he'd been task to retrieve as hostage, "I want to know...how do I wake myself up from my coma?" if it was a coma, Elliot had never heard of people going on grand adventures such as this one when they fell into a coma, and far be it from him to claim to be the first.

Slomoe grinned even wider,

"Ah, so you figured it out. Alright, alright, it's not like I was keeping the info from ya, ya know? I just thought it really was something you ought to figure for yourself." He looked Elliot up and down, "Trinket sensed it in ya too. You aren't quite dead, you're nearly there, but not. Bit like a dream. Probably why he sent ya to me. As to how ya ought to wake yourself...well, how do ya normally wake up from a dream?"

Elliot frowned, he had a feeling that Trinket was trying to get at something, but he didn't quite know what.

"Well, when I get really scared, I guess?" Elliot figured, "Or when my alarm goes off, or someone shakes me awake."

Slomoe nodded,

"Exactly! That's what you need, Elliot Crow. A bit of a shock."

Elliot wasn't so sure about that. Was that even what he'd said?

"But, I've been through so much already. If it wasn't a shock to find out this whole world exists, then..."

"No, no." Slomoe interrupted, shaking his head with exasperation, "You can't just wake up at anytime. People don't *choose* when they wake up. Ya need a good shock, and of course, to make matters more interesting..." Slomoe's grin turned almost vicious, "Ya can only waken on the night the moon is full in the sky. Truly full."

"You mean..." Elliot said slowly, "The full moon?"

"Oh yes." Slomoe agreed, "See, the only reason you're a spirit right now, is 'cause of that magic of yours. Probably saved you too, it's what's keeping you tied to this plane right now. However!" he suddenly exclaimed, nearly causing Elliot to jump, "You do still have a body. The moon is full of healing properties, ya know? Full of them! On a full moon, your body and magic should properly sync up again."

"When's the next full moon?" Elliot asked him eagerly.

Slomoe looked a tad puzzled at this,

"A week from Wednesday, I do believe...Wednesday is the day after the day after tomorrow, so...ten days? Yup, that sounds about right. Ten days and ten nights."

Ten days, Elliot thought to himself. He'd only just managed to communicate with his father about the danger Casper was in. But was it enough? Would Casper be well protected for ten days?

He'd have to find some other way then, to communicate with his family before then. Just because he was alive didn't mean he had to completely change his goals, after all.

Elliot took off the crystal pocket watch and handed it to Slomoe who looked at it with excitement,

"Perfect! Perfect! By those with responsibilities, it's just what I need!"

he exclaimed happily, "A crystal heart! A genuine crystal heart!" he was jumping up and down now, literally.

It was almost amusing to watch him, but Elliot still had so many questions. The first one that came to mind, of course was,

"Will you still take me as your apprentice?"

Slomoe looked at him, a grin split his face and he nodded his head,

"Of course, of course!" his eyes traveled to the sword once more, then back to Elliot's face, "You have far exceeded my expectations, Elliot Crow! By far! You defeated Miranda and even drew the Sword of the Worthy. The first, I would only expect from anyone who wished to be my apprentice, the second, well, that was of course, a happy surprise."

Elliot looked down at the sword, as though only seeing it for the first time,

"Oh...I forgot to return it."

"Return it?" Slomoe looked amused, "No, no! There's no need to return the sword to anywhere, Elliot Crow. That sword chose you, you are its master now. And let me tell you that it is very picky as to who it chooses. Besides, I've the sense you'll be needing it sometime soon."

Well, Elliot certainly wasn't sure he liked the sound of that. The fact that he would need the sword spoke of a future with certain danger. Although he knew he had handled himself rather well, especially for someone who didn't really know what they were doing, he didn't actually *like* danger. Or rather, he told himself that he didn't like it. A small part of him did find his adventures of the past couple of days to have been rather exhilarating if he did say so.

"Your highness..." Elliot began.

Slomoe raised a hand,

"Just Slomoe." Slomoe told Elliot, "You are my apprentice now, to you, I am the master, not the king, ya know?"

Elliot didn't know, but he figured it would be alright if that was what Slomoe wanted. Slomoe, in the short time he had gotten to know the man, was not the sort that conformed to formalities.

"Alright, Slomoe," Elliot tried again and the king smiled, "In the mirror world, I met a boy there, though he wasn't really a boy, I knew he was far older than he looked. His name was Toshi and...I got the sense that he and Miranda were somehow connected."

A look of understanding passed over the king's face,

"That they are, Elliot Crow. That they are." Slomoe agreed, "Miranda is known by many as a witch. That, however is a lie, one that anyone with good instincts can see. Toshi is one with responsibilities. The ruler of the Kingdom of Mirrors and Realm of Reflections. But, for some reason, he was never able to learn to believe in himself. Miranda is the embodiment of all of Toshi's fears. I believe it started with his fear that someone would someday come to take his father away, the previous King of the Realm of Reflections. Miranda seduced him, and then murdered him. She is Toshi's fears, but she is also the realm its self, crying out in pain. Do you understand, Elliot Crow?"

That sinking feeling in his gut that Elliot had felt earlier came back ten-fold. It was horrible and twisted.

"Does he know?" Elliot whispered, he couldn't imagine what Toshi was going through, to be thrown out of your own home like that, or to be so utterly helpless because of your own disbelief...or maybe he could. After all, was it not his own inability to believe in himself that had gotten him killed (Or sort of killed) to begin with?

While he had been sent into a coma and had cut himself off from his family and loved ones, Toshi had gotten his father killed and had achieved much the same thing though far more permanently. The only difference was that Elliot might have another chance to do things right.

"He might know." Slomoe said finally, "I personally believe that he does. Whether he is consciously aware of this or not, I can only guess. For years, centuries, in fact, Toshi has been running around his realm, fighting off the shadows, and helping those that happen to stumble through a mirror. They see him, ya know? Running about in the glass. But they usually forget soon after. Sometimes though...sometimes, he's that bit of movement ya see, in the corner of your eye when you're by a mirror, or that movement in the glass that ya might notice in the background a moment before it's gone. Of course, if you believe he exists, then you'll never really forget him. That's why people forget so quickly, because obviously, that little bit of movement, or that sense that something doesn't quite match up in the mirror, it's all a trick o' the light, no?"

Elliot thought on this, and then thought about it just a little bit more. He had seen Toshi before. He'd seen him several times, actually.

Those small moments in his memory where he'd seen exactly what Slomoe was describing, suddenly became less hazy, as insignificant memories like those ought to, and he saw him. He saw Toshi fighting off the shadows, playing his never-ending game of words.

"Happy endings do exist, Elliot Crow." Slomoe's voice cut into his thoughts and Elliot knew that he knew exactly what he was thinking and what he had just remembered, "But not all endings will be that. No...not all stories are happy ones."

CHAPTER TWELVE

Lessons on How to Dream

The sun didn't seem to set in the Kingdom of Dreams, nor did it rise. It just sort of hung there in the sky all day long without any sort of rest, reflecting off the silver grass and leaves. It wasn't particularly hot though, as one might think it would be with the sun blaring down on them all day. In fact, it was rather cool. It had been somewhat disorienting for Elliot when he realized he and Slomoe must have been talking for hours, yet, the sun hadn't moved at all. Had he not seen the sun rise when he'd arrived? Or maybe that was his mind playing tricks? A dream? Something in between?

Furthermore, Elliot was quite sure that he knew just about as much about Slomoe as he had when they'd first started their conversation, and that was to say, nothing.

He was a rather illusive speaker, weaving his words like an expert, until Elliot would realize that he had somehow started talking in circles, and Slomoe would send him an amused look, as though having just won some sort of game. It had taken Elliot a whole hour to realize that one didn't simply *talk* to Slomoe. Oh, no, talking with Slomoe involved playing a strange game of wits and words. Or maybe that wasn't entirely accurate. Chess was a game of wits. Slomoe played a different game and he didn't bother telling his opponent the rules first. He would start off first, and then change the rules about half-way through, just when Elliot thought he was getting the hang of it. When that happened, Elliot felt like he was being forced into a conversation where everyone ought to talk backwards if they wanted to make any sense. Ironically enough, their "leisurely" chat really did end with Slomoe attempting a backwards conversation, which had been the incentive Elliot had needed to give up.

"Alright, alright, then." Slomoe finally clapped his hands together when he noticed Elliot's worn out expression. He'd had his fun.

"Let's start with your first lesson about dreaming."

Elliot looked up at him from his spot at the table. He'd long since finished drinking his tea (there really was only so much he could drink before he got sick).

"You're going to teach me now?" Elliot wondered, a tad disbelieving as he'd thought the conversation would never end.

"Well, I am your master." Slomoe puffed out his chest rather proudly.

Elliot recalled once again that Trinket had told him Slomoe had been quite eager to get an apprentice. He seemed quite happy about the relationship.

"So then," Trinket once again clapped, "Let us talk about dreams, Elliot Crow." He got up from his chair and headed to one of the nearby bookshelves. He reached up, taking a thin, red volume off of the shelf, then moving to sit down at the table once again, though this time in the seat beside Elliot instead of at the head of the table, where he normally sat.

He opened the red book where a strange conglomeration of words formed. They seemed random at first, but they shifted about and changed in an almost purposeful way. Finally, they seemed to settle down from their excitement, forming words that made very little sense outside of rhythm, perhaps.

Starved Twilight,
Brings lights of bright,
Snakes of white,
Slither right,
Settling in the tombs of the night,
Angry knights,
Cry for their rights,
To go off to fight,
Those naughty serpents that bite,
Because their tombs are far too tight.
They say, "Let's finally go to bed tonight."
Goodnight.

Elliot furrowed his brow in confusion, then looked up at Slomoe,

"I'm afraid I don't understand." He said slowly, then looked back down at the words to find they hadn't changed again while he'd briefly looked away, as he'd feared they would.

"You aren't supposed to." Slomoe said simply, "You see, Elliot Crow, people like to analyze dreams. People think there's some great, deep meaning, and there usually is." He added in, "But that meaning is buried under a whole load of not-rules. Rules that don't conform with reality, ya know? In a dream, anything can happen if you believe it will happen. 'Bit like Miranda."

Elliot nodded, he could at the very least understand that. But he *knew* now, or rather, he knew better the sort of world he was getting into and why dreams were so very dangerous. Especially if they were like Miranda.

"There are a couple of things that you must remember when entering a dream." Slomoe raised a single finger in a factual sort of manner, "The first is that you're dreaming. The second is that you ought not expect it to follow the same rules you're used to and that those rules can change," he snapped his fingers, "in an instant. The third is that *you* are in control. If you're falling, simply believe you have wings and fly away, if you're drowning, believe you're part fish and breathe under the water. You're only limited by your own imagination. It's a lot easier to realize you're in a dream world when it's someone else's dream, when it's your own dream however, even though you *can* do the same, it's far more difficult."

"Why's that?" Elliot inquired, ever so curious and even forgetting momentarily that the entire reason he was learning from Slomoe was to save his brother.

"Because when you go into someone else's dream, you are still awake, giving you a little more control." Slomoe explained, smiling excitedly, this was *his* subject after all, his domain and he took great pride in what he did, "But, when you're in your own dream, you're asleep. To accomplish those same things, you would have to use a special technique called 'lucid dreaming.' Realize you're dreaming, then control the dream. It's far more complicated than it sounds."

Elliot nodded, it certainly did sound complicated, and it would have to be difficult otherwise he probably would have heard about it from his friends or at school. Though the term 'lucid dreaming' did sound vaguely familiar. Maybe something else his mother had mentioned at some point? No, it was something his father had mentioned, Elliot recalled. He nearly smacked himself when the realization hit.

His father had talked about lucid dreaming, about thinking up poems while he slept. Of course, he always said they seemed like such a good idea at the time, but that they rarely turned out all right. But, when they did turn out, they certainly turned out.

"My father," Elliot said, catching Slomoe's attention, "The song he wrote for me. That was from a lucid dream of his, wasn't it?"

Slomoe raised an eyebrow,

"It certainly was." He agreed, "Your father is something of a master at dreaming. Been practicing his whole life. It started when he was really young, ya know? He had a dream that he was drowning, and in his slumber, he believed it was true, so while he was sleeping, he wasn't breathing, holding his breath the whole time. He might tell ya, to this day, it was the most horrific dream he'd ever had, being in the water while the surface was covered in thick ice. But then he couldn't hold his breath any longer and he took in a breath, only to realize that he could breathe. That was the first time he ever realized he was dreaming while he was dreaming."

Elliot hadn't known that, and he felt a pang of...something...hurt, maybe? That certainly seemed like a word, he felt a pang of hurt at not knowing about his father's lucid dreaming, it seemed like something he really ought to know. His mother would know, Elliot thought. Now knowing more about dreams and having visited the Kingdom of Dreams, Elliot couldn't help but think that it was actually kind of cool.

"It was also during that dream," Slomoe continued, "That your father invented a technique to wake himself up when the dreams got too scary. He'd squeeze his eyes as tight as he could, then slowly peel them open. He'd wake up right away, but then, as he got older, he learned not to be afraid of bad dreams and started to stay asleep through all of them on purpose. A curious man, your father, but certainly someone who can respect a good dream." He gave a nod of approval.

Elliot could remember his dad saying something like that before as well, about how to best wake yourself up from a nightmare. But he'd been little and had far too much trouble trying to figure out when he was dreaming that it hadn't really mattered at the time.

"Dreams are important." Elliot recalled his father saying, "In a dream, you can see your characters, analyze your story from all angles, then go back to the beginning if you must and make sure you didn't miss anything."

"Yes, he can respect a good dream." Elliot thought out loud. He talked about his dreams often, but he hadn't made the connection right away between that and what Slomoe was talking about.

His stomach clenched with a bout of homesickness. Then he thought back to the realm of reflections and how tired his dad had looked. How worn and how desperate he'd been to communicate with him. He was waiting for him to wake up. Him and his mother and maybe even Casper. They were all waiting for him, visiting him in the hospital and watching him, waiting for his eyes to open, to know at last that he was okay.

From his own perspective, Elliot was waiting for when he could go home. He had so much he wanted to say to them. He wanted to apologise to his mum, for being so cruel to her over the years when she had only loved and cared for him. He wanted to learn more about her world when he saw her again, because all that she knew, it was helpful! Magic was real, and so were spirits. She would love to know about his strange adventures, whether she believed them or thought them only a dream (though Elliot got the sense that she would most definitely believe him). He could imagine her, looking up in the sky in the hopes of seeing the Youfoe flickering into existence, or looking into the mirror just a moment longer to get a glimpse of the boy forever trapped inside the mirror.

His father would listen to his story, maybe even gain a bit of inspiration to write a strange and quirky story about his adventures. His brother...well, he'd probably ask if he had some sort of concussion. He'd tell Casper, because he was a part of his story too, whether he liked it or not. But everything else, it could be his secret. He didn't have to say a thing if he didn't want to.

Could he return to living the same existence as before? Probably not, Elliot decided. He'd changed a lot in the last few days.

When would the week be over and Wednesday come? Just how much would he change by then?

"Well, then, Elliot Crow." Slomoe stood up so suddenly that Elliot was rather startled by the sudden movement. He bumped up against the table, causing the tea sets to rattle and his chair to fall over, although he didn't appear to notice any of this. He clapped his hands together.

"It's about time that we take you to experience exactly what you'll be doing now, my apprentice."

Elliot looked up at him, uncertain as to what he ought to say. So, he simply nodded. Slomoe's behaviour was quite bizarre to the point that if he did anything even remotely ordinary, Elliot would have to start questioning his identity, or health, whichever really.

He slowly got out of his chair, and unlike Slomoe, was quite cautious about bumping up against the table or breaking things.

As soon as Elliot had gotten around his chair, Slomoe grabbed his hand.

"Let us go!" he pointed towards the divide of bookshelves to their right, and then, promptly took off skipping to the divide directly to their left, as Elliot had predicted (though he was still at a loss as to how he predicted such things).

Elliot struggled to keep up with the overly-enthusiastic king, jogging, then walking, then sprinting at times, before they finally reached a bunch of tall bookshelves positioned in a square. These shelves were painted a bright yellow.

Elliot was beginning to think that there must be some sort of organizational system going on here, but he couldn't for the life of him come up with any sort of clue as to what that might be. While at first glance, Elliot might have thought things were somehow divided by colors, all of which were put together properly, a lot of them were put into shapes that certainly had to be intentional. Yet, there were also shelves that appeared to completely lack color, and sometimes those that had matching colors were very far apart from one another.

Elliot couldn't pretend to know how Slomoe's mind worked, in fact, he would have some serious doubts about anyone who could make such a claim. He found it very unlikely that, if there was such a method of organization that Slomoe was using, that it certainly wasn't something he was going to be able to learn.

"This," Slomoe interrupted Elliot's ponderings, "This is the square of custard colored dreams."

Elliot could only offer him a puzzled look, and when he realized this wouldn't be enough to get Slomoe to explain, he decided to speak,

"I don't understand."

"These are the milder dreams." Slomoe elaborated, "The dreams that aren't particularly happy, but aren't particularly sad. They aren't frightening in any way, or particularly interesting. But they're quite safe for someone just learning about dreams and how to enter them."

"I'm going to enter a dream?" Elliot asked him. He couldn't help but feel a little bit of excitement at the prospect. After all, how many people could say that they had entered another person's dream?

"Well, you are my apprentice." Slomoe said with a proudness to his voice that often appeared when he made that statement, "And it's only expected of the apprentice of the King of Dreams to enter a dream himself. So, you'll be entering the dream world with me for your first time. Even if these dreams aren't as intense, they can still be dangerous if one isn't careful. If you believe the dream will go in a different direction, it's very possible that it will, then the dream changes see. You will have influence on how the dream goes, and you will certainly have power there, considering you're awake, ya know? But that can still be a double-edged sword, Elliot Crow."

Elliot nodded slowly, he could understand that. Dreams could be scary things.

"Why don't you pick one out." Slomoe suggested, "Pick a book, any book you want. It will be your first dream, or rather, the first dream you'll be experiencing as the dream walker and not the dreamer."

"Um, okay." Elliot said, looking around at some of the books.

They were all the same custard color as the shelves. Some were big and thick, some were small, some were piled up in a case which held a bunch of books about the size of a deck of cards.

One of them did catch his eye, however. It was a thinner book with a worn looking cover made out of leather. He had a peculiar feeling that it was something his father would enjoy, at least in appearance. As he pulled it out from the book case, he noticed that it smelled strongly of red peppers and not of custard as it's cover deceptively suggested.

He brought it over to Slomoe who looked at the book fondly,

"Ah, that one. That is one I haven't seen in quite a while."

He nodded appreciatively at Elliot's choice, then took it in his hands gently, as though cradling a baby.

He ran his hand over the spine, then looked up at Elliot.

"Grab onto my arm, Elliot Crow." He ordered, "I don't want you getting lost at a different point in the dream than I. Make sure you do not let go."

Elliot grabbed Slomoe's arm. He seemed to wait, to make sure that Elliot wouldn't get away, then he opened up the front cover.

Elliot felt a strange tug and a sudden feeling of vertigo. The book glowed a soft silver, but then the light grew brighter and brighter. It wasn't blinding, and it didn't hurt his eyes, but it did seem to encompass all of his surroundings, drowning out all the scenery. Then he felt a brief moment of bliss.

He couldn't put the exact feeling into words, but if he were to describe it, he would have to say that it really did feel like he was entering a dream.

CHAPTER THIRTEEN

Casper's Torment

There was a girl who fell to her knees in a world of rubble. She was dressed up in rags and crying behind broken glasses. Then, out of nowhere, a boy came, looking just about the same age. He wore a crown on his head and Elliot new that he was supposed to be some sort of prince. It was a bit like a fairy tale. The dream had that sort of quality to it.

Was the girl the dreamer or the boy? He wondered to himself, observing as the world seemed to swirl and they plunged into the water. It didn't really feel cold or hot or uncomfortable, however. But Elliot automatically held his breath, only to take in a huge gulp of air when his lungs could no longer take it.

This was a dream, and just like his father's dream of drowning, this one would be the same and he would be allowed to breathe, just as he had.

The boy was swimming and the girl was nowhere in sight. So, this was his dream, then? Elliot wondered.

"This is his dream."

Elliot nearly jumped out of his skin, turning to see Slomoe, floating in the water beside him.

"Of course, not all dreams are experienced by the dreamer. Sometimes, when we dream we are merely observers, floating above the world. You need to remember, Elliot Crow that in dreams, anything is possible."

Elliot gave a slow nod, then found the water had become far shallower. The boy was in a swimsuit, drifting about in the waves by an island.

"Hold on," Elliot said, looking at two very familiar figures, "Are those...my mum and dad? Why are they here?"

"They aren't." Slomoe said with some amusement, "You haven't figured it out yet?"

"Figured it out?" Elliot repeated, looking back at his parents. They were younger than he remembered and a boy, a little boy with dark hair and brown eyes was playing in the sand by his mother.

"That's me." Elliot realized, "Then the boy..." he turned back to the boy. The boy with sandy blond hair and green eyes, identical to his mum's. It was Casper.

"This is Casper's dream." Elliot looked at the small boy with awe. It was almost like watching a memory, of days that had long since been forgotten, but not. He shot Slomoe a suspicious look,

"Did you do this on purpose? Using my brother's dream?"

Slomoe's smile grew, he shook his head,

"No. You chose this dream all on your own, Elliot Crow. You, who came to me with the purpose of saving your brother. You, who have thought of nothing but your family. You, who went to the realm of mirrors, only to take a detour so that you could warn your father of impending danger. All this time, Elliot Crow, all this time you have thought of your family. So, when you went to pick a dream, you chose the only dream from the custard section that belonged to one of your family members. Your brother's dream."

Elliot didn't ask how Slomoe knew about his 'detour' in the realm of mirrors, he had a feeling he'd been watching him in some way or another. Had he really unconsciously sought out his brother?

His eyes traveled to the happy, sandy haired boy. He couldn't have been more than six years old.

"He looks so happy." Elliot murmured. He hadn't seen Casper so carefree like that in a long time. Now he was different, always a little on edge. Why had someone wanted to kill him anyways? It just didn't make any sense to him. He and Casper might not talk all that much, but he was a nice person. Even Elliot, his brother, recognised that.

The dream seemed to grow dark and Elliot felt himself being pulled back into the realm of dreams. He was standing back on the silver grass, his eyes traveling to the book in Slomoe's hands.

"That's it?" Elliot wondered.

It had been rather short. Slomoe shrugged his shoulders,

"Most of the dreams here are boring." He said, "And many of them are short. Dreams vary in length, of course. Those dreams there," he pointed to the ones that looked about the size of a deck of cards, "Those are so incredibly short they're almost not dreams at all, but simply ideas that came in a bout of unconscious thought. So short that most wouldn't even remember them. I love all dreams, of course." Slomoe extended his arms outwards, as though he wanted to give every dream out there a big hug, "But I love some more than others." He finished with a grin.

Elliot would have thought from the way he spoke that he was a father admitting to having a favourite child out of one hundred and fifty kids. Like he might have had something to be guilty about.

Elliot thought back to the dream, there'd been a darker undertone to it in the beginning, and the feeling had lingered a bit, leaving him with a sense of unease.

It was a normal dream, now that he thought about it. Casper had been a kid at the time, probably, dreaming that he was a prince, saving a princess. The girl had made him think of Cinderella a bit, though she hadn't really been anyone he'd recognised. Maybe just someone Casper had made up. Elliot had had similar dreams when he was younger, about a fairy tale world where he'd go off on adventures, although, they were more often than not, terrifying as the situation seemed to worsen or even spiral out of control, until Elliot woke up in a right fright.

He'd stay up in his bed for a little while longer after that, sometimes with his lamp on with his eyes closed as he tried to come up with a different ending. One that had a happy ending. Maybe it was his own way of giving himself closure.

His father had always told him that when he was little, they'd rarely have problems with him waking them up due to bad dreams, so he must have been practicing that method for quite some time. Even though he couldn't recall how long it had been.

He had noticed that as he grew, his endings tended to grow a little more complex. Most dreams didn't have happy endings, or endings at all, because Elliot would wake up far before his dreams ever ended. But he could make a happy ending in his own mind, one that would make his heart stop pounding. A story that he could fall asleep to when the darkness seemed far more malicious than it really was. Where everyone got a happy ending and all those peculiar people he'd created could rejoice and escape the fears of his created world.

Maybe his fascination with happy endings had come from his father. He'd write him and Casper stories when they were growing up. The stories he usually wrote, dark fantasies, Elliot had read some of them, mostly out of a childish sense of curiosity and adventure. He was surprised to find that his father's stories were nothing like those fairy tales he'd been exposed to growing up, and they often ended in despair for the hero who had tried so very hard to achieve his goal.

He'd been confused at the time, wondering if his father didn't like happy endings. He never asked. Maybe it had been his pride, not wanting to admit that he'd read his father's books, or maybe it was a strange lingering sensation in the back of his mind, a feeling of having actually enjoyed those tragic endings that had prevented him from ever speaking of it. Maybe it was because he was afraid that if he admitted to liking a tragedy, that he'd be acknowledging he was more like his mother than he pretended to be.

"Well then, another dream, Elliot Crow?" Slomoe broke through his thoughts, his voice utterly cheery.

Elliot gave a hesitant nod. It would do no good for him or his family if he continued to stand there doing nothing. He needed to save Casper, and that was what he was going to do.

Instead of being offered to pick another dream off of the shelf, Slomoe started walking again down the rows of book shelves, out of the Custard Section. Elliot quickly followed behind him.

"Dreams are the window into the subconscious." Slomoe ran his hand along a stack of red books but continued on into yet another section of pink shelves.

"They can show us our desires. Our fears, and the inner self that we most desperately wish to hide from all others. Nightmares are not true terrors, Elliot Crow. It is that self that we wish most desperately *not* to face that scares us the most. Anyone would take a nightmare any day. That is why dreams are so dangerous, so terribly so. I've known of men that have gouged out their own eyes or lopped off their own ears facing that madness. You know how to handle yourself in a milder dream. Now how about something darker?"

Slomoe grabbed Elliot's arm, and even though he had no book in his hands, Elliot felt the same pull he'd felt before. But this time, as he descended, he felt something chilling. Like being dipped into an ice-cold vat of water. Like he was being drenched to his very bones.

Was it perhaps Death, finally coming to claim him? Or perhaps it was something else, the dread of seeing something that really ought not be seen.

It only seemed to get worse and worse, like all the horrible things in the world were crashing down at him at once. All Elliot could feel was despair and a horrible empty coldness that gripped at his very being. For a moment, he wanted to scream. But then he just didn't have the will to make any noise as he dove deeper and deeper into the pits of dread, fear and loneliness.

He could hear something, someone chanting, *why, why, why?*

Why did it have to be him? Why couldn't he have been born normal?

Elliot shook his head, pulling at his hair.

"Snap out of it, snap out of it, snap out of it." He chanted to himself. It wasn't his emotions, but the emotions of whoever was dreaming.

He needed to focus.

But he felt like he was suffocating. Never before had he felt like he *needed* to breathe so badly, even when he was alive.

There was no pain. He just felt cold and numb. Pain would actually be welcome. To feel anything would be welcome.

Then, the dream seemed to shift. The painful feelings were still there, but at the same time, it had lessened enough that Elliot could think a little clearer. His thoughts, which had only been focused on the despair that this person had felt, started to move. Albeit was more like he was trying to trudge through a pond of molasses. It was still enough for him to process that he was in something like a warped version of his brother's bedroom.

The first thing he noticed were the walls which were a light purple, unlike the blue he knew them to be. The next thing he noticed was the window. He had to double-take when he looked towards the glass. He could see trees outside, and houses, and though it might have looked a little bit like seeing an object from a distance, there was something not quite right about it. Like someone had grown lazy and not bothered to fill in all of the details.

And then the room changed in the blink of an eye. The desk was ravaged, broken in half with the table top slumped in a downward V. There were clothes, papers, bits of fluff, sheets and blankets all scattered on the floor.

Elliot turned suddenly, jumping like a frightened cat at the sound of shattering glass.

Casper was laying in bed, panting and looking over at the window with fear. Elliot froze, then slowly turned around. The window was different now. It had changed. The curtains were drawn and there was a strange rattling sound that caused Elliot to feel a similar sort of fear to his brother. He swallowed hard, then slowly moved towards the curtains.

"Don't do it, Elliot!" Casper shouted at the top of his lungs.

But Elliot was frightfully determined. It might have been the dream egging him on, or maybe his newfound courage that he'd managed to gain during his journey through this strange world. But he drew the curtain back, only to jump as something came crashing down to the floor. Elliot's eyes widened. They looked like human bones. He felt panic clawing it's way up into his throat when he realized something rather peculiar. The bones weren't covered in that much detail. A bit like the trees outside of Casper's window.

Right, Elliot thought to himself, trying to make sense of it. Casper had probably never seen real human bones before. Not in close detail anyways, so it was logical to assume that these bones would be very...sketchy. Very unreal in appearance, since Casper himself had nothing to draw on.

It was then that the door to Casper's room opened, causing Elliot and his brother to spin around. A man with slicked back black hair and a neatly trimmed moustache dressed up in a suit stood at the doorway. His eyes, not unlike Elliot's own brown eyes, blazed with righteous fury. He looked a lot like an old-fashioned gentleman, actually, and the woman that stood by his side in a Victorian style dress certainly supported that image.

"It was you!" The man pointed his finger at Casper, "You murdered him!"
"I-I didn't –" Casper was practically hyperventilating now, his fear was evident and for some reason, he couldn't finish his sentence.

Elliot turned back to the skeleton by the window and covered his mouth, trying to resist the urge to throw up. Although the bones had not been particularly detailed, something far more detailed and morbid seemed to have taken their place.

It was a corpse. His own corpse.

Elliot walked towards the body shakily and with a morbid fascination, staring into his own lifeless eyes and the pool of blood that seemed to be endlessly pouring out of the hole in his stomach.

Then the world around him vanished. It felt like he was being pulled, up and up and up, until he was back in the kingdom of dreams. He looked over at Slomoe, not sure what to say just yet.

Slomoe raised an eyebrow, surprisingly patient. Elliot looked down at his hands where a book with a black cover was clutched in his hands.

"This is...Casper's dream?" his voice was little more than a whisper, but Slomoe had heard.

"Indeed, your first collected dream." An almost greasy looking smile made its way across Slomoe's lips, "Sometimes ya need to send people in unprepared to see what they can do, ya know? Ya found the key to capturing a dream. Ya have to first become a part of it, that's how you take it, and in a dream ya can be anyone. An old lady, a superhero who saves the day, a face in a crowd of faces. The possibilities!"

He twirled around like a ballerina and Elliot wondered if maybe his presence had been forgotten, until the book was plucked right out of his hands.

"A tormented dream." Slomoe hummed, stroking the binding thoughtfully, as though it were some sort of precious treasure, "A bit rarer than a nightmare...or perhaps ya could call this a 'true nightmare,' ya know?"

Elliot actually nodded,

"Yeah, I think I do know." His eyes traveled back to his brother's nightmare. He wondered if maybe the book's delicate, falling-apart look might be a reflection of Casper's state of mind. Knowing this world as he did, he wouldn't be surprise if his deduction was accurate.

"Well, a rough first go." Slomoe said, "But that can't really be helped. Dreams are a bit like lotteries, ya know? If you want to enter one person's dream in particular that is, and ya did say ya wanted to enter the dreams of Casper Crow, no?"

"I wouldn't have minded anyone in my family." Elliot told him slowly, "But yes. Thank you."

His 'thank you' was a bit tentative, mainly because he had his doubts that Slomoe didn't know what Casper had been dreaming at the time. He was the King of Dreams, after all. He saw all dreams, all of them. That included the bad ones.

But at the same time, Elliot got the sense that he also wasn't lying, in that for any apprentice, or anyone that worked for him might find it to be a lottery if they were aiming to enter the dreams of a particular person.

He also wondered how much control Slomoe might have over dreams. He'd said he could manipulate them, in that case, had he also manipulated Casper's into being forced to confront his darkest feelings?

Even his 'instincts' were strangely silent at the mental accusation, and normally they were quite loud when it came to such mental inquiries. The last time they'd been this silent was in the Realm of Reflections, and Elliot was certain there'd been some sort of reason for that. He didn't know what that meant, but it certainly wasn't something he'd dismiss anytime soon after coming to know just how precious and important his ability to sense these things really was in accordance to his own survival in this world.

Whatever Slomoe's motives, he had, technically helped Elliot. He reached down to the ground, picking up his sword which he'd dropped at some point, just before he'd entered Casper's dream. He felt more comfortable having a weapon in his hands, even if his instincts were telling him he was safe at the moment. Who was to know the next time Slomoe would throw him into a dream without warning if this kept up? A sword could well come in handy *when* that did happen again (not if).

"That dream," Elliot began, "That was...I mean, they say that dreams are a reflection of things that people are going through in real life, and...and the corpse, in that dream, it was me and it looked like how I am. The same stab wound and everything. I mean...but why would Casper feel guilty?"

Slomoe stared at him a moment,

"I think you've forgotten, Elliot Crow. You did tell me the killer was after your brother, did you not?"

Elliot nodded, starting to piece things together. His father had written a few mystery novels in the past. He'd always said he didn't really have the talent for it, which Elliot had never really understood. To him, all stories were the same. But in a murder mystery, usually the killer had a motive for murdering the victim. That was a bit strange, Elliot realized. The person that had stabbed him had been after Casper specifically. Which meant that he had a motive for killing Casper. But he didn't know what he looked like?

It didn't really make a lot of sense now that he thought of it. But Casper was guilty. He felt guilty over Elliot's murder. Which meant that his brother must know something, or have some idea as to why someone would want him dead.

What was really going on?

Elliot started walking after Slomoe again, following down the rows and rows of books and towards shelves made of glass.

"Crystal dreams." Slomoe hummed happily. He seemed to ponder on something a moment, before he came to a quick decision, "Elliot Crow, as your master, I must insist you run an errand for me."

A little taken aback by the randomness (he must have still been dazed from the dream, since Slomoe was all about randomness), Elliot gave a small, curt head dip, indicating that he'd do whatever Slomoe wished for him to do.

"Just an errand." Slomoe grinned, revealing nice, shiny white teeth. "I need you to deliver something for me, to Time."

"Time?" Elliot repeated, he'd gotten the sense that he'd end up meeting Time again. He rather hoped he wouldn't have to do something crazy, like jumping on a moving train from a blimp.

Trinket had said that all those with responsibilities had to have some way of accessing their realm. Elliot figured it was some sort of law, though he couldn't help but wonder who it was that upheld such laws. It certainly wasn't a job he would ever wish to have.

Elliot gave himself a mental shake, now was not the time to repeat words. Slomoe wanted him to deliver something to time, so he'd best try to figure out how he ought to get there and what needed to be delivered. It bothered him that he'd barely had time to think on what he needed to do to get back home again.

"What do you want me to deliver?" Elliot asked him, "And how do I get to the realm of Time?"

Slomoe reached into the pocket of his pastel-blue dress pants, pulling out what Elliot identified immediately as the crystal heart he'd been sent to retrieve.

"I want you to deliver this." Slomoe said simply, then, he placed it around Elliot's neck. The pocket watch, which was still silent of any sounds of life or ticks hung just below his chest.

"So, you don't lose it." Slomoe elaborated, "Now then," he said walking back and forth, his long legs not bending as he raised a finger in the air as though he were a cartoon character about to make some sort of point, "I think you can find a way into Time's realm on your own. It's really quite simple when you think about it. And then you, being my apprentice, can return to this realm by entering in through a dream. All dreams connect here, see, just like all mirrors connect to the Realm of Reflections. Now the thing about our realms is that you can only enter the Realm of Reflections through a mirror if you've been invited. Like you can only enter the Realm of Dreams through a dream if you've been invited by me. The same goes for time."

Elliot looked at him in confusion,

"But I haven't been invited into Time's realm."

THE MURDER OF ELLIOT CROW

"Oh?" Slomoe raised an eyebrow, "You say you haven't, but either you're lying, or you're unaware. You stink of Time. More than you stink of dreams or reflections. It's rather off-putting actually."

Elliot furrowed his brow in confusion,

"I smell?" he wondered if he ought to be insulted.

"Well...smell might not be the most accurate term." Slomoe relented, "But yes, you do. Now then, chop, chop." He clapped his hands together, "Best get to it, Elliot Crow. I need that crystal heart delivered, and Time waits for no man. Rather odd considering he has all the time in the world."

Elliot nodded, he'd certainly thought that odd himself when he'd first met Time. It took him a moment to realize Slomoe appeared to be waiting for something, staring at him as though he were expecting something to happen. It was then that Elliot figured, he wanted him to leave.

But how was he to do that?

He supposed, he could always enter through a mirror again, then go on through another mirror into the real world.

Oh, wait! Maybe he wasn't supposed to use a mirror, but a dream. Hadn't Slomoe said that in order to enter his realm again, he'd have to enter through a dream? In that case, perhaps it was a two-way street, much like with the mirrors.

But then, Elliot thought, how was he supposed to do that?

He felt something brush up against his leg and looked down. It was Cairo, his cat. She was looking up at him with the same expectant look that Slomoe was looking at him with.

Okay, Elliot tried again, Slomoe had said that all dreams led to the Kingdome of Dreams, that every dream could be reached here.

Thinking back on it, when Slomoe had pushed Elliot into Casper's dream, he hadn't opened a book like before. But that was because his brother had been dreaming already. He'd been asleep and dreaming, which meant that the dream had been taking place before Elliot had entered, then he'd gotten a book after the fact.

So then, Elliot continued to reason, in order to exit the Kingdom of dreams, he would have to enter the dream of someone who was already dreaming. How was he supposed to do that? Should he think of a specific person? Were there magic words that needed to be spoken?

No, he was overthinking this. This was the Kingdom of Dreams, and dreams were all about belief. No matter he tried to believe there was a dream, directly in front of him, but that simply didn't seem to do it.

Cairo brushed up against him again and Elliot looked down at her. She appeared to be annoyed with him, as though he'd forgotten to consider something.

Wait a minute, Elliot's eyes widened as realization struck. Cairo could find other realms, or at least, Elliot knew she could find Trinket's realm, and then, back on the train to the Kingdom of Dreams, how had she gotten there again? And then in the Realm of Reflections...That was it!

His instincts told him that he was quite correct in his assessment, that Cairo could aid him with his travel between realms. It probably wasn't what Slomoe wanted, but that didn't make it any less true, and maybe this would be a good opportunity.

"Cairo," Elliot looked at his cat, "Could you lead me to Trinket? If I'm leaving anyways, I ought to make sure he and Gear survived the blimp crash." Slomoe let out a laugh,

"As though Trinket Deadlock would ever die from a blimp crash!" He whipped a tear away from his eye, "That's rich, ya know? Oh...I ought to tell that one to Blue later."

Elliot tried to hide a frown. He didn't much like being mocked, but Cairo looked up at him, as though believing it to be a good idea. She started running off and Elliot followed after her.

They wove through the bookshelves of the dream kingdom, leaving Slomoe behind, and out of view. Even though they didn't appear to go far, and even though Elliot was certain he'd traveled in this direction before, he knew something was very different.

The book shelves were thinning far too soon, and before he knew it, Elliot was in a grassy field, and not silver grass either, but ordinary green grass. Cairo had slowed down, passing over a bridge over a small stream where rainbow fish played in the waters. Elliot looked back but found that he couldn't see even a hint of the Kingdom of Dreams at all.

Elliot followed Cairo, now at a walking pace over a cobblestone road. He was led into a familiar looking square towards a familiar looking house. Cairo finally stopped, cleaning up her face with her paw.

"Thanks, Cairo." Elliot shot her a grin, he looked back at the door, then he knocked.

CHAPTER FOURTEEN

Magic

Elliot grimaced as he heard the sound of what he thought was some sort of explosion, then the sound of metal against metal.

"I've got it~" Elliot heard Trinket's voice sing.

"Like *** you're going out like that you *** *****!"

There were more peculiar sounds behind the door, like something falling into a pile of metal parts. Finally, the door opened, revealing Gear. Her face was covered in black soot and grease, and her hair looked even more wild than usual, held back by green goggles.

"Oh, it's you." Gear said flatly.

"Who is it, Gear?" Trinket asked in a whiny voice.

"It's that Crowfood kid!" Gear shouted back.

"It's Elliot..." Elliot trailed off, not sure how he liked Gear's nickname for him.

Trinket popped up from behind Gear, smile still on his face, as usual, although his face was covered in soot and grease, much like Gear's. His hair, which was usually neatly kept, looked wild. He wondered if maybe this had something to do with the explosion he'd heard earlier.

"Elliot Crow!" Trinket greeted happily, his eyes then fell on the pocket watch hanging off of Elliot's neck, "Oh my...is that a crystal heart?"

Elliot nodded, then Gear's eyes found the crystal pocket watch as well. Her eyes widened,

"How in the *** did you manage that, kid?" she looked rather impressed.

"Well, Slomoe said that if I wanted to be his apprentice that I needed to go to the Realm of Reflections first." He looked at Trinket, "Sorry. I know you warned me against that..."

"It's alright." Trinket wiped away his concerns, "It seems I underestimated you, Elliot Crow...You must have seen Miranda, I presume?"

"I did." Elliot nodded, "I fought her off with the sword I pulled from the..." Elliot paused and looked down at his empty hand which had previously been carrying the sword.

Where had it gone? Had he let go of it? No. His hand had been grasping the sword only a second ago. As though the thought itself was some sort of trigger, the sword appeared in his hand.

"My, my..." Trinket tilted his head to the side, and Elliot got the sense he was impressed, "The Sword of the Worthy. I haven't seen that one in a long time."

Gear looked surprised, then looked at her mentor,

"Wasn't that your sword, Trinket?"

"That it was." Trinket nodded, a hint of thoughtfulness in his voice, "You're headed to Time's realm, right? Knowing the King of Dreams, he wouldn't want to make Time upset by keeping a crystal heart from him."

"Yeah." Elliot nodded slowly.

"Do you know how to get to Time's realm?"

"No." Elliot admitted, "I've been thinking about it. Slomoe says that I smell like Time, and that I should be able to get there. But I've only been there once before and it was only for a few minutes before he kicked me out."

Trinket tilted his head the other way, and Elliot wondered if maybe saying 'he smelled like Time' might actually have been peculiar enough to give him pause.

"He said you smell like Time?" it seemed Elliot was right in his assessment, "Hm...I suppose he would know. How odd, and you said you were only in his realm for a few minutes?"

"Yeah." Elliot nodded his head, "But Slomoe says I smell more like Time then dreams or mirrors. Does that mean something?"

Gear looked over at Trinket, and Elliot got the sense that she already had a good idea.

"Perhaps..." Trinket hummed again thoughtfully, "You are new to this world, Elliot Crow, but you also exabit signs of magic. I wonder...Oh, where are our manners, come in, come in." He gestured as Gear gave him an incredulous look.

"Don't just leave us hanging you ***!" Gear shouted at him.

If anything, Trinket's smile only seemed to widen. Elliot wondered if Trinket actually enjoyed Gear's yelling at him. He walked into the 'house' cautiously, much like the first time.

The place looked exactly the same as it did before, like a giant warehouse. The Youfoe appeared just the same as it had when he'd first seen it, without any damage appearing to have been sustained from the lightning storm or the fire.

"Come, come." Trinket gestured, "I'll start the tea and we can talk a bit."

"Oh, um, thanks." Elliot said politely, following behind Trinket and onboard the large ship. He was more aware now, and smart enough not to lose sight of Trinket this time as they walked up the stairs and down into the long, thin hall.

Gear mumbled something as she walked behind Elliot, but he didn't hear what it was she'd said as it was likely something no one was meant to hear other than herself.

Elliot and Gear both took a seat in the sitting room as Trinket went off to prepare some tea.

Although Elliot was normally patient and he certainly didn't want to rush the man, he was feeling a tad fidgety and nervous. Just what other strange revelations was he going to face during this talk?

After a few minutes, which felt like hours to Elliot, Trinket returned to the room with a tray of tea. He sat down in the chair to Elliot's right.

"Alright," Trinket began, "I suppose I should begin, then. To start off, do you know the difference between wizards and witches, Elliot Crow?"

Elliot shook his head,

"No, I don't. I just know that both of them can use magic and that Miranda isn't actually a witch."

"Correct." Trinket agreed, "Though she might appear to be one at first, she's a manifestation of fear from one of those with responsibilities. That might be a good place to start, actually. See, magic is everywhere. Witches have the ability to see it, the pulse that travels through the earth, skies, rivers, even living things. They can...syphon off, I guess you'd say, some of the magic from that pulse and use it, manipulate it how they see fit. Wizards, we derive magic from inside ourselves."

"Inside ourselves?" Elliot repeated.

Trinket nodded,

"It's because our souls are a bit off-beat from everyone else's."

"If you want the technical term." Gear rolled her eyes, but Trinket ignored her.

"Souls are constantly being reused and recycled, but, sometimes a quirk occurs, or sometimes we take back something a little extra. You know...how yin and yang are perfectly balanced? Well, that's kind of how souls are. A complete mesh of five elements. Sometimes something extra is added and that causes the balance to no longer be a balance, and all that extra stuff has to manifest its self somehow, or in some way. You can usually see the signs begin almost as soon as a child like that is born, strange things happen around them."

"Like...how I know things before they happen?" Elliot guessed.

Trinket nodded,

"That's how your magic manifests itself, by giving you hints or glimpses into the future. For me and Gear, it's an understanding of all machinery, just by touching it. Our powers are, of course, linked to those with responsibility. Ours is from the Realm of Machines. Yours, if I were to guess it, comes from the Realm of Time." Trinket picked up his tea cup and took a sip.

Elliot picked up his own cup and did the same. It tasted quite good, as always. Trinket's assessment made a certain amount of sense in Elliot's mind,

"Was that how I wound up in Time's realm?" Elliot wondered, "After I was stabbed, I mean?"

Trinket put his tea cup down,

"It's possible that you instinctively used magic to try to save yourself. That might explain why you're not like normal ghosts."

"Actually," Elliot said, "I'm alive...or at least, my body is. I'm in a coma in a hospital back in my hometown."

Trinket's eyes sparkled with intrigue,

"Fascinating. Perhaps, you must have sent your soul to the Realm of Time as a means of...recharging. That would certainly be enough to sustain it for a while, but it won't last forever. Perhaps some sort of shock would do it. Send your soul back into your body, that is."

Elliot nodded, recalling that Slomoe had said the same thing.

"Gear, we're leaving tomorrow morning."

Gear let out a groan,

"For once, can't we just visit a realm where we're actually welcome?"

"Now, Gear," Trinket said in a chastising tone, "you know there's no fun in that."

"I *** hate you."

"Come now, Gear. Lots to do, lots to do." Trinket said fondly, "We need to do our final repairs before tomorrow, then we'll do our checks in the morning and...oh, I suppose..." he looked over at Elliot, "How would you like me to give you a few lessons on how to properly use that sword of yours?"

Elliot looked down at his empty hand, noting the sword was once again gone. He looked back up at Trinket. This was probably the first time someone had actually offered him some lessons. Slomoe's idea of 'teaching' was more like, 'through him over the cliff and see if he climbs back up,' and Elliot was hesitant to call that teaching. The more knowledge and skills he had at his disposal, the more likely he was to make it home again before he really was dead.

"If you're willing, please teach me." Elliot agreed quickly.

Trinket's smile seemed to widen and Gear rolled her eyes. She got up from her spot on the edge of the sofa, then patted Elliot's back as she passed,

"Yeah, good luck, kid. You're gonna need it." She turned to Trinket, "I'm going to start on the repairs."

"You're not going to have some tea?" Trinket asked her.

Gear snorted,

"You *** know I won't."

She turned back towards the hall and started making her way in the direction that led to the exit. Elliot guessed she was going to do some repairs to the outside of the ship, which he was quite sure she and Trinket had been doing before he had gotten there.

Trinket took another sip of his tea, then Elliot picked up his own cup and took a sip.

"Were you guys hurt?" He asked Trinket and Gear, "I saw the engine room glowing before I got on the train to the Kingdom of Dreams. It was on fire, wasn't it? The Youfoe, I mean." Elliot added.

Trinket chuckled,

"Gear and I were perfectly fine, I landed us safely. The one that took the most damage was our pour ship. Thankfully, that stuff is ridiculously easy to repair and this isn't the first time she's been on fire, and probably not the last either." Trinket laughed outright, "Actually, I'm the one that caused most of those."

Elliot wondered why he was laughing about that. It certainly would explain the sounds of all those explosions though. Part of him wondered if Trinket set the Youfoe on fire on purpose. He didn't really seem to care all that much for damages.

"Don't sound so proud of that, you ***!" Gear's voice shouted from down the hall.

Trinket looked to the hallway,

"I guess she heard me."

Elliot had to resist the urge to give the man a strange look and instead took a sip of his tea. He was really starting to miss food and sleep, and everything else that made him feel alive.

As night fell in the Youfoe, Elliot found himself spending the lonely hours of the evening on his own. He'd been next to useless helping out Trinket and Gear with their repairs. Only being able to clean up a little bit around the warehouse, and even then, he didn't know where most of their equipment was supposed to be stored. Elliot started reading a peculiar fantasy novel in the library. It wasn't a particularly good story, and he soon found himself growing tired of it.

He never had been much of a reader, but whenever he found himself spending a night with Trinket and Gear it seemed about the only the he really could do, what with not needing to sleep and all. Cairo had fallen asleep in the corner in a space between the two book shelves.

Elliot took a breath, then closed the book and set it down at his side.

He didn't really understand Slomoe sometimes. The man seemed to make everything out to be some sort of game. It frustrated him, and he sort of understood how it was that Gear didn't like him. He could imagine Gear shouting at him as the king pranced about his bookshelves, smiling and laughing all the while...wait, wasn't that like her relationship with Trinket?

He breathed out a sigh, wondering if they might have something on sword fighting. Trinket had said he wanted to teach Elliot how to use a sword, after all.

He was more than a little disappointed when he couldn't find anything. Elliot had never really been one to study much, though his grades hadn't been good, they hadn't necessarily been bad either. It just would have been nice to actually be prepared for a change, or to have the feeling that he was actually doing something useful. The feeling of helplessness was becoming a rather constant companion during his travels. Like he was only being pushed along by the different forces he happened to cross and going along with it because that was easiest. He didn't feel confident, not even in himself. Wasn't that what Trinket had said was important? Believing in one's self?

Elliot let out another sigh and sat back down on the couch. He closed his eyes and listened to the hum of the ship, then...the repetitive beeping of a heart monitor.

His eyes opened slightly, but his mind became hazy as he noticed a woman with gothic dress and long, black hair. She was immediately by him. She heard her call out his name.

"Mom."

A man came in. He was dressed in a doctor's garb, but Elliot wasn't able to stay awake for much longer. His eyes closed...then opened again. He was back aboard the Youfoe.

He swallowed back a lump of emotion which had somehow managed to lodge itself in his throat while he wasn't paying attention.

That was the second time he'd managed to catch a glimpse of his home, and the first time since that he'd caught a glimpse of his mother.

The door of the library opened up, revealing Trinket, dressed up in a tux of sorts and a top hat, his usual outfit (one which Elliot had no idea as to how he worked in as it seemed quite uncomfortable to wear all the time).

"Elliot Crow." Trinket's smile seemed even wider than usual, "You've a big day today. A big day indeed...Come on, then. Let us get to work." He gestured for him to follow.

As soon as Elliot rose to his feet, Cairo woke up and jumped down off the couch, following behind Elliot in a show of her usual loyalty. She exited first and Elliot followed after, closing the door behind them. When he turned back, Trinket was already half-way down the hall and Elliot had to jog after him before he could catch up. The man didn't appear to notice and Elliot wondered if maybe he was actually excited. Not every tell needed to be a facial expression, Elliot thought to himself, and the way that Trinket insisted on walking far faster than his usual pace seemed a good indication as to his mood.

Trinket led him up a flight of stairs and down another hallway,

"So, read anything good last night?" He asked Elliot curiously.

Elliot shrugged,

"Just some fantasy novels." He admitted, "Although, I did try looking up some books on sword fighting, I couldn't find any."

Trinket hummed thoughtfully and nodded his head, as though that were to be expected. He didn't confirm or deny whether or not he actually had a book on the subject, however.

Because, of course, Elliot thought dryly, that would be entirely too easy.

They stopped by a ladder and Trinket began to climb up, opening up the hatch door at the top. Elliot could see the sky momentarily, and the wind ruffling Trinket's hair and threatening to blow off his hat. How was that even staying on anyways? He wondered with fascination.

He'd never considered it before, but maybe Trinket's hat was magical?

He decided not to voice the thought out loud. It would likely earn him an amused look and no other explanation outside of that. Elliot followed his lead and climbed up the ladder. Trinket helped him up onto what must have been the very top of the blimp.

Though how they had managed to get there made no logical sense. They would have had to have passed through the balloon part of the blimp, and Elliot knew they hadn't. Though he wasn't entirely sure about Trinket's hat, he was positive that the blimp was magical, and if Trinket denied it then he was lying.

The area was a spacious one, and considering how fast they were going, Elliot would have expected the wind to be much harsher. It was very plain, looking like a cement arena with a black, metal fence that surrounded it, as though to assure the safety of whoever climbed up.

Trinket knelt down and closed the door.

Elliot nearly jumped out of his skin when he felt something brush up against his leg. He looked down to see Cairo shooting him a look of amusement.

Really, Elliot wondered, how did she do that? There was no possible way for her to physically get up on the deck...and the train too...

Elliot wondered if he should even question such peculiarities anymore.

"Elliot Crow."

Elliot's attention snapped back over to Trinket.

"Today we'll be working on stances."

Elliot blinked in confusion,

"Stances?"

Trinket nodded,

"There are many different ways to fight with a sword. Many different branches, and many different styles within those branches. When it comes to a stance, you want to use something solid, something that will leave you unmoving if pushed, for example." Trinket moved his right foot in front of his left, his left foot pointed directly to the side, though his heels lined up perfectly and his knees bent.

"This is a standard fencing stance." Trinket explained, "You'll see this stance in tournaments all the time. Try it out."

Elliot did and Trinket got out of his stance. He moved Elliot's leg slightly so that his heels were more in line, then had him crouch a little bit more. After only a minute, Elliot was starting to feel the strain on his muscles.

"This particular stance makes it very difficult for your opponent to attack you from your front. It's more offensively focused, however. You'll notice," Trinket got into the stance again and moved back and forth in a sort of shimmy, "It's easy to move back and forth rapidly. There are, however, a couple of downsides to this stance. If I were to attack you from the side, for instance." Trinket got out of his stance, then pushed Elliot from the side, causing him to fall back with a small scream of surprise.

"You'd fall right over." Trinket said as though nothing had happened.

Elliot knew right then that Trinket was going to be a tough teacher, but he didn't realize how tough until Trinket had him holding a stance for exactly one hour, then switching to a different stance an hour later. He was pretty sure his legs were going to give out only ten minutes in, and they did after the second stance.

Elliot didn't think of himself as being unfit. He played soccer, and that generally took a lot of work. It just happened that the work Trinket was giving him was that much more difficult, and it didn't appear to be letting up either.

Elliot hadn't even realized his muscles could hurt, what with him not being alive. Elliot paused, noticing something...strange.

"I'm breathing." Elliot murmured.

"Well," Elliot's head snapped up to Trinket who had been the one to speak, "It certainly took you long enough."

"But...I'm a spirit, right?" Elliot panted from his spot sitting on the ground.

"You are." Trinket agreed, "But you're a little more alive than you were before. The mind, the body and the spirit are all connected, Elliot Crow. You can't really train one without training the others. The more you work yourself, the more connected to your body you'll become."

Elliot stared at him blankly, wondering at the double meaning to Trinket's words. Most of what the people in this world said seemed to have a double meaning. His body was at the hospital, which meant...he was growing more connected to it somehow? Had Trinket planned that?

Elliot tried to get up, only to fall back down when Trinket poked him in the chest.

"Take a break, Elliot Crow." Trinket said, sitting down beside him.

He looked like he hadn't broken a sweat! It was almost frustrating, and once again, Elliot was reminded that he had been wearing a tux through the entire ordeal and putting in just about the same amount of work that he had.

"His breath is laboured." Elliot heard a voice coming from nowhere.

"He seems to be losing fluids."

Elliot's eyes opened in a room that looked much like a hospital room. His thoughts seemed to be a bit clearer and for the first time, he knew where he was.

"He's coming to." A man's voice said with disbelief.

"Elliot? Elliot? Can you hear me?" It was his mother's voice.

Now was his chance. If he wanted to get his message across it was now or never.

"Cas-per." It was difficult to speak and his thoughts seemed to be getting hazier, "Casper." He tried again, "Casper is...in...danger..."

"He should be brain dead!" The doctor gaped, not believing what he was witnessing.

"I'll wake...again." Elliot mumbled, as the vision of his mother became blurrier and clouded by black dots.

His eyes opened again and he was back on top of the Youfoe. Trinket was staring at him through his squinted eyes. Elliot's own eyes wandered down to Trinket's left-hand side where two swords were rested and a mountain of padded gear.

"If we had more time, I'd take at least another week on the stances." Trinket pushed himself up off the ground, "But alas, we do not. So, I'm going to teach you how to properly hold a sword. I will teach you how to parry and how to properly attack. Stand up, Elliot Crow."

Elliot stood up, all the while thinking that his moments in the hospital must last far longer than he'd originally assumed.

Trinket handed over his practice sword and adjusted his grip, showing him a few defensive techniques, how to attack and so on until he deemed Elliot ready for a practice round.

The practice spars were disastrous to say the least. He couldn't hit Trinket at all while the man easily disarmed him, made him fall to the ground, and even thumped him over the head a few times. Needless to say, Elliot knew that Trinket was only playing with him. It made him feel a little mad, though he also knew it was ridiculous to think he could ever match up to him. Trinket had likely been at this for years while Elliot had been at it for a few measly hours.

"Tell me, Elliot Crow," Trinket said, all the while pointing the practice, dull sword at his chest, "Why do you want to learn the art of the sword?"

Elliot looked at him puzzledly,

"Because...I want to save my brother."

Trinket lowered the sword, nodding,

"Protection, then. That's a good reason."

Elliot had thought he had always been honest and clear about his reasons.

Trinket knelt down, looking him in the eyes once more,

"You still seem to have a bit of trouble believing in yourself. You've been practicing, but you don't quite have the hang of it yet, do you?" It wasn't really a question. Trinket got up again, his sword over his shoulder, like some sort of marching band leader, "Always believe in yourself." Trinket said easily, "If you do that, then nothing is impossible." He tapped Elliot on the head once again, "You've been using that brain of yours to work through your trials. That's always a good thing. Learn to trust those skills of yours."

Elliot rubbed the top of his head where Trinket had bopped him.

"Now, then." Trinket said, "I'm getting rather hungry, so I'm going to go eat. Keep practicing with that sword of yours until I come up to tell you to stop. Then, you'll be taking a break until morning. If you strain yourself too much, that will be detrimental." He warned.

Elliot nodded, having learned to take such warnings to heart. He picked up his sword once more and started to practice, just as Trinket had told him to.

Trinket didn't return until the sun had set and by then, Elliot was exhausted. By the time he was allowed to break, he returned to the library with Cairo and lay on the couch all night not doing anything.

CHAPTER FIFTEEN

A Waste of Time

T he next day was spent sword fighting. Elliot was given very few moments to break and offered a nice cup of cold tea twice, which was rather refreshing, admittedly. Elliot had never had tea cold before, though he realized that the super sweet ice tea he was used to was certainly not real ice tea as actual tea, served cold from the fridge was. It must have been a Canadian thing, since Gear said that this was pretty standard, even in America.

Elliot never scored a point on Trinket, but on the fourth day of traveling, he knew he was at least getting a little bit better. He wasn't getting knocked down as much. In his own contemplations during his nights by himself he started to realize that the reason he wasn't knocking him down wasn't due entirely to a lack of effort, but rather to his own adjustments of his stances during their fights. Trinket seemed to have noticed too, and probably before even he had that Elliot now had fewer holes to exploit.

Of course, if Trinket were really trying, and Elliot knew he was holding back by a lot, he would wipe the floor with him.

Then came Elliot's next realization, though he'd felt rotten about Trinket knocking him down constantly and thought he was going hard on him, the truth was quite the opposite. No wonder Gear had found it so funny the first day. She obviously knew her own mentor's methods.

Elliot looked out to the window where the light of the stars and the moon were pouring in, offering him some light. There wasn't much time, only three more days until the full moon. It wouldn't be long until he got back to his family and then...then what?

Elliot closed his eyes and found himself in a hospital room. He saw his mother in a chair by his bed, her arms were crossed on his bed and her head was rested on top. She moved a little bit, as though sensing his consciousness. She looked up at him.

"Elliot?" She whispered.

"The full moon...I'll wake up."

"The full moon." She repeated.

Elliot closed his eyes again, then opened them. He was back on board the Youfoe. It felt like waking up from a dream. It was strange, how his life was like a dream...wasn't there a poem about that? Elliot thought to himself, getting up from his spot and running his hands along the book shelves until he found the volume he was looking for.

He opened it up to the fourth page, skipping over the copyright and title page.

All of life is gold,
In streams of silver,
In grasses green,
All of which aglow,
In vivid shades of dreams.

Elliot closed the book. He'd never really been one for poetry. Nor had he ever considered himself a poet, but now, he found himself enjoying those playful words which had long ensnared his father in their workings. Maybe that was how it started, he mused to himself, looking at the cover which had no words on the front or side leaving the title to the imagination of anyone who happened to pick it up.

He got up and put the book back on the shelf, then sorted through the far desk and pulled out a paper and pen. He sat down tentatively, staring at the blank piece of paper. How did someone write a poem anyways? His father made it look easy. He could just whip up a series of words, each one coming out brilliantly. He did that often, actually. Spewing out verses at the table, then lighting up and going off to write what he said down.

"All of life's a dream." Elliot murmured.

That sounded good. It was a line he could use, maybe work on. He wrote it down, but soon found himself staring at the words on repeat, playing them over in his mind. His father had said something about that once.

"Make it a story. The words aren't your enemy, play with them a bit and see what happens. You won't get something right off."

"A story..." Elliot thought out loud. Cairo had perked up from her spot on the couch. He turned to look at her after a moment and realized she was looking at him.

"I bet you dream, don't you?" he said to her.

Cairo shot him a look that said something along the lines of, *Silly human, of course I do.* Elliot's lips twitched.

"I bet you dream about chasing birds and rabbits, don't you? I see your tail and paws twitch when you sleep."

Cairo let out a big yawn, then nestled back down to sleep, as though the very thought of dreaming was making her drowsy. Elliot smiled, then started to write,

All of life's a dream...

Elliot let a small chuckle escape him, thinking that it wasn't a terrible first attempt. He allowed his eyes to shift back over to Cairo who, funnily enough, was twitching about in her sleep.

Probably chasing dream rabbits, Elliot thought amusedly.

There was a gentle knock at the door. The person on the other side didn't wait for an invitation before the door opened, revealing Gear. Her hair was even more wild than usual and she had a look about her that indicated the knocking was about all the politeness he'd get. She really wasn't a morning person.

"Trinket's waiting for you, Crowfood." She said curtly, then turned and walked down back down the hall she'd arrived through.

Elliot put the pen away but folded up the paper before putting it back in the drawer. He rather liked what he'd written, even if it wasn't really that great. He set it in the corner so that he'd recognise it when he got back, but that anyone who saw it was likely to mistake it for an ordinary sheet if they caught a glimpse of it. He closed the drawer and noted that Cairo had stirred from her dream. Elliot shot her a grin,

"I wrote a poem about you last night."

Cairo looked up at him questioningly.

"All of life's a dream,
Even for a cat,
She prowls about the garden,
Chasing tasty rats.
But when she pounces on one,
She finds it is in vain.
The silly cat wakes up,
In a tangle of colored string."

Cairo actually looked somewhat amused by his attempt, and Elliot took that as a good sign.

"I guess we should go back up to the deck." Elliot said out loud absently, walking out into the hall. He closed the door behind him and Cairo, then walked down the hall towards the usual training area.

As usual, when climbing the ladder up to the deck, he left Cairo behind, only to find her already waiting for him up top. He looked back down on instinct, wondering if Cairo might have a twin and had, in fact, been pulling the wool over his eyes through their entire relationship. It seemed that wasn't the case, however. He closed the door then looked back up at Trinket who appeared to have caught on to his thoughts.

"Cats have a tendency to show up wherever they feel. Especially bonded familiars. I find they also have a tendency to enter places people generally don't want them to enter."

It was then that Elliot realized that Trinket didn't have the usual equipment out and waiting for him.

"Now then." Trinket said, "I thought we'd take our morning to learn something other than sword fighting."

Elliot felt both excited and disappointed. He hadn't even realized that he'd been looking forward to the grueling exercises and spars against Trinket until then. It was actually rather funny. He'd never really looked forward to much in his life, really. Even though he played soccer, since it was what most guys his age seemed to enjoy, he hadn't felt the same thrill he had gotten from sword fighting. Yet, the prospect of learning something else from the eccentric man also intrigued him. Trinket might have been a tough teacher, but he was also a very good one.

"I don't know much about time magic." Trinket admitted, "But I do know it's a powerful sort of magic. One that can decimate a mountain, heal wounds, and even cause the world to freeze if the user knows how. Those visions of yours are only but the tip of the iceberg, so to speak."

Elliot swallowed hard, wondering if he could really do something like that. He found it a bit tough to believe.

"Of course, Time magic, just like any magic, can be terribly dangerous when mishandled. So, we'll have to try not to mishandle it."

Elliot wondered if Trinket really knew what he was doing, or if he was just pretending. It felt much like the later. Why was it that everyone in this world was so utterly insane?

"We'll start with something simple." Trinket said, smile playing on his lips. He threw something into the air. Elliot caught it automatically.

"You've got good reflexes." Trinket complimented.

Slomoe had said something along the same lines, Elliot recalled before looking down at the object in his hand. It was a square package that looked like it had been store-bought. Still, it looked very familiar.

"Tarot cards." Elliot read the script at the bottom. His mother had several decks of tarot cards back at home, hidden away in her room.

"My gift to you." Trinket said, "You aren't allowed to buy your own, after all. It has to be gifted to you by someone."

Elliot nodded, he remembered something along those lines. His mother had once asked him if he wanted his own deck, but he'd shot her down. Was that irony? He wondered vaguely. He found it rather funny that something bought and sold at one of his mother's favourite stores might in some way actually be magical. He tried to remember what his mother had said.

It was best to choose your own deck, as people had affinities for different things. It had something to do with the spirit of the cards, although Elliot had thought that had sounded like a cheesy line from one of those Saturday morning cartoons he'd watched when he was little.

So, it was best to pick the deck, but have someone else gift it to you. Elliot had always thought that if you were too specific in your request that it wasn't really a proper gift. There was something about the mystery of presents that had always been genuine to him. But then again, he knew nothing of affinities and such other than the meager bits and pieces of scattered information he'd managed to get from his mother.

His mum didn't like people touching her tarot cards either, he recalled. Something about tarot cards easily absorbing different energies. She did, however, allow him and his brother to touch them. Her family seemed to be the exception. Although, if that whole thing was true, about energies, then Elliot couldn't help but feel a little bit bad for his thoughts during the very few and rare moments that he had picked up one of her decks (normally to put them away after his mother had left them out).

Trinket had said that the mind, body, and spirit were connected. And with all his negative thoughts about his mother and her interests, well...

"Do you know how to use them?" Trinket asked Elliot curiously.

"Um, I've seen my mom use them before." He admitted, trying to recall the different layouts he'd seen. He could remember a bit. His mother had said that it also depended on the deck as well.

"Well, try it out then." Trinket gestured, taking a seat, cross-legged in front of Elliot.

Elliot took this as his cue to sit down as well.

"I've never actually done this myself before." He murmured, opening up the deck. He started looking through the cards individually, recognising a few of them automatically and feeling a little bit proud. He had been listening to what his mother had told him after all.

He paused, thinking about something,

"You aren't supposed to read your own future though, right?" he looked over to Trinket who gave a nod.

"Quite right." Trinket agreed, "But, you can ask the cards about events, or about present problems."

Elliot thought on this,

"Like...how to get to Time's realm?"

"That would be an excellent question." Trinket added, "So long as you don't ask about *how you will* enter the realm of Time." Trinket warned, "You need to make your own decisions. Divination is a contract between the diviner and that which is being divined. You will be told what you *need* to know, but not necessarily what you *want* to know."

Elliot thought on that. It felt like some sort of word game. His teacher had told him the difference between need and want. But did he really need to know anything about the future? He paused, thinking about all he'd been through on this crazy journey, then nodded his head. Well, any sort of advantage he could get, he would take.

He started shuffling the cards, thinking about his question and thinking about it hard. He lay the first card down in the center, then he drew another card and put it to the right, then the last card went to the left of the center card making a total of three.

He'd seen his mother do something along these lines when she had a simple question she wanted an answer to.

Trinket watched him carefully, as though ready to help if something went wrong. He turned over the center card.

The Tower

He'd once heard his mother refer to this card as the 'disaster card.' Though it usually talked about some sort of destruction or disaster, this time Elliot wasn't so sure that was what this card was saying. A vision of white invaded Elliot's sight and he caught a glimpse of something. The name of which was on the tip of his tongue, though only because he'd seen it in books.

"Stonehenge." Elliot whispered, eyes widening. He looked back over at Trinket, "That's the entrance?"

"This time it is." Trinket said thoughtfully, "Time is a bit like the King of Dreams in that he likes to make getting to his realm terribly difficult. However, unlike King Slomoe, Time doesn't enjoy watching people struggle, but rather doesn't want anyone to get to his realm at all. He moves around the means of getting to his realm, which is allowed, according to the rules, so long as there are a few consistencies."

Elliot regarded him puzzledly, before realizing Trinket was expecting him to turn over the next two cards. He turned over the one on the right, going in the order in which he'd lain the cards down.

The Queen of Swords

Elliot scrunched his forehead,

"You need to want to get there to actually get there." He said slowly, he saw Trinket nod out of the corner of his mind, but he didn't really need the confirmation. He knew he was right. He turned over the last card.

The moon

This actually caused Elliot's breath to catch,

"And...it can only be accessed on the night of a full moon."

"Ah," Trinket nodded, "That is one of Time's constant rules. Always a full moon. I never really took him as a fan for the clichés, but then again, those with responsibilities can be full of surprises."

"But...but that's when I'm supposed to wake up." Elliot said worriedly.

"It is." Trinket agreed, "Which is why we aren't heading to Stonehenge." Elliot shot him a confused look,

"Then...where are we heading?"

"Blackstone." Trinket answered.

Elliot didn't know what to stay. Why were they heading to his hometown? "That's where you live, correct? At least, that's what I've managed to gather."

"Um, yeah." Elliot nodded uncertainly.

"You have a piece of Time's realm inside of you." Trinket said as though it were obvious, "You can access his realm all on your own. You don't need a full moon to do that."

"Slomoe said something similar." Elliot recalled, thinking about how the king had expected him to leave the Kingdom of Dreams all on his own, but how he had chosen Cairo to get there instead...could that be it?

Elliot's thought process came to a halt, then sped up ten-fold. Trinket had told him before, hadn't he? That cats could get into all sorts of places that people didn't want them to, and she was his familiar.

"Cairo." Elliot stated, looking over at Trinket, "She's my familiar, and...and she's connected to my magic, right? Which means, she's probably connected to the realm too."

Trinket nodded and Elliot gave a mental fist pump. He'd guessed right.

"You said before that cats could travel where they wanted, so then...then she could probably get there."

"She could." Trinket agreed, "And you could follow her. Then, you could follow her back to me. There are other ways you could go..." He paused, "But, those are things that are mostly learned with experience."

Elliot almost felt silly. He could have gotten there whenever he had wanted. Trinket had known, obviously. He just hadn't said anything. He'd wanted Elliot to figure it all out on his own, though he had no idea as to why.

Was that just a quirk of the people in this world? Elliot wondered, to act all mysterious and say strange things when they're actually giving out a riddle? It was somewhat annoying, but he had to admit that he was rather proud of himself for actually figuring it out. He took the crystal heart from out of his shirt, allowing it to hang down over his chest. He gathered up the tarot cards.

"I should do it now, then." Elliot decided.

Trinket nodded,

"It's best not to put these things off." He agreed.

Elliot packed the cards up into their cardboard package and stuffed the into his front right pocket. He paused a moment as he looked at his familiar, then he looked back over at Trinket.

"I wrote something down earlier and left it in your library." He told him, "I hope you don't mind me fetching it before I go. I don't want to forget it, is all."

Trinket nodded,

"You don't need my permission. It's always a good idea to be prepared." Elliot wasn't so sure that the poem would prepare him for anything. It was, after all, just a silly poem about his cat. But he was reluctant to let it go, and so, he opened up the hatch door and climbed down. He wasn't at all surprised anymore when Cairo was already down there, waiting.

It was like she vanished whenever she was outside of his field of vision, Elliot mused absently.

After fetching the paper out of the desk drawer in the library and putting it in his pocket with the tarot deck, he turned to look down at Cairo. She seemed to have already been expecting this.

"Alright, Cairo." Elliot said, "I want to get to Time's realm. Could you please lead me there?"

Cairo let out a meow, then turned and started running off. Elliot had expected this, and took off running after her. She took a left, then an immediate right, then another right. Elliot groaned when he realized they had arrived right back where they'd started. Then, Cairo took another turn, this time going in the opposite direction. She ran into the library, only for Elliot to find that it wasn't actually the library inside, but rather, the kitchen.

"Crowfood?" Gear wondered. She seemed to be preparing something on the stove.

"Sorry, following my cat." Elliot quickly said as Cairo scratched at the cupboard beneath the sink. Elliot opened it up and Cairo entered.

"You *** serious?" Gear asked incredulously as Elliot followed Cairo, noting right away that inside the cupboard was completely different from before. He doubted even Trinket would put an entire room underneath the sink. Which meant that this was Cairo's doing.

Somehow, she seemed to be warping the space around them. Or at least, that's what Elliot thought she was doing. Thinking back, she'd probably been doing that all along.

Were all cats really like that? Elliot wondered, thinking back to what Time had said and the hint he'd been given to reach Trinket's realm.

Follow the cats.

Maybe, Elliot realized, Time had already seen his bonding with Cairo from the start, and wasn't that a strange thought?

He found himself standing on a bridge, floating precariously in the middle of nowhere. A man in a dark cloak was looking directly at him from his seat in the very center where his small workshop sat.

"You are not incorrect." Time spoke in his deep voice.

Elliot froze, wondering if he was talking to him. Then he felt rather silly, because unless he was talking to himself, he and Cairo were the only two in the large room that went on endlessly with ticking and humming gears and trinkets.

"I knew." Time continued in his same raspy voice, "You would meet your familiar, Cairo who would lead you to Trinket Deadlock upon delivering the package I had asked you to give. Inside the package were a bunch of useless metal parts that had fallen off my wall. It was not the contents of the package."

Elliot stared at him, disbelievingly as everything, his entire journey began to unravel.

"It was about you going to the wizard who refuses to keep his nose out of other people's businesses. He would help you no matter if you had something with you or not, because Trinket Deadlock likes to meddle. *Chivalry*, I believe he calls it."

Elliot got the sense that though Time and Trinket must have a very dynamic relationship. One that he might never understand if the tone of slight fondness behind his words was any sort of indication. Like how a kid might talk about their favourite toy while pretending all the while that it was no big deal so as not to upset their friend.

"You would then meet Slomoe." Time interrupted his thoughts, "He would take you as his apprentice, and he would give you a test. Because you are of this realm, he would ask you to retrieve a Crystal Heart. He would ask this of you because he finds giving impossible tasks to those that wish to apprentice themselves to him to be amusing. Then, you would come back here."

Elliot took the crystal heart from his neck, looking at it uncertainly,

"What is it?" He wondered, looking into the crystal and getting a strange sort of shiver. He'd thought all along that the crystal heart was something precious, but he hadn't been able to figure out why or how.

Though Elliot couldn't see Time's eyes, he knew the god-like being was smiling. His pale lips twitched upwards, though barely and only for a moment.

"You still haven't figured it out?"

He was silent, and Elliot realized once again that he was being tested once again. Time was silent, and even if he asked, Elliot knew he'd receive no answer. It was another riddle that needed to be worked out on his own.

The crystal heart had been found inside of the Realm of Reflections, Elliot though to himself. Inside of the Kingdome of Mirrors and guarded by Miranda. There, he had met Toshi. He looked back over at Time. He'd been surprised when Elliot had entered his realm the first time. Back then, he'd caught him fiddling with pocket watches. Those watches, which were, apparently souls which Time fixed.

"This is someone's soul." Elliot realized.

"Those with responsibilities cannot enter the realm of someone else with responsibilities."

"You couldn't reach it on your own." Elliot realized, "You weren't surprised to see me arrive in your realm. You used me to get you the crystal heart, because you couldn't reach it!"

Time nodded and Elliot couldn't help but feel a little upset,

"But why didn't you just tell me?" He wanted to know.

It was then that Elliot thought that Time was amused, yet had, of course, expected the question.

"If I had asked, would you have gotten it for me?"

Elliot paused at the question. Would he have gotten it? Probably not. It wasn't as though it were any of his business, right? Elliot was starting to realize how horrible that sounded, especially after having met Trinket, a man who seemed very intent on helping just about everyone, as Time had pointed out. A man who made other peoples' businesses his own and seemed really quite happy to do whatever needed to be done, enjoying his meddling all the while.

"No. I wouldn't have." Elliot admitted, realizing just how horrible he'd been. He'd done that to his father too, and his mother, and to his brother who, in hindsight might have actually needed someone to meddle in his life.

"Not back then." Elliot finished, meeting Time's eyes with a new conviction.

"But you would now." Time stated, and it was, in fact, a statement.

He would do it. Because it was the right thing to do and because he had a pretty good idea that he knew exactly who the watch belonged to.

"That's Toshi's father, isn't it?" It wasn't really a question because Elliot knew. That was the King of the Kingdom of Mirrors, King Kagami.

"It is." Time said curtly, "None of those with responsibilities has ever died before. But because Toshi was born, the King of Reflections became vulnerable. His own realm killed him."

Elliot shook his head,

"It's not Toshi's fault." He defended. It wasn't fair to put that on Toshi. Toshi who had fought for his life inside of the Realm of Reflections for who knows how long. Toshi, the boy who looked far younger than he was, playing his endless game of words.

"No, it was not." Time said simply, "King Kagami did not have the necessary time to teach his son. That is all."

Elliot looked at him, a little stunned. But he knew, and he had no doubt that Time knew,

"If someone dies where you can't reach them, I'll help." He thought that it needed to be spoken out loud anyways, even if they did both know. Because now, the words were like a contract between them. His father had talking about that a few times.

*"A promise isn't something that necessarily has the word **promise** in it. It's a contract between two people. But it needs to be spoken out loud for it to be put into effect. That's how words work. They're funny like that."*

Time dipped his chin, acknowledging the offer, and Elliot knew instinctively that Time would one day call him on that promise. When that day came, Elliot would answer it. He would live through this, and he would make sure his brother lived through it too. Then he would gather those souls that Time couldn't reach and help them.

Although Elliot certainly couldn't say he was a fan of other people manipulating him, and that Time's goal, in the end, had been the crystal heart, he had managed to get out of the whole thing a much better person. It might not have been Time's intention. But it still felt like, in a strange sort of way, that Elliot owed him something.

"Thank you." He said.

This time, it actually seemed like Time really was surprised. He walked down from his workshop, down the platform, then took the watch that Elliot had been holding. He said nothing, turning his back to Elliot and walking back to his workshop where he set the crystal pocket watch on the table and opened it up, taking out some tools and working on the device with expert hands.

He wasn't going to say anything more and as his silence droned on, it became apparent that Elliot had been dismissed.

He looked down at Cairo,

"Could you lead me back to Trinket and Gear's blimp?" He asked her.

Cairo gave a nod, then, to Elliot's shock, she jumped right over the ledge and into the abyss of time. Without even a moment's hesitation, Elliot jumped off after her.

He didn't even scream as the world changed around him. But he did let out an "Oomph!" as he landed on his butt right on the top deck where Trinket and Elliot had had their sword practice.

Elliot blinked in utter confusion before noticing Trinket, sitting behind him and leisurely sipping tea.

"Well then," Trinket looked up at him, his face unchanging from its usual smile and Elliot noticed that there was another cup sitting there and knew instinctively that it was for him.

"How did it go?"

CHAPTER SIXTEEN

Trick and Treat

Blackstone was a small town that rested in the northwestern part of the province of Alberta. It was a quiet sort of place with mostly prairie surrounding it and no hills. It was extremely flat and seemed to go on forever and ever with very little in sight save for the surrounding farm houses and fields of grain.

It almost felt like the end of a story. There was a feeling of fulfillment, coupled with a feeling of nostalgia and acceptance.

Elliot watched with awe over the railings of the deck of the Youfoe as they descended right outside of town. Trinket was smiling knowingly,

"Your adventure isn't over yet, Elliot."

Elliot looked up at him in confusion.

"You still have to save your brother. Once you wake up, it's all over." Trinket told him solemnly, "You saw the killer's face and you alone can identify him."

"You think he'll come after me again?" Elliot asked Trinket.

"Well, I don't know." Trinket said, although it sounded like he certainly knew, "But if you were the killer, Elliot Crow, what would you do?"

He did have a point, Elliot thought. The killer had been after Casper, but things hadn't gone according to plan. If that happened to him...Elliot thought back to the mystery novels he'd read. If someone wanted someone else dead enough that they would actually try to kill them, then they usually tried again, didn't they?

He had two days before the full moon.

Elliot slowly made his way down into the Youfoe, following after Trinket. When he arrived at the exit with Cairo, with Trinket and Gear standing nearby, he knew this was farewell.

At least it was better than last time, Elliot comforted himself, thinking about the flaming blimp falling out of the sky.

"Well," Elliot said, feeling a little awkward all of a sudden, "I'll see you two later. If...if you ever need me, although I can't really think of a reason you'd need me, you can ask me for help."

Trinket's face didn't change at all, as expected. Although Gear rolled her eyes,

"We don't want nothing from you, Crowfood. We did this because we wanted to...and because Trinket's a nosy ***."

"Aw, but you love me anyways, don't you, Gear dear." It wasn't a question and his tone was just teasing enough to make Gear snort with derision, then storm off.

"See you, Crowfood. With your track record, it won't be too long."

"That's a bit insulting." Elliot grimaced, trying to at least keep up some illusion of competence.

Trinket shook his head,

"I think you've grown on her. Gear doesn't like goodbyes." He looked down at Cairo and gave her one last pet, "Make sure to treat this little lady well. You're lucky to have such a clever familiar, Elliot Crow. And...for Gear's sake of course, please stop by again after all this is over."

Elliot froze a moment, before a smile made its way onto his lips. He hadn't even thought about that. For some reason, he'd been operating under the notion that once this was all over...well, that it would be over. But he could see them again, couldn't he?

Cairo purred under Trinket's touch. The gentlemanly wizard looked up at Elliot.

"I think I'll have to stop by then." Elliot had to resist the urge to laugh, "For Gear, of course."

Trinket nodded, realizing Elliot had caught the joke.

"For Gear." Trinket nodded solemnly, or, as solemnly as Trinket could look with such an unchanging expression.

"I'll reach you when this is all over." Elliot promised, "Thank you, Trinket, and give Gear another thanks from me." He added in, "The invites open for you guys too, you know, if you're ever in the area."

"I'll keep that in mind. Until then," Trinket chuckled, "Adventure awaits!"

Elliot gave one last nod, before making his way down the steps, landing for the first time in several days on solid ground. He hadn't realized how much he'd missed it. Ground that didn't hum or shake or go through any turbulence. Cairo appeared just as relieved to be out of the air as him. She looked up at Elliot with her own little message.

It's about time! What were you thinking? Who's ever heard of a flying cat?

Elliot shrugged,

"If it's any consolation, I promise to never put you in a carrier."

Cairo shot him a terrified sort of look (and even though she was a cat, she could pull it off rather well).

"Come on." Elliot said, "Let's get out of the way of their lift off."

Cairo followed him away from the blimp. But it wasn't very long before they heard the Youfoe humming to life, then growing even louder. The wind around them picked up and Elliot picked up Cairo to shield her from the flying debris of grass and twigs as they achieved lift off.

His eyes widened as the ship flew up and right over the two of them and towards the city. He could see Trinket in the open doorway giving him one final wave. His hat remained steady on his head causing Elliot's suspicions to come back once again at full force. It had to be magical. There was no other explanation for a hat like that to remain on anyone's head during such violent winds.

The ship flickered out of existence but briefly, as it passed overhead, high in the sky, he saw it flicker into existence. Twice.

Unable to contain himself, Elliot laughed, allowing Cairo to jump out of his arms.

"What do you think, Cairo?" He asked the orange tabby, "Do you think we'll be seeing news reports about UFO sightings in Blackstone?"

Of course, she didn't answer him, simply walking on ahead towards the city. Elliot followed behind her. He couldn't say he understood why he was smiling, only that he couldn't stop. The adventure wasn't over. It was a startling realization that after his brother was saved that he would still have his magic and that this world would still be here for him after the killer was caught. What's more, he found something he actually wanted to do with himself. He'd never had something like that before, something that was entirely his that he alone could hold onto. Not to forget that he was also apprenticed to the King of Dreams. He got the sense, when he left the kingdom that Slomoe had no intention of letting him go. At least, not yet.

His father had said something about that once,

"No story really has an 'ending.' Not until death and even then...who really knows?"

It would be a long walk into the city and as the sun started to fall into the sky and Elliot and Cairo were on their fourth break, Elliot started to wonder if maybe he ought to just carry her for a while, considering it was just about the time that she usually went to sleep. Cairo came back with a dead mouse in her jaw. Elliot had to look away, discovering that he wasn't so fond of watching cats play with their meals.

After she'd devoured her kill, Elliot picked Cairo up and walked with her for a while, continuing to follow the highway, passing by a farm.

Cairo appeared to be drifting off in his arms, when suddenly, she tensed. Her fur prickled and she started to hiss at...something.

From the shadows of the tall grass, two black cats came running out.

For a moment, Elliot thought that maybe it was some sort of territorial thing, only to feel a strange niggling in the back of his mind that told him it wasn't.

"Spirits?" Elliot wondered, looking at the black cats curiously.

The sound of children laughing filled the air. It was actually a bit creepy and vaguely reminded Elliot of some sort of horror movie cliché. Maybe that was why he didn't feel so afraid.

In a ring of black smoke, the cats seemed to grow, and grow. Limbs stretched, bodies became larger and thicker and taller. Their paws extended out into fingers and their fur turned into flesh and fabric.

Two children, one boy and one girl with pale skin and black hair stared out at him with glowing yellow eyes that looked much like a cat's as they seemed to reflect the light in the same way.

Yet, Elliot wasn't afraid. Cairo had stopped hissing, apparently satisfied that Elliot had caught on to their deception.

"Aw, no fair." The girl whined.

"You had a familiar's help." The boy pouted.

They looked like they were youngish. Maybe eleven? But considering how young Toshi looked and how old Elliot suspected he really was, he had no doubt in his mind that these 'children' were not as young as they appeared.

"Did, um, you two want something?" Elliot asked them uncertainly.

They were dressed oddly (though at this point Elliot supposed he oughtn't be surprised), in black ponchos with cat ears on top of their hoods which they wore over their heads, an orange collar was strapped around their necks and a wiry tail attached to their orange shorts and skirt.

"I'm Trick." The girl introduced proudly.

"And I'm Treat." The boy grinned.

"Like..." Elliot paused, "Trick or treat? Like on Halloween?"

"Of course." The boy said, as though it was strange that someone didn't know about them.

There was a gleam in the cat-girl's eyes,

"Are you a new spirit?"

Elliot nodded and the girl clapped her hands together,

"I should have known. Everyone knows about us. We're the reason the fleshies think that black cats are bad luck, see."

The boy, Treat nodded his head solemnly,

"We can't even cross their paths without setting people on edge."

"But of course," Trick continued, "The real fun starts on Halloween, well, that's what they call October thirty first now."

"That's when everyone can see us." Treat grinned.

"And when our powers are highest." Trick shared her twin's expression.

Elliot wondered momentarily if maybe the two of them were having him on, but his instincts were telling him that no, they weren't. They were being completely truthful.

"Pranks galore!" Treat jumped up and down excitedly.

"Until they discovered we have a huge sweet tooth." Trick added in, "Then it became a game."

"No sweets, then we'll come up with our own way of having fun. Trick! Prepare the whoopee cushions!"

"Whoopee!" Trick jumped into the air, then giggled when a farting sound was made. She took a whoopee cushion out from under her butt, then fell back laughing.

It seemed that these two spirits weren't entirely sane, Elliot deduced. Then again, they did seem to conform to the pattern of insane spirits and wizards in this world.

"So, now you know about us." Trick said, "You need to give us something in return."

"I need to give you something?" Elliot wondered cautiously.

"Yes!" Treat crossed his arms, eying Elliot suspiciously, as though he were some sort of suspicious customer at a restaurant getting ready to dine and dash.

"We told you our story." Trick said, as though it were obvious, "So, if you don't want to be pranked, you'd best tell us a good one."

"Well," Elliot thought out loud, "I'm not much of a story teller, or a writer. But my father is. He actually makes a living off of it. I remember some of his poems, if you'd like me to tell you one?"

"A poem?" Treat scrunched his nose, "But those are all fluffy and boring. Like – like that guy, remember that guy, Trick?" Treat turned to his sister.

"Oh yeah, that guy." Trick nodded, obviously knowing exactly who her brother was talking about, "The one that talked about his golden love?"

"Yeah, that guy." Treat confirmed.

"My dad doesn't write about that stuff." Elliot shook his head, "Well, not usually. He likes to make poems that have stories in them."

This at least seemed to catch their interest. Trick straightened importantly,

"Very well then." She said, "Tell us this not-boring poem your father wrote."

"But if it's bad, I'm going to turn your hair blue." Treat warned.

Elliot nodded quickly, deciding it might be best to just get on with it before his audience grew bored. He cleared his throat, then began to recite,

"*Soldier boy walked through the snow,*
Through the rain,
"*What a silly boy, don't you know you'll be maimed?*"
His eyes do not fall,

A calm in his step,
He passes them by without a single regret.

Soldier boy watched them, no turning away.
"What a silly boy, are you not in pain?"
He ground his teeth,
His hands balled into fists.
He said nothing,
Any answer, ridiculous!

Soldier boy listened,
Not a word out of turn,
Not a sound from his mouth.
"What a silly boy, he's too young not a doubt!"
But he stands in his line with the same steely gaze.
No word to persuade him,
No word to dissuade him.

Soldier boy Falls,
No dignity lost.
Winter gathers the many to see,
A daring, young solder asleep in the frost.
"What a silly boy, to fight such a war."
And they'd proceed to deny as they did once before.
The poor little soldier boy,
Asleep on the moor."

He knew that one by heart because his father used to sing it out loud every now and then. It wasn't really a song and the rhythm, like most of his songs, had been rather odd. But it had still been memorable.

"A rather dreary ending though, isn't it?" Trick tilted her head to the side looking contemplative. Her brother looked much the same.

"Well," Treat said, "I suppose it wasn't boring. Not like that lovey stuff. But I want something happy. Tell us a poem like that."

"A happy poem?" Elliot wondered. His father hadn't really written any 'happy poems.' Many of them had a certain hint of darkness about them that, admittedly, might throw a child off.

"Tell us a poem about tentacles!" Trick exclaimed.

"Tentacles?" Elliot repeated, never having heard such a peculiar request before in his life.

"Yes! Like the ones you might see on an octopus!" Treat agreed with his sister.

The decision appeared to be unanimous, although Elliot was certain he knew no poems about tentacles. His mind raced, trying to come up with something. Anything to latch onto.

"Tentacles..." Elliot murmured. He looked down at Cairo momentarily. His eyes glazed over as he tried to find...something, some words...something about jellyfish maybe? Or octopi? The twins appeared to very much like octopi for some reason.

And then it started to come to him. A strange memory that played in the back of his mind about an English class he'd had on repeating words and patterns. This was what he managed to come up with:

"Was a kraken or an octopus?
Was a squid or a jellyfish?
Was time to admit we were wrong.
Was tentacles all along."

Apparently, his endeavor was rather successful as both of them fell back laughing. Treat fell to the ground making a fart noise, then removing yet another whoopee cushion.

"Tentacles!" Both of them exclaimed during their fits of laughter.

Elliot felt himself calm down a little, realizing that no, he was not about to get mugged by two eleven-year-olds.

"That was funny!" Trick said, wiping away a tear, "Your dad wrote that?"

"No." Elliot shook his head, "I thought it up, just now." He wasn't even sure that he'd be able to remember that one later.

"Really?" Trick asked him, looking Elliot up and down appraisingly, "That was very good. You should keep writing those."

Treat nodded his head fiercely in agreement,

"Far better than that man who liked to write about flowers."

"And gold." Trick added in.

"And women with alabaster skin."

Elliot could sense that Treat had no idea what the word 'alabaster' meant and that he had only said it because it was a nice, smart sounding word. People seemed to do that a lot, use words they didn't know because they thought it made them sound smart. With children, it was actually kind of funny and many adults found the behaviour to be cute.

"Does that mean I might pass?" He asked them.

The two of them put their fingers to their chins, putting on a show of thinking, when finally, they nodded their heads.

"Very well." Trick said, straightening once again.

She and her brother moved off to opposite sides and gestured in an exact mirror movement to each other, that Elliot might pass and continue on his walk into town.

"We'll see you again, Mister Poetry Guy!"

Elliot hoped that nickname didn't stick. He wasn't *really* a 'poetry guy.' But even he had to admit that he was proud of himself, coming up with a poem like that on the spot. Maybe he had inherited some of his father's talent. He had always done rather well in English...

By the time Elliot had finally managed to make it into town it was night time and the stars were out. One of the things about small towns in isolated areas was that there were many visible stars. Cities often blotted them out from the strength of their own light, and though that was certainly a problem in Blackstone, it wasn't that bad compared to others.

Elliot was growing tired. His muscles ached from days of strain and long hours of walking. He set himself down by one of the buildings, then closed his eyes.

Elliot's eyes opened slightly, but he saw no one in the hospital room. He felt so tired, like he could just go to sleep...that's what he ought to do...His eyes clouded with black dots and then, he woke up.

He was right back to where he'd been on the sidewalk. Cairo jumped up onto his lap and started licking his face.

"Geeze! Cairo, cut it out!" Elliot laughed a little bit as her rough tongue scraped at his cheek, "Have you ever noticed that you've got dog breath?"

Cairo stopped licking him, she looked rather offended. Elliot chuckled again. No cat wanted to be compared to a *dog*!

"I'm kidding." He told her, "Do you want to keep going?" he asked her, "Or do you want to sleep here?"

Cairo got to her feet and meowed.

"Alright then." Elliot said finally, getting to his feet as well.

It was still dark outside, but now ominous clouds had crept their way across the sky, blotting out any form of natural light. He didn't really know where he was going, not at first anyways. He saw a man getting on a bus and followed him quickly. Much like the first time, no one seemed to notice him. Even Cairo seemed to elude the senses of the other passengers. She fell asleep for a bit in the seat next to Elliot.

A drop of water fell on the bus window. Then another droplet and another until it was pouring rain, blurring the passing colorful lights into an abstract painting that constantly changed as the bus continued on its route.

He didn't get off until the bus had reached its final stop and there were no more people on board. Cairo followed behind him. It was only a few paces away from the bus that Elliot observed Cairo's foul mood. She did not like getting wet. He caught sight of what looked like the train station.

"Cairo, let's go there." Elliot decided.

It was sheltered, at the very least. It looked like, somehow, Elliot had managed to find himself at the mall's train station. He'd always enjoyed ridding the train, even though it did have very few stops, it was still used by those odd people who needed to travel those odd distances.

The familiarity of the station, or maybe the normalcy of it all after what felt like a lifetime of strangeness and of not really knowing what he was doing made him feel safe. It seemed fitting somehow, that this place, the place where it had all started would somehow make him feel like he was back home.

Home, Elliot thought, maybe that was where he was trying to go. Home to his family. Even if they couldn't see him yet, he wanted to see them anyways. He missed them terribly and it had felt like a lifetime since this whole thing had begun.

He needed to go home.

When he and Cairo stood at the station, sheltered from the rain, Elliot wondered if the train was even running that late. It did seem a bit of a delayed reaction to start wondering now, but he hadn't actually been out this late before to take the train. Elliot looked up at the black screen which read the time.

It was four twenty-three in the morning. Maybe it wasn't late, just very, very early. The trains had to start at sometime.

He heard the sound of a bell dinging, of wheels on clattering tracks, and the white of a headlight approaching down from his left. The train pulled up, right at the station. Elliot pressed the button to get on. Surprisingly, it took a lot of focus to actually do as much. He was reminded of his limitations in his ability to interact with the solid world.

He and Cairo both got on. The doors closed behind them and they took a seat. Cairo jumped up on the seat beside him, once again falling asleep. The rain continued to fall and Elliot heard the rumbling of thunder in the distance.

The storm seemed to be picking up. By the time the train had come to a halt, it was absolutely wild outside. Elliot got off with Cairo, thinking that maybe the two of them ought to just stay in the shelter and wait for the storm to pass.

The two of them were well covered. There was a wooden gazebo of sorts over top of a glass square full of seats for waiting people. Elliot sat down by the door and Cairo cuddled up in the seat beside him.

He'd never realized just how grateful he was for all those nights he'd had a nice, comfortable room to sleep in during storms like this one. He hadn't realized how much he'd miss it when he didn't have it.

He didn't have a book to keep him entertained, but Elliot got the feeling that even if it was available to him, that he would have been unable to concentrate anyways. He pulled his left knee to his chest, slightly turned as he watched the rain and flashes of lightning illuminating the dark sky.

To think he'd been admiring the stars only minutes ago.

CHAPTER SEVENTEEN

A Sailor with a Big Mouth

It was morning by the time the rain stopped. Though the long night had probably been the loneliest Elliot had faced so far, he was a tad reluctant to wake Cairo up from her sleep. He still did anyways. There was very little time before the full moon and he still didn't really know what he was supposed to do to 'shock' himself back into his body. Both Trinket and Slomoe had been vague when Elliot had asked for a little bit of elaboration. He rather hoped they weren't talking about an actual shock. Even the thought of it was painful.

Cairo and Elliot continued their walk, crossing a busy street, into an alley, taking a right then headed down to Elliot's home.

It seemed quiet. Elliot stared at his house. For some reason he'd thought it would be different somehow but it was very much the same as it always was.

"I suppose we're going to have to investigate." Elliot straightened a bit.

He didn't really have a plan. All he knew was that Casper was in danger and that someone wanted him dead. So then, the best course of action would logically be to investigate his older brother.

"What would a detective do in this sort of situation?" Elliot thought out loud, "Maybe go through his room? Casper doesn't like it when people go in there. Maybe there's a reason for that."

Cairo shot him a plain sort of look and Elliot crossed his arms,

"Don't give me that." He huffed, "I know that no one likes other people snooping around their things, I'm just saying that maybe Casper has another reason aside from the obvious."

When Cairo's stares didn't let up, Elliot rolled his eyes,

"Come on, Cairo. If I'm going to be waking up from my coma, then it will have to be tonight. I don't really have all that much time."

Cairo let out a scolding meow. Or at least, it sounded scolding. Elliot let out a sigh,

"I know I should be trying to figure out a way to wake myself up. But it's not like we're really going to be able to test out any method until night time. Besides, it's kind of an opportunity, isn't it? Casper can't see me, and there's quite a bit you can get away with when people don't see you." Elliot looked up at the door to his house, staring at it a while, "We're going to have to find some way of getting in so that no one catches us."

He walked out onto the lawn. When he'd been running from Miranda's shadows, he'd kicked out the screen of his window. He could probably use the shed to hoist himself up there to his bedroom. Deciding it was a good plan, Elliot walked along the top of the fence, then climbed up to the higher fence around the back yard. The roof of the shed was just a step up from there. The window sill was slightly taller than Elliot had remembered and he had to jump up to reach it. He started pulling on the window frame.

"Come on." He grunted, only to lose his strength and fall back down onto the shed roof.

Even though he'd failed, he smiled a bit, realizing he'd gotten it to budge, though only slightly. That meant his plan was possible. He gave himself a small break before trying again.

He jumped up onto the sill. His fingers caught the ledge, then started to pull again at the frame. He'd managed to get it open wide enough that he could stick his fingers inside and pull, making far easier work of it than before.

He pulled himself up awkwardly, rather happy, once again that no one could see him. It would be rather embarrassing being caught breaking into his own bedroom.

He lost his balance part way in and fell on his head, rolling into a summersault of sorts.

"Mraw."

Elliot's eyes shifted over to where Cairo was sitting, right by his head. He felt his face heat up with embarrassment.

"It's not that funny..." he trailed off.

He shifted a bit, pushing himself up off the ground. He was inside now, which was probably the most difficult part.

He tiptoed across the floor to the door into the hallway. It was an old house, and the floor boards had a tendency to squeak, especially on the main floor. Since his and Casper's bedrooms were on the upper floors they didn't really have that same issue. He looked over at the alarm clock by his bed.

It was seven thirty in the morning. For some reason he thought it would be later. Maybe it was because he'd passed the hours before morning watching the rain and waiting for it to let up that it had felt like such a long time. Whatever the case, Elliot slowly opened the door, peeking into the hall. He didn't know why he was being so cautious. No one could see him, after all. Maybe it was just habit due to his getting ready to do something he knew he wasn't supposed to do.

He crept towards his older brother's room. The door was closed, indicating that he was still in there, probably still asleep.

Elliot crept back into his bedroom, then silently closed the door. He looked over at Cairo who was sending him a questioning look.

"Casper's still in bed." Elliot explained. He made his way over to the window and closed it, "We're going to need to pretend we aren't here, or, well, you will." He admitted, "You're the only one anyone can actually see, after all."

Cairo jumped up onto his bed then looked back over at him. Elliot smiled amusedly,

"Yes, you can go back to sleep."

He had no doubt she was tired. They'd been through a lot together over the past week and a half. It was tough to believe that it had been so little time since he'd left.

He lay back in his bed as Cairo curled herself up into a ball. He could hear the sound of movement and muffled voices coming from the floor below. His mother and father would be up. His father had a book due in a couple of weeks and he'd been working quite hard recently to get it all done before the due date. He was always scrambling like that in the final month, though he was far from being a procrastinator. His mother owned a book store. Fitting, considering her husband's occupation.

Elliot didn't know what Casper was doing. It was the heart of summer vacation and though he generally, as a rule got up earlier than Elliot, his version of 'early' was normally somewhere around ten o'clock.

He was in for another long wait, and this time, he didn't have the rain to entertain him. He simply lay there, watching the alarm clock as Cairo snoozed away. He rather wished he could sleep in times like these. Although not getting sleepy seemed to have its benefits, sleep was something he missed greatly.

When I wake up, Elliot thought, I'm going to take a nice long nap.

It wasn't until after he'd had this thought that he realized how silly it was. The reason he wanted to wake up was so that he could go to sleep.

The sound of giggles filled the air causing Elliot to tense at the sudden noise. He jolted out of bed and saw two very familiar black cats in orange collars sitting at the foot of his bed.

"Trick? Treat?" Elliot wondered, "What are you doing here? How did you get here?"

In a cloud of black smoke, the two cats transformed into the two familiar 'children' in their cat costumes. Their blue eyes alight with the promise of mischief and mayhem.

"We followed you!" They both cheered excitedly.

Their loud voices roused Cairo from her sleep. The ginger tabby shot them a look of annoyance, but opted to stay awake. Perhaps worried about the trouble Elliot might get into without her there to keep an eye on him.

"You told such a funny story about tentacles!" Trick said excitedly.

"So, we thought that someone with such funny stories must have a funny story of his own." Treat said proudly.

Trick crossed her arms and sent her brother a glare,

"I believe *I* was the one who said that."

"No, I'm quite sure it was me." Treat said with a grin that indicated it was most certainly *not* him who had thought that up.

Trick inflated her cheeks like a puffer fish. It must have been her way of getting across her frustration. For some reason, it made Treat laugh as though it were the most amusing thing in all the world.

Elliot felt himself tense a little bit at their antics. He certainly didn't want the two of them alerting his family to his presence. Not now, at least, and he had no doubt that they would if he didn't find some way of handling the situation.

Stalling seemed like a good idea, and telling a story, well, it wasn't as though he minded them knowing about his strange adventure through the spirit world.

"Alright." He relented, deciding that he should try to at the very least make the story last long enough so that his mother would leave, or so that Casper would get up.

"My name is Elliot Crow." Elliot introduced, "This is my familiar, Cairo. About a week ago, I was just an ordinary human. Or, at least I thought I was..."

Trick and Treat quickly sat down on Elliot's bed, listening to his story with rapt attention. They seemed to recognise the characters that Elliot brought up, though they didn't seem to have known about Toshi's situation in the Kingdom of mirrors. He found himself skipping over a few parts when he realized his story was taking up well over two hours and it was going on nine thirty.

Yet, Trick and Treat didn't seem to be getting bored, and actually laughed when Elliot spread his arms out trying to emphasize the ridiculousness of words like 'anteater' and 'koala' being some sort of kryptonite for creatures like Miranda the 'witch.'

That finally led him to this very moment, in which Elliot was waiting in his room, waiting for his brother to wake up so that he could investigate.

"Oh! Like a detective!" Treat clapped his hands together excitedly.

"Trick, let's be detectives too!" Trick decided, a decision which Elliot tried to protest, though the words seemed to die on his lips. He couldn't really think of an excuse *not* to have the two, crazy spirits tag along. Well, nothing that wouldn't end well for him.

"Why don't you try to enter his dreams?" Treat asked Elliot curiously, "You can enter them, right? King Slomoe gave you power over his domain, which means you should."

Elliot hadn't thought of that. Could it really be that simple?

Elliot thought back to all those stories he'd learned, about detectives and mysteries. Casper was feeling guilty over what had happened, because he'd been stabbed. That meant that there was a good chance, that if they did come face to face again that he might just confess everything.

"But that's no fun, Treat!" Trick whined, placing her hands on her brother's shoulders and moving him back and forth. His head bobbing comically from side to side with the motions.

"Alright." Elliot decided, "I'll do it. Hopefully he's still out of it."

He probably only had a few minutes before Casper woke up. He got up again, then opened up his bedroom door. Trick and Treat followed him, although Elliot had rather hoped not to have an audience he couldn't exactly argue with them now. It would be a waste of time, and they *had* been the ones to come up with the idea.

Elliot slowly opened the door to Casper's room. Surely enough, his older brother was still asleep. What really caught Elliot's attention, however, was the floating green threat that spun around and changed slowly to purple as it hovered around Casper's head.

"Is that a dream?" Elliot murmured.

He got the same feeling from it that he did from those books Slomoe liked to collect. This was one of Casper's dreams. One that was still being dreamed.

"Alright." Elliot said, reaching forward and touching the strand.

How was he supposed to do this exactly? He wondered.

"Meow."

Elliot looked down to see Cairo sitting there on the floor. She got up, then jumped onto Casper's bed and with one more swift movement, she lunged at the floating thread, which opened up and seemed to engulf her. Elliot quickly did the same, copying her movements, he got up onto Casper's bed and jumped into the dream world.

The feeling was much the same as entering one of the books Slomoe had had him go through. The only problem now was whether or not this one would be a nightmare.

Thinking back on his own track record of good dreams and bad dreams, Elliot got the sense that this was not going to be one about anything particularly non-threatening.

He was right.

As soon as he entered, Elliot felt like he was falling. Then, he was flying. Cairo was floating beside him in the air. The world around them appeared out of focus, especially in the distance. It was a bit like looking out at a drawing. A distant drawing, but still, a drawing.

His attention focused on the river. The only discernable landmark around. He got the sense that that was where he was supposed to focus.

Someone below them was floating as well. It was Casper, flying just above a yellow, rubber raft. The sort you might see as a means of evacuation on an airplane or larger boat. It screamed of danger and the sound of rushing water and chaotic lapping of stony shores added to this perception.

The sound grew louder. Suddenly, Elliot, Cairo, Casper and an older man with white hair were all in a boat which rushed over white water.

With the wind in his hair and the quickly passing scenery, Elliot got the sense they were either in a lot of trouble, or in for a thrill.

"Elliot?" Casper looked at his brother with surprise, "You're okay?"

The focus of the dream shifted onto Elliot who felt the rapid water become a little bit calmer. It was because Casper's fear had shifted onto him. He was afraid about what he'd say. Whether he blamed him for what had happened perhaps.

"Casper, I'm fine." Elliot told his older brother, "But you need to listen to me. I'm going to wake up tonight."

"Tonight?" Casper looked confused, "But aren't you awake now?"

Elliot shook his head,

"I'm not. But I can contact people through their dreams. It's...kind of a long story. One that I don't have a lot of time to tell just yet, since you're going to be waking up soon."

"Wake up?" Casper repeated, obviously not yet understanding.

"Casper, you need to tell me, what happened? Why is someone trying to kill you?"

"Kill me?" Casper repeated.

"Yes!" Elliot felt a bit of his own frustration leaking into his voice, "The reason I was stabbed, they were after you and I think that you know that."

Casper froze, he looked down at the floor of the raft which now appeared to be incredibly still.

"Well, laddie, it's no pleasant tale."

Elliot's attention shifted to the older man who was paddling the boat. *Laddie?* Elliot wondered.

"Don't tell him." Casper hissed, looking at him sharply.

This man seemed quite intent on revealing all of Casper's secrets if the malicious grin that formed on his face was any indication. Elliot had once heard, from his father that everyone you meet in your dreams is really just yourself. That meant, this man was the part of Casper that secretly wanted to cause himself pain by letting this secret be revealed, or maybe the sort of man that wanted to get everything out in the open so that he could finally be free. Whatever the case, he opened his mouth again and spoke.

"There was a fund raiser in Casper's class. The teachers wanted the lad to hold all the money. The task was on him, but he screwed up!" the man laughed.

"Shut up! Shut up! You don't know what you're saying!" Casper yelled.

But yelling seemed to be all he could do. His feet sunk into the rubber of the raft and his hands seemed to be stuck in a very similar fashion, despite how much he struggled against his restraints.

"I remember that." Elliot spoke out loud.

He remembered how Casper had taken the large, yellow envelope home with him every day, always keeping it in his sights.

"But then, one day." The man continued, his voice now very harsh and spoke of a grimness that could only lead to an unpleasant revelation, "Poor Casper looked inside his desk and found the money gone. He was so sure that he'd put it there just before gym class. He searched everywhere, his locker, his bag..."

Why hadn't he heard of this? Elliot wondered. Surely the teachers would have contacted their home if that had actually happened.

"But Casper managed to avoid trouble, o' course." The old man laughed heartily and Casper seemed to sink deeper into the yellow raft.

"The idjit took money from Kyle Redwood!" The man cackled.

"Kyle Redwood?" Elliot repeated.

It really was a small town. In total, there were about twenty kids in the same year as Elliot. Less in Casper's year. He'd seen Kyle before and though the two of them had never actually interacted, Elliot had always gotten a bad vibe off of him. He'd always told himself that he was being ridiculous back then, though now that he knew what his 'vibes' actually were, he knew now that there had to be some sort of reason for the uneasy feeling surrounding Kyle.

"He gave Casper the money, then, Casper took the cash from his dad and mum and used that to pay him back, thinking all the while that he'd get a job and pay *them* back later. But Kyle wanted more money. Casper hadn't known about the 'interest' he needed to pay. So, the money from his job went to Kyle while Kyle made him do things he didn't want to do. It all got worse and worse, until finally, Casper had enough and threatened to come clean. Twitchy said he'd killed Casper, but when Casper showed up again..."

"Twitchy?" Elliot repeated the strange sounding name.

It was only then that Elliot realized he was sinking into the raft as well. Cairo walked over to him and rubbed up against him.

"I know, Cairo." Elliot murmured to the cat. She was telling him that this was only a dream. He had nothing to fear. Not if he believed he had nothing to fear.

"*That's why dreams are so dangerous.*" Slomoe's voice reminded him.

He couldn't help but wonder if Slomoe really was communicating with him, or if it was just those psychic voices in his head giving him another hint at how to best survive yet another ordeal.

Casper let out a scream and they both fell down into darkness.

Elliot felt himself being pulled. Like he was really just waking up, and then, the world melted away. Like sidewalk chalk being washed away by a garden hose. He blinked his eyes as he found himself back in Casper's room. He fell over when his older brother shot up out of bed, causing Trick and Treat to laugh. Cairo let out a hiss and yowl, not at all enjoying the sudden motion. Casper let out a scream of surprise when he saw the cat there.

Cairo shot him a glare while Casper stared at her in confusion.

"What the heck?" Casper wondered. He obviously recognised her from the dream, but he didn't really know what to make of her.

It was then that a very strange look came over his face. He paled considerably, his usual tanned features appeared considerably white and his breathing sped up slightly.

"E-Elliot?"

CHAPTER EIGHTEEN

Elliot the Ginger Tabby Cat

Elliot?" Casper tried again, his voice came out a little bit squeaky, "Y-you're a cat?"

"What!?" Elliot shouted.

Trick and Treat burst out laughing, as though the whole thing was some sort of joke. Cairo shot Casper another glare. To Elliot, the message was quite clear,

I'm not your brother, you silly human!

How Casper had managed to misinterpret that one was anyone's guess.

"O-oh god, you're mad at me, aren't you?" Casper shook slightly and Elliot realized, with fascination that he looked dangerously close to a panic attack.

Cairo looked over at Elliot with exasperation on her feline face.

"Don't look at me, I got what you said loud and clear." Elliot defended, then realized just how ridiculous the whole thing was. Cairo was his familiar, of course he would understand her. As for other people, especially humans, or people of the solid world, well, that was another story entirely.

Even so, going back to normal world logic, it seemed like a bit of a jump to assume that he was somehow possessing a cat.

"Knock it off, you two." Elliot said half-heartedly at the giggling twins who were now rolling about on the floor of his brother's bedroom floor.

"It's funny!" Trick said, letting out another scream of delight.

"I knew it!" Treat shouted, "I knew if we stuck with you we'd get to have a bit of fun!"

Elliot made a mental note to make sure he bought Halloween candy that year. Now that he knew what was at stake, it suddenly seemed like a very important task.

"Mister Story Teller the orange cat!" Trick announced through her giggles.

Hadn't they called him 'Mister *Poetry guy*' before? Elliot recalled absently. Casper picked up Cairo, cursing all the while. He looked around wildly, as though not entirely certain as to what he ought to do with the poor cat.

"Okay...okay." Casper decided, "Maybe...maybe mum will know what to do? She likes paranormal stuff like that. Maybe she'll know what's going on. Just...just wait for a bit, okay, El? I need to get changed."

"Seriously?" Elliot wondered as Casper started rifling through the pile of clothing on his floor, picking out whatever was close by and slipping it on.

Treat covered his sister's eyes as he changed, causing Trick to give a look of disappointment from behind her brother's fingers. Casper finished up, then picked Cairo back up again. The ginger tabby let out a yowl of surprise as the two rushed out of his room. Elliot ran after them.

"Casper, what do you think you're doing!" He shouted after him.

This could be problematic. He really needed Cairo's help if he ever hoped to wake up again. She was just about the only help that he had at the moment, and she was his means of travel.

Casper was pretty fast, maybe even a little bit faster than his younger brother who ran after him, only barely managing to make it through the door. Trick and Treat seemed to be quite out of luck as the door slammed in their faces. Casper quickly opened up the door of his car and placed Cairo in the passenger seat. Elliot ducked under Casper and flung himself into the car after his precious familiar and friend.

Casper buckled himself in and started the car.

"Casper, where are we going?" Elliot asked his brother, knowing very well that he couldn't hear him.

The sound of giggling caused Elliot to turn his head where Trick and Treat were strapping each other into the back seats.

"Ooh, someone's gone coocoo." Trick laughed.

"It's not a joke!" Elliot groaned, feeling his frustrations at the two of them coming back in full force.

"Of course, it's not a joke!" Treat echoed his sister's laughter.

"Yeah!"

"Everyone knows it's not a joke..."

"Until the punchline!"

Elliot was slammed against the window as the car took off. Cairo let out a yowl, complaining about Casper's recklessness.

"Sorry, Elliot." Casper said quickly, looking over at Cairo briefly to make sure she was okay.

Elliot gave an exaggerated shrug when Cairo shot him a dirty look.

"Just because we're related doesn't mean I know what's going through his mind, you know...I don't think I've ever seen Casper act like this before."

"Maybe it's a guilty conscience?" Treat suggested.

Trick snorted,

"And what, dear brother, would you know of a guilty conscience?"

"Touché."

Although his driving was a tad reckless in the beginning, Casper seemed to regain himself a little bit, slowing down as they neared their mother's shop. Elliot finally let go of the chicken bar, not even realizing he'd been gripping it the entire way until he had let go.

Casper opened up the car door of the driver's side then picked Cairo up again who was growing agitated at her treatment.

"Just bear with it a little longer, Cairo." Elliot said, trying to sooth her, "I swear, once I've woken up, I will feed you so many cat treats, you'll be in heaven." Cairo seemed to calm down a little bit at the promise, but Elliot knew that if they were going to stay friends that he had best deliver.

The shop was a small one, resting cosily between a mainstream clothing store and a Vietnamese restaurant. Margret Crow did rather well for herself, and the shop, though not always busy, did pretty well for itself with people always coming in and out. It was very unique compared to the line of businesses that occupied its section with its dark-grey color coupled with its black shingles. The roof twirled inwards at its sides, giving the impression of a strange cross between something classy and something disturbing. Elliot used to think it looked a touch like a haunted mansion when he was little and would often hide among the books with his brother during their games of pretend.

Elliot followed Casper into the store. Their mother looked up from her spot by the counter. Her face was powdered white, just as it always was. She wore a black dress and dark red lipstick. Her green eyes found Casper, though they didn't at all see Elliot, much as he had expected.

"Mum!"

She must have seen the fear and panic on his face and had she not, then his voice hinted heavily at something being very wrong.

"Casper?" She crossed her legs and stopped fanning herself with the large, decorative black and navy fan she'd been waving in front of her face, "What seems to be the matter?"

Margret Crow had a very peculiar way of speaking. Her voice was almost always calm. Elliot had never heard her raise it in anger or fear. Though he'd never seen his mother during a time of crisis, he suspected that even then her voice wouldn't waver for even a moment.

When she did get angry, she grew very quiet. That was always how she got Elliot and Casper to do things when they were younger. It was also how she tended to express her displeasure.

"Mom! I–I turned Elliot into a cat!"

Elliot slapped his hand to his face. There was no way that anyone, even his mother would believe something like that. As predicted, she regarded her eldest son calmly, eyes finding Cairo momentarily.

"Why do you think that?"

She never had been the judgemental type, though Elliot wondered why she was humoring Casper's theory at all.

"I saw Elliot in my dreams last night! He said someone was after me and that...and the cat was there in the dream, and when I woke up it was on my bed!" It was right about then that Elliot realized his mistake. With all the peculiar things that had been going on lately around his family, and the attempts he'd had to communicate with them, maybe, in their minds, it really wouldn't be all that far fetched to think that he really *was* a cat.

"I highly doubt that your brother is a cat." Margret Crow regarded Cairo curiously, "But that doesn't mean your instincts are wrong."

Casper paused,

"What do you mean?" he asked her slowly.

"Your father saw Elliot in the mirror. He said there was a cat with him. Perhaps it was this one."

Elliot stared at his mother with a bit of surprise. He wouldn't have thought anyone would be able to get so close to the truth.

Casper went silent and Elliot had a feeling that they'd discussed this before, how their father had seen him in the mirror. This might have been the first time he'd actually believed it to not be a work of fiction produced by their father's imagination and grief.

"Who's that?" Trick whispered to Treat who gave a shrug.

"That's my mum." Elliot said absently.

Trick and Treat stared at him a long while. Long enough that Elliot thought they might be expecting him to say or do something.

"What?" he asked defensively.

"She looks like you." Trick commented.

"I think she does." Treat agreed, "They've got the same nose and chin." Elliot shrugged, wondering why they were talking about this. Even though he had his father's brown eyes and dark brown hair, he'd always been told (mostly by his dad) that he looked like his mother. Something Elliot had never really appreciated. In his defense, there weren't a lot of guys out there who wanted to be told they looked like a woman. Especially when Elliot thought his mother looked quite feminine and beautiful, even when she was dressed up in her usual gothic wear. There was a certain elegance about her that spoke of someone obsessed with the classical.

"So," Casper said looking at the cat as though she were some sort of fragile glass figurine, "Elliot's inside the cat?"

"Possibly." Margret got up from her spot at the counter while Elliot contemplated banging his head against a wall.

She gently lifted Cairo from Casper's grasp. His mother had always been a cat lover. She didn't dislike other animals, but cats had always been her favourite. They'd even had a cat when Elliot and Casper had been little. A black girl-cat named Minuit. She had been their mother's cat before she'd gotten together with their father. Sadly, Minuit had died when Elliot was only two-years-old and he didn't remember much about her save for some blurred recollections of visiting a vet during a dark, rainy evening.

"But I don't think so." She continued, regarding Cairo curiously, "Cats have always been said to have a strong connection to the supernatural. I've no doubt that Elliot is trying to communicate with us somehow. Dreams have always been said to be very close to the realm of death. Mirrors have also been said, in legends all over the world to be connected to the spirit world. In some faiths, it's believed that if one dies in front of a mirror that their spirit becomes trapped inside."

Elliot had never seen Casper actually express a belief in their mother's faith in the supernatural, but now he appeared to be drinking in her words like he couldn't get enough of them.

"Then...then the cat, she's somehow..."

"A medium." Margret Crow offered, "A connection between this world and the spirit world, perhaps. Possibly a familiar. In either case, Elliot could be nearby."

"Then...should we try to contact him?" Casper looked around the room nervously.

Margret Crow offered a hum, as though contemplating this herself,

"Perhaps. Or perhaps not. Elliot plans on waking up from his coma tonight. We can ask him then what happened to him."

Casper gave her a strange look,

"Elliot's out there and...it's weird, we don't know if he's in trouble or anything, maybe we can help though? I mean, what if he needs our help?"

"If Elliot says he'll do something, he'll do it." She said simply, "That's just how he is. It's how he's always been, ever since he was a baby."

Casper frowned, obviously wanting to protest. Elliot could understand why he was upset. He'd just been opened up to a whole new world of possibilities. A world where spirits existed and the world was just a little bigger than he'd originally realized. But he was being blocked off from that world. Not sure what to do with the knowledge he had and otherwise feeling useless because he didn't seem to know enough to be of any use.

"So...what do we do with the cat?" Casper looked at Cairo who was now in his mother's arms, purring as she was pet.

"Let her be for now, I suppose." She decided, "Whether Elliot's inside of her or whether she's acting as a sort of medium, we won't truly know until Elliot tells us, and until then, I'm sure she has a job to do." She set Cairo down and Elliot gave a mental fist pump. He'd never thought that having a mother with knowledge of the supernatural would come in handy but lo and behold, here it was making the situation that much better.

Cairo jumped down to the ground, she looked over her shoulder at Margret Crow, then to the surprise of both her and Casper, she gave a small head bob that looked suspiciously like a bow of thanks. She didn't travel very far, however, opting to stay. At least, for as long as Elliot planned on staying.

"You saw that, right?" Casper looked at his mother questioningly.

"The cat thanked us, yes." She agreed, moving back behind the counter and taking her seat. She spread out her fan so that it covered half her face, then started to fan herself, much like she'd been doing before.

"Do you not have work, Casper?"

Casper turned around without saying a word. He left the bookstore, letting the door slam behind him. Elliot winced a little bit. It was obvious that he was angry. Casper got angry at their mother very often. It wasn't an uncommon occurrence. Although, it had been far more common as of late. Maybe he should have taken that as a hint. There was a lot of hints actually. So many that Elliot felt a little guilty that he hadn't seen it sooner.

A look passed over his mother's face. It was something like sadness, and maybe something like hurt. But it was gone rather quickly, like it always was. He knew that Casper was oblivious to their mother's feelings on the matter, but he had known, and out of the two of them, that made Elliot the worst in his opinion.

"Elliot," she spoke, looking around the empty shop. There were no customers at this time of the day. They were all out working, while the younger people who were off of school didn't usually come to this sort of shop for a good time. That left the two of them alone, save for Trick and Treat who were unusually silent.

"I know you're here." She said, "I understand how Casper is feeling." Her voice grew a little quieter, "I feel the same way. I never thought I would end up in a situation where I'd be talking to you like this." She ducked under the counter, obviously looking for something. After a moment, she pulled out a large, rectangular box that looked much like a package for a board game. There was no cover on the top. In fact, it looked very familiar. Like something he'd seen once before in the past.

"You were always very different, Elliot." She spoke again, "Always...I was convinced, when you were little that you might possess some sort of sixth sense. You knew things that you shouldn't know, sometimes, things that hadn't yet happened."

"Because he's a wizard." Treat whispered to his sister who nodded knowingly.

"A wizard of time, probably." Trick agreed with her brother.

"You'd cry when I brought this out." Margret Crow looked down at the box, "I couldn't blame you for that, considering the stigma surrounding these things. I swore I would never use this, however...sometimes we need to take risks." She opened up the box and pulled out a wooden board.

She unfolded it across the table. It was only then that Elliot recognised exactly what he was looking at. A spirit board, also known as a Ouija board.

"Ooh, she's serious." Trick looked rather surprised at the sight of the thing.

"Those things can be dangerous if not supervised correctly." Treat commented.

"Dangerous how?" Elliot asked cautiously.

"They invoke spirits." Trick explained, "Any spirit. Because you never know who or what you're going to get, it can cause a lot of bad things. You're basically taking a random spirit into your confidence."

"It's a bit like...grabbing a nearby stranger and forcing them to do something they may or may not want to do." Treat explained, "It could go well, or it could go horribly. Usually the latter, especially when the one invoking the spirit invites them into their own body. They aren't happy, so they lash out."

"Like any stranger would." Trick added in.

"But it's pretty rude to begin with." Treat shot back.

"We don't mind though." Trick added in helpfully, "We've been summoned plenty of times."

"Usually on purpose." Treat said proudly.

Elliot looked over at his mother who picked up an extra chair, then moving it around the counter across from where she had been sitting, then returned to her seat.

"I hope you're here." She said, taking a deep breath. She placed a wooden chip down on the board, then pressed her two fingers up against it.

"Go." Trick pushed him towards the table, "It should be safe. Since she's not invoking you."

Elliot hesitantly approached the table. He sat down in the chair opposite his mother, then put his fingers on the wooden chip. He looked back over at Treat.

"Am I doing this right?"

The twins both shrugged. So much for their help. And they'd said they'd done this before too...

Elliot slowly started to move the chip across the table, surprised at how easy it was compared to moving and touching other solid objects. He set the chip on the word which read *Hello*.

"Elliot?" His mother asked, "Is that really you?"

Elliot bit his lower lips, swallowing back his emotions, he moved the wooden pointer towards the word *Yes*.

"Okay." She breathed, obviously revving herself up to do this. Elliot had never seen his mother shaky before, but she certainly looked it now.

Cairo jumped up onto the counter, eyes looking over at Elliot, watching him steadily as their communication continued.

"What I need to know," She tried again, "What I need to know is why do you think your brother's in danger?"

Elliot looked down at the board. It had every letter of the alphabet spelled out for him and numbers, zero to nine on the top with yes and no written below the numbers. It was everything he needed to talk to her, but it was still a bit annoying that it would take so long.

He looked over at Cairo who dipped her head.

"You're right." Elliot nodded, then looked back at the board, "There's time for this."

This was what he'd been hoping for from the start, a means of communicating with his family. What did the method matter if it worked?

Elliot started to spell out his message.

H–E pause G–O–T pause T–H–E pause W–R–O–N–G pause B–R–O–T–H–E–R.

"He got the wrong brother." His mother repeated the message out loud, "I'm confused, what do you mean?"

Elliot scrunched his forehead, not sure how he ought to best elaborate that one. He thought the message was quite clear. He started again.

H–E pause W–A–I–T–E–D pause F–O–R pause C–A–S–P–E–R pause T–O pause L–E–A–V–E pause T–H–E pause H–O–U–S–E pause B–U–T pause S–A–W pause M–E pause L–E–A–V–E pause A–N–D pause T–H–O–U–G–H–T pause I pause W–A–S pause H–I–M.

"He waited for Casper to leave the house, but saw me leave and thought I was him." His mother repeated. Her eyes widened ever so slightly with comprehension.

"Then whoever tried to kill you was never after you, he was after Casper. But why? Do you know?"

Elliot had to think again on what he wanted to tell her.

C–A–S–P–E–R pause I–S pause B–E–I–N–G pause B–L–A–C–K–M–A–I–L–E–D.

"Casper is being Blackmailed." Although her voice was even, Elliot knew his mother well enough to tell that she was horrified, worried, and a little bit afraid.

"So then, it was the blackmailer who wanted Casper dead?"

Elliot moved the wooden chip to *No.*

"No?" she wondered, "It's not the blackmailer who killed him? Is it related, then?" she asked puzzledly, wondering why Elliot would bring up a blackmailer if he wasn't the killer.

Yes.

Elliot moved the wooden pointer again down to the letter part of the board.

H-E pause I-S pause T-H-E pause B-L-A-C-K-M-A-I-L-E-R-S pause F-R-I-E-N-D.

"He is the blackmailer's friend." She repeated faithfully.

"Could you tell me his name? The name of the person who tried to kill you?" she pressed.

Elliot moved the wooden chip to the word *No.*

"Do you know his name?" she asked Elliot once again, wanting to know if he was simply refusing to tell her or if he really didn't know.

No.

She hummed, taking out her fan again and letting out a small sigh, as though facing only a small inconvenience. Anyone who actually knew Margret Crow would know that she was terribly upset at the equivalent of yelling, screaming and maybe even throwing a tantrum for most ordinary people.

"I do wish that your brother would just tell me the problem. It would all be so easily solved. What could he possibly have done that would make him keep silent like this?"

At this moment, she was talking to herself, not Elliot.

He eyed the board curiously, wondering a moment why she even had that at work with her. It was then he was hit by a peculiar realization. She hadn't been keeping the board at work with her. She'd been carrying it around with her, waiting for him to arrive so that they might have a chat. While Elliot had been running around trying to communicate with his parents and with Casper, his mother had been running around trying to get to the bottom of this whole ordeal. When Elliot had started showing signs of trying to communicate with them, she had prepared herself for when he would try to seek her out.

Elliot sat there a while longer. He looked over at Cairo.

"Should we go?" he asked her.

Cairo didn't appear to care whether they stayed or left.

"We should go." Trick said.

"Yeah! I'm getting bored." Treat whined.

"Alright." Elliot nodded, getting up from the chair, before pausing a moment. He put his fingers on the wooden pointer, then slowly moved it down towards the corner. His mother watched from behind her fan, her expression remaining blank.

Goodbye

Cairo jumped down off of the table as he started to leave.

"I'll see you tonight, Elliot." Margret Crow said causing him to pause momentarily on his way towards the door. "You promised, Elliot. Tonight, you're waking up. I will be most cross if you go back on your word."

Elliot felt the corners of his mouth twitch upwards.

"I'll wake up tonight." He confirmed, even though he knew she couldn't hear him.

Then, much like a ghost, he passed right through the glass of the door. It would only be when he'd managed to make his way outside that he'd wonder how he had done it.

"Where to now?" he looked over at Trick and Treat, deciding that for now, he'd let them take the lead. He didn't want them to be bored, knowing it was quite possible they'd take out their boredom on him if it got too bad, and it wasn't as though he had anything else to do just yet anyways.

"We're bored." Treat pouted.

"Yeah." Trick mirrored her brother's expression, "This is the boring part of the adventure and we don't care for that."

"So, we'll leave." Treat decided.

"But we'll come back." Trick added in.

"When things get exciting again."

"Because you're interesting."

"Oh." Elliot said, blinking in surprise. He was quite glad to see them leave, but still, it was rather sudden. Suspiciously so.

"We'll see you, Mister Adventure guy!" Trick started skipping off.

Treat ran after her and they looped their arms together, then started skipping with her at the same pace.

"Bye..." Elliot trailed off, then realized that once again, they had changed his nickname.

Well, at least they were consistent in their inconsistency. He watched them for a little while, until they had turned the corner, out of sight.

CHAPTER NINETEEN

A Bond Forged in Blood

Casper had gotten a job, about a year ago, serving frozen yogurt at the mall. The place got a lot of business, what with people going in and out and the mall being one of the few attractions their town possessed. Their father had once talked about how he could remember the frozen yogurt place opening up as a kid and how it had been a favourite of pretty much all the teenagers in Blackstone. That hadn't changed, even after around thirty-five years. It was probably the oldest store there. Elliot had always preferred the Cat's Eye. It was a quiet little café that sold some of the best smoothies. Something that both he and his best friend, Sam had both agreed on. It wasn't nearly as busy as the frozen yogurt place, so, at some point, it had turned into their own little hang out. That wasn't to say that the Cat's Eye did poorly, only that it didn't do as well as the frozen yogurt place. No one did as well as them, actually. It was a little bit like a monument at this point. Even the older generation looked at the place with a certain sort of pride, as though it had been through their own hard work that the place remained open, or that it had even opened at all.

Maybe it was a quirk of a small town, but even if Elliot himself didn't frequent it, he could understand the pride, at least a little bit.

Casper had never missed a day of work. His brother rarely got sick and when he did, he covered his nose and mouth with a mask, so as not to spread his cold, then went out anyways. He prided himself on his attendance. Casper was a little bit like that, even in school. Although Casper, like Elliot prided himself on being 'normal,' he had his own inspiration and incentives. His father had said that Casper was very 'money driven.' Although this behaviour was new, Elliot figured that it made sense that Casper was 'money driven' if he was being blackmailed.

It was due to these little facts that Elliot immediately knew that something was wrong when he couldn't find Casper working at the register, as he normally did. He didn't panic. Casper not being there could mean a variety of things. He might have gone off to use the bathroom, or maybe he was stocking shelves in the back. He decided to wait for a bit.

His wait turned into nearly half an hour before Elliot decided it was best that he just go looking for him. He nearly forgot that he was invisible once again (which was really a difficult thing to forget when you had people walking through you every couple of minutes) before he opted to check the door marked 'Employees Only.' No Casper.

Elliot tried the washroom. There were two in the mall and he decided he might as well try both when the one closest to the frozen yogurt place was empty.

Still no Casper.

That left him with the question of where exactly Casper would go? Had he gotten into a car wreck? That was the only thing he could think of that would keep his brother from his work. Elliot walked out of the mall and out onto the street. He tried to follow the rout he'd seen his parents take when he was asked to help them with the groceries or other errands. He didn't know if Casper took the same route or not, but he would guess so. He was careful to look for any signs that a car might have crashed on the road, only to come up with nothing. Not even a single skid mark that suggested a sliding vehicle (and Elliot knew that some newly licenced teens enjoyed that sort of thing).

Cairo let out a meow, drawing Elliot's attention back to her. They stared at each other for a rather lengthy amount of time. He started to feel a weight in his back pocket growing heavier and heavier. He slapped his forehead,

"Why didn't I think of that?"

Cairo let out another sound, looking rather smug.

"Oh...shut up." Elliot said, knowing it was a weak comeback. Now he got the sense that she was laughing at him.

The park was close by. It might not have been the best place to do a reading, what with the screaming kids running about, hopped up on summer energy. But there were plenty of benches where Elliot and Cairo could sit, and Elliot had a terrible feeling in the pit of his stomach that he needed to do this and that if he didn't...something terrible might happen.

He took his tarot cards out of his back pocket and sat down on the bench, trying to ignore the kids soaking their heads in the large fountain in the center of the field. There were some families there, but it mostly consisted of inconsistent groups of adults that had been dragged down there, mostly nannies and sitters, watching the children play while they read or played on their phones pretending they were doing something important.

Elliot took the cards out of their packaging and shuffled through them until he was satisfied he'd gone through them enough times that he wouldn't draw the same hand as he had before.

He lay them down in the same order as before. He placed the first in the middle, then the next to the right, and the last card went to the left of the first card he'd set down.

Cairo leaped off the bench as a group of kids started trying to pet her. She tried to get away, since they were all sopping wet and one of the kids looked a little bit sticky, Elliot observed passingly before looking back down at the cards.

He flipped the center one over, all the while thinking, he needed to find Casper. He needed to know that he wasn't in danger.

The Magician

Elliot stared in confusion. For a moment, it was almost like he was looking into a mirror. He looked over his shoulder, trying to figure out if Casper was nearby. He looked back at the cards puzzledly. It was like the card he'd turned was trying to say that Casper was looking at him, that he was in his sights. But Elliot couldn't see him, and even if he could, why would Casper be at the park when he was supposed to be at work?

He turned over the next card.

Two of Swords

The sound of clashing metal reverberated through his head. Someone was shouting something, but he couldn't make out the words. Like an echo that had made its way through a cave, only for the message to be garbled once it had reached the exit. But it sounded familiar. Like someone he'd heard before. Maybe in passing, but not someone he was familiar with. It was almost taunting him. Daring him to figure it out.

Elliot turned over the final card, the one on the left.

Death

The card of Death didn't always indicate an actual death. In fact, it rarely did. His mother had always said that the Death card was one of the most interesting ones because it was a card that signified, not endings, but beginnings. With it, Elliot got no vision. No hints as to what it might mean, other than the picture of the bony figure in a black hood and carrying a scythe.

Death was the card with the most balance. The card of loss and the card of gain. The card where the line between good and evil became blurred. He felt like the card was trying to tell him something. Something important all on its own. He put the other two cards back in their packaging, then spend a moment staring at it, wondering if maybe he'd pick something up if he stared long enough.

"Death." He spoke out loud.

Nothing happened of course, but he still couldn't help but be disappointed, even if he knew nothing would happen.

"Death." He spoke again.

He got up from his spot, returning the package of cards to his back pocket. All except for the Death card which he opted to keep separate, as though he was afraid that he might forget about it if he didn't.

It was important. He was firm in this belief. So much so that he knew it was true. That was what his instincts were telling him, so that was what he would believe.

Cairo's yowls broke Elliot from his trance, causing him to snap his head over to see his cat edging away from a group of kids. Elliot put the Death card in his other pocket.

"Let's go, Cairo." He said, "I think I'm a bit stuck anyway. I won't be able to get anything more from the cards right now."

She was more than happy to leave, trotting away quickly, away from the 'hell spawn' (her words) and onto the sidewalk. Elliot had to give a small jog to keep up with her, listening as one of the parents or nannies went over to the kids to scold them for tormenting the cat.

Once they seemed to be a safe distance away, Cairo gave Elliot a questioning look.

"I don't know." He said, "The cards I drew were *The Magician*, *Two of Swords*, and *Death*."

Cairo looked alarmed, but Elliot shook his head,

"No, Death isn't really a bad thing. Not always anyways. It can be renewal or even...awakening..." Elliot's eyes widened with realization, "That's it!"

His sudden exclamation caused Cairo to jump and shook him a dirty look.

"Sorry." Elliot apologised, "But that's it! I saw myself when I was trying to think about Casper. I thought that meant he was close to me or...but that didn't really make sense, did it? Why would Casper be at the park, right? Unless he wasn't at the park."

Cairo shot him another look that said something along the lines of, *No, duh.*

"No need for the attitude." Elliot said, but he was too caught up in his reasoning to really care at the moment, "Listen, I'm not completely here, am I? This is just my spirit right now. I'm also lying in bed in a coma at the hospital."

Cairo nodded her head, understanding what he was getting at. Casper was at the hospital, probably in Elliot's room.

"But what about the swords?" Elliot spoke out loud, then looked at Cairo who appeared to be wondering why Elliot was looking at her at all.

Don't look at me, I'm not the wizard.

"Well, you do tend to have some good advice." Elliot defended.

Cairo looked proud of herself. Elliot wondered if maybe he ought to hold back on inflating her ego anymore than it was.

"Let's see..." Elliot trailed off, "The hospital is a little way away."

He could remember being there a couple of times. Once for a bad ear infection, and another time when Casper had broken his arm playing on the play equipment when they were little.

"We might need to take a bus or something." Elliot thought out loud.

It was getting a bit later in the day. It was long past lunch time, going on four o'clock and just about going on supper. Not that Elliot was hungry. He hadn't been hungry in what almost felt like an eternity. That didn't mean that Cairo wasn't though.

"Are you hungry?" He asked her, "I don't have anything." He said upon her expectant look, "But if you want to break for a little while..."

When did visiting hours end anyway? It wasn't like he knew anything about that stuff, seeing as his last two visits had been considerably short. Now that he knew Casper wasn't in trouble, it wasn't like they were in any sort of rush.

"But maybe you can go catch a mouse or squirrel or something."

Cairo nodded. She looked a little bit relieved, reminding Elliot that he really ought to go a bit easier on her. Cairo trotted off to do a bit of hunting, while Elliot sat down on the ground, leaning up against one of the boulevard trees. His muscles were aching slightly. He hadn't realized that he had needed a rest as well. He was almost used to strained muscles, what with all the sparring he'd been doing with Trinket aboard the Youfoe. Of course, it wasn't nearly as bad as a day of sparring. This was a welcome break in comparison.

It was nearly an hour and a half later that Cairo came back with her kill. It looked like a sparrow, but Elliot looked away as soon as he saw it. He still didn't like watching Cairo eat.

In order to avoid looking at his cat devour a small bird, he looked up at the sky, opting to watch clouds for a time. Cairo had finished with her meal and the two of them waited a while before Elliot made the first move to get up. He stretched his arms up high, then stretched out his legs before he started on his walk down to the bus station.

"I know a route that goes to the downtown area." Elliot told Cairo, "The hospital is a short walk from there."

Cairo followed after him. They walked at a leisurely pace for some time. Their walk took them back towards Elliot's house where he spotted someone standing by their yard. He didn't really pay any attention at first. They appeared to be talking on a phone, maybe lost. It didn't seem like anything worth noting.

Until he got a chill.

He froze, turning his head towards the figure. A man, or at least, Elliot had thought it was a man, with a baseball cap brought down over his face.

"Cairo." Elliot whispered, causing his cat familiar to pause and look up at him, noticing his pale expression.

"That's him." He said, "That's the person who stabbed me."

He really was young, Elliot observed. He might have been able to pass for twenty, maybe. But Elliot had a feeling, after going through all the clues, and after hearing his brother's story, that he was the same age as Casper. Somewhere in his late teens.

Elliot didn't move from his spot. His father was the only one at home right now. He worked from there and knowing him, he was probably still typing away at his computer, trying to get his final draft finished before he sent it to his editor.

What was he supposed to do? He couldn't really fight. Well, he couldn't fight a person that was solid, or apart of the material world. The killer pulled the phone away from his ear, then hung up on whoever he'd been talking to, slipping it into his back pocket.

Getting a bad feeling, Elliot watched as he turned around, then walked right past his house.

"Where is he going?" Elliot whispered.

His instincts screamed to go after him. So, he did. Elliot followed him down the walkway and down towards the one of the busier roads which was just across an alley way, offering a pretty good insulator against the sound of rushing cars that passed.

There was a bus stop on the other side. It was nearly ten minutes before the bus showed up and the killer got on. Elliot followed him and Cairo padded in after. While the killer sat near the front, Elliot and Cairo got on at the back. Neither of them wanted to be particularly close to him, even if he couldn't do Elliot any harm and even if he seemed to be ignoring Cairo completely, or hadn't actually noticed her yet as they had gotten on through separate doors.

Elliot played with the fabric of his shirt, his senses alert in a way that could only be caused by fear and anxiety. He jumped at every sound and at every little bump the wheels jumped over. It wasn't long before Elliot had started to recognise the route they were taking.

"Cairo." Elliot said quietly, "I think...I think he's heading to the hospital."

The universe is a very strange thing, and though sometimes it gave people incentive to believe it was working against them, it was sometimes very focused in its own artistic manipulations and machinations that it completely disregarded good and bad. Was it fate that Olivia Sharp, a young woman working at the hospital part time during the summer had been vomited on by one of the children with a case of the stomach flu the day before? Was it fate that the next day, on the job, she started to feel ill and show the same symptoms that day during the evening and had to ask another part time worker to cover her after allowing Casper Crow inside to visit his brother?

Was it fate that the girl who took over hadn't known that Casper Crow was in to visit his brother, nor what he even looked like, and so, when Elliot's killer made his way over to the counter and asked if he could visit his younger brother, Elliot Crow, she had no reason to believe that he was lying?

Had Olivia Sharp not have gotten ill that day, she would have known, and she would have called the police. But, as things lined up, the new girl who had only just taken over and the person who had stabbed Elliot to begin with didn't know about Casper Crow being there.

When later asked, Elliot would say something along the lines of it all having been inevitable, whether fate or not. It had happened, and it was always going to happen like that, because that was just how the universe worked. Just another one of those strange little things that no one really understood and would likely never understand.

To Elliot, he thought it to be an awful big coincidence that he just so happened to be there when he had just been about to go over to the hospital himself and see how Casper was doing.

"Ooh...looks like you're in trouble now."

Elliot nearly jumped out of his skin upon hearing Trick speaking. Her brother giggled and she soon joined him in his amusement.

"What are you two doing here?" Elliot wondered. Because really, there was no reason for them to be at the hospital. Hadn't they left him?

"We were hoping to see you wake up." Treat admitted, "It is almost out, you know?"

Elliot regarded him with confusion a moment.

"The full moon." Trick elaborated.

"It's almost out." Treat repeated.

"So, I can wake up." Elliot realized.

"Not yet." Treat said in a slightly teasing voice.

"You have exactly five minutes before the sun goes down and the power of the moon fills this part of the world."

"Five minutes?" Elliot repeated fearfully, "But the person who tried to kill me is heading to my room now! I don't have five minutes."

"Mister Coma Guy." Trick gently patted his back.

Once again, Elliot noticed his nickname had changed. Treat's hand joined his sister's in what was supposed to be a 'comforting' gesture.

"Don't you know who you're talking to? Trick and Treat, masters of pranking!" Treat announced, now striking a pose with his sister.

"Leave it to us. You just work on the shock."

"Shock?" Elliot repeated. He hadn't even thought of the shock. It took his brain a moment to compute the fact that he did, in fact, need some sort of 'shock' to wake himself up. He thought he would have all night to shock himself awake, but now...

He had five minutes.

Trick and Treat ran off, laughing heartily and chasing after his killer, ready to unleash all the havoc they could upon him.

Trick jumped up onto her brother's shoulders and the two of them teetered back and forth as she started running her hands through the killer's hair. Just as they'd threatened to do with Elliot, slowly, his hair started to change to blue. It was almost amusing to watch, or it would have been, had the situation not been so dire. He stopped upon seeing his reflection in the glass of one of the windows.

"The ***?"

His curse had caught the attention of one of the passing doctors who gave him the stink eye.

"Young man, I suggest you hold your tongue while you're here. There are children in this part of the hospital."

The killer looked thoroughly rebuked, and yet, Elliot felt something. Like...like a slimy and dark aura that seemed to wrap around him, and the doctor as he gave an embarrassed smile.

"I'm sorry. I...I stubbed my toe and it just sort of slipped out. I promise I'll be more careful next time. I'm here to visit my younger brother, see."

The doctor seemed to relax a little, taken in by his charm,

"Well, make sure it doesn't happen again."

Elliot had once read a story in English class. In the story, there was a child in it who didn't seem to have any emotion. He was charming, intelligent and people were always taken in by him. But he had no morals. His teacher had once talked to them about the character. A 'textbook' psychopath, she'd said. You often found them in literature. Those people who worked for personal gain, or those people that hurt others for the sake of hurting others. His father had talked about them once. One of his main characters had been a psychopath so he'd done a ton of research.

Elliot didn't even know this person's name, but he did know then that this person would qualify. He continued on his walk, as though nothing had happened. He'd been stalled for nearly half a minute! Elliot decided to start looking for his room. Maybe he could warn Casper somehow.

He peered through open doors and glass windows, sticking his head inside when he could and running ahead of the killer.

It was then that he heard a small shout of surprise and rage.

"I'm sorry, I-I don't know what happened!" a nurse stuttered.

Elliot turned to see the teen covered in blood. It looked like one of the bags had exploded, coating the walls and part of his arm and neck.

"It's alright." He said, although Elliot got the sense that he was, in actuality full of rage on the inside, "Could you point me to the bathroom so that I can clean up?"

"Oh, um, it's right down that way, just take a left." She pointed it out to him.

"Thank you." He nodded his thanks, then went off to wash off.

That would certainly buy him some time. Elliot continued his search, hoping beyond hope that he'd be able to find the room he was looking for. It was during his fifth attempt that he found it. His brother was inside, sitting on a chair and staring into space.

It was strange to see him like that. He entered the room, going right through the door as though it wasn't there.

And that was the trick, Elliot had discovered, believing it wasn't there, or believing that he would reach the other side.

"You've got two minutes before the sun is down." Treat said, "Trick's standing guard outside. She'll distract him while you find a way to wake up."

Elliot let out a sound of frustration and impatience,

"But how am I supposed to do that?"

Treat shrugged his shoulders,

"Up to you."

Elliot closed his eyes, trying to come up with a solution.

That's right, he could tell Casper about the danger if...He felt himself return to his body. His thought processes slowed, like every word he needed to come up with lay beyond a pool of molasses, and he needed to reach them individually.

His eyes opened slightly.

"Cas-per..."

Casper jumped out of his seat.

"Elliot? Elliot, are you awake?"

"No...can't wake...t'ill sunset. Casper...danger."

"Danger?" Casper repeated, he furrowed his brow in confusion, "What do you mean? What danger?"

"He's here." Elliot said, feeling his time in his body shorten once again,

"The...killer...here."

"What do you mean?" Casper asked him again.

Why couldn't he figure it out? It wasn't as though Elliot could make it any clearer than that. His eyes closed, only for the door to the hospital room to open.

His warning had come too late.

Elliot opened his eyes, once again outside of his body.

"Whoa." Treat said, "I've never seen someone possess their own body before." Elliot didn't bother answering. Now really wasn't the time to be impressed. Casper had frozen, eyes wide and face pale.

"You." He said softly, voice surprisingly weak.

The killer looked at him, then smiled. To Elliot it looked like an utterly terrifying sight, yet to anyone else, he supposed it might look friendly.

"Casper, I'm assuming." He greeted, "Just thought I'd check in with Elliot and see how he was doing." Casper tensed, eyes widened as realization struck him. Elliot could practically hear his mind working as the pieces of the puzzle fell into place.

"I'm Elliot's friend, from school."

There was a long silence, as though he were expecting Casper to welcome him. But it never happened.

"Only family is allowed to visit right now." Casper said slowly. He might have fallen for it if he hadn't heard Elliot's message only moments ago.

The killer's smile never left his face, just as it hadn't the day he had tried to kill Elliot.

"You're the one that did this, aren't you?" Casper realized it was too late to get out of this now. He couldn't leave Elliot alone, unguarded. Not now.

As soon as he turned around he had a knife in his hand. He didn't say anything as he tried to stab Casper, just as he had his younger brother. But Casper had already been on guard, more so than Elliot had been at the time. He fought, he kicked, he screamed.

He grabbed his killer's hand and tried to keep the blade away from his chest where his heart beat rhythmically, filling his ears with blood.

"Come now, Casper. It's not like you can live much longer anyways, right? Not after what you did to Elliot. What will your parents think? Well, it's not like you have any friends who think much of you anyways. You're lucky you don't need to worry about them."

"Don't listen to him, Casper!" Elliot shouted, even though he knew he wouldn't be heard.

"Wake up, Elliot!" Treat shouted, "You need to wake up!"

"I won't let you hurt him!"

People were banging on the door now. The doctors had crowded, and it sounded like they were trying to break it down now.

Elliot caught a glimpse of something in the reflection of the glass. It was a boy, he was shouting, but there was a certain determination in his eyes.

"Toshi?" Elliot wondered, before Toshi raised his round mirror and the glass of the window broke, sending shards scattering off in every direction.

Elliot didn't know why he'd done it. Maybe it had been meant as some sort of distraction. It had worked, but not in Casper's favour.

The eldest Crow brother let out a horrible, choked scream of pain. The knife had imbedded itself into his forearm. Blood dripped everywhere. On the floor, on the pristine white sheets of the hospital bed, and onto the face of Elliot Crow.

He reached up shakily, touching the drops of his brother's blood when he suddenly came to the realization that he wasn't standing up any longer, but lying down.

The shock of seeing Casper get hurt for him had sent him back into his body.

He was in the hospital bed, and he was wide awake for the first time in a very long time. Before the killer could take the knife out of Casper's arm, Elliot flung himself at him, tackling him to the ground. He was so surprised that Elliot was actually awake that he had no means of reacting. Elliot punched him in the face with all of his might. He'd probably broken his hand, but he didn't really care at this point. He punched him again and noticing passingly that two of his knuckles had turned purple.

"That's for me and my brother you psychopath!"

"Elliot..." Casper looked over at him, eyes wide with something kin to disbelief, "You're awake."

"I am." Elliot agreed, "Can you open the door? I've got him."

Casper nodded, getting up off the ground, his blood dripping down his finger tips.

"I'm going to open up the door." He called out to the people outside.

The banging stopped and Casper turned the lock, then the door knob. The doctors rushed inside, some wanted an explanation, while others took the boy that had tried to kill the two of them away. Their mother and father arrived, wanting to know what had happened, embracing Elliot and making sure he was alright. Like they didn't really believe he was actually awake.

Out of the corner of his eye, Elliot saw Trick and Treat give him the thumbs up.

"Way to go, Mister Wizard Guy."

Elliot's lips twitched wondering if the two of them would ever settle on a nickname...probably not.

CHAPTER TWENTY

The Life of Elliot Crow

Casper Crow let out a low groan as he rolled around in his bed and pressed the snooze button on his alarm clock. He'd fallen right back to sleep, only to let out another groan as his alarm went off for a second time.

It was soon after Elliot's recovery that the leaves on the trees had started to turn yellow, signalling the coming of fall. In Casper's opinion, the summer wasn't officially over until school started again. Today was their first day back. It would be Casper's last year of high school, and Elliot's second year of high school.

The excitement of 'back to school' had long since lost its glamor. He could remember looking forward to the new school year when he was little, but now...now the summer just seemed far too short. Casper gathered his things and made his way downstairs to eat some breakfast.

He was startled when he saw Elliot already downstairs, drinking tea of all things with their mother. He looked up and over at Casper,

"Morning." He greeted.

"Morning." Casper said.

Elliot had always been a late sleeper. On weekends, he slept in until noon, and during the school days, he wouldn't wake up until someone went up to his room and dragged him out of bed.

"Since when do you drink tea?" Casper wondered, preparing some breakfast for himself.

"Elliot's been waking up early to have tea with me." Margret Crow said fondly.

Casper looked back over at Elliot and his mother as he put some bread in the toaster. Elliot had been different ever since he'd gotten back from wherever he'd been. Even now he was a bit fuzzy on the details, only knowing that he had been a spirit and that he had memories of the time he'd been unconscious.

"Oh, right." Elliot said vaguely, "I found a couple of sprites living up in our attic, is it alright if they stay?"

Casper was used to his brother saying strange things by now. He'd never seen 'sprites' before or any sort of spirit, but he had no doubt that they existed, because Elliot, the boy who had lived in the world of spirits, believed that they did.

"I don't see a problem with it." Their mother said, lifting up her cup of tea and pausing a moment. She stared down at her cup curiously, as though surprised there was anything in it at all, "Do we need anything to take care of them?"

"No." Elliot shook his head, "They just might make a bit of noise every now and then. You know, footsteps or creaking floorboards. But I think it's a good thing they're here. Sprites are generally very protective or their territory, you know? So long as they're welcome here, they'll protect us from dangers like fires or floods."

"That's quite convenient...this tea is different from the last batch." She commented, changing the subject.

"I never make the same type of tea twice." Elliot said, a smile twitching at the corners of his lips.

"Why not?" Casper couldn't help but ask at yet another discovered oddity.

"That would be boring, and who can be bothered to remember a tea recipe anyways?" he wasn't really a tea drinker. He just did it, because his mother liked tea. That being said, it wasn't like he disliked it either.

Elliot had searched high and low for a fencing club, alas, Blackstone didn't have one. It was simply too small a town, garnering too little an interest in those that enjoyed the art of sword fighting. He'd heard that Edmonton had a very good fencing club and even a couple of kendo dojos (that was, Japanese sword fighting).

In the end, he had to settle for traveling to Trinket's and Gear's realm and continuing his practices there. After his first week of school, he and Cairo found their realm and took a knock on their door.

He heard the sound of something shaking, and then a hissing noise.

"Huh, I really did think that would explode." He heard Trinket's voice from behind the door.

"You ***! You wanted it to *** explode!"

"Ouch! Gear, dear, there's no need to be violent."

"Just get the *** door."

"Ouch."

There was a pause before the door was opened and Trinket came out, his face in it's usual pokerfaced smile.

"Elliot Crow! It's been a while."

Elliot grinned,

"It has, hasn't it?"

"Would you like to come in? My, you look far more solid since the last time I saw you."

"Thank you." Elliot said, knowing it was supposed to be a compliment. Trinket's way of saying 'way to go, you did it.'

He walked into the large space, noticing Gear was there, being hung up by her harness with what looked like a welding torch in hand and a large mask over her face. She stopped what she was doing and lifted up the mask.

"Oh, it's you. What are you doing back here, Crowfood? You got another *** problem that needs solving?"

Elliot shook his head,

"Nope. Trinket said I could visit when I wanted, so here I am."

"Here he is." Trinket said, presenting him with a wave of his hands.

Gear scowled at her mentor's attitude, although she always did that. Elliot couldn't say he'd ever seen her without a scowl on her face save, perhaps for the time she'd lowered him onto the train to the Kingdome of Dreams.

"So, has King Slomoe contacted you?" Trinket asked Elliot curiously.

"Nope." Elliot shook his head, "But I've been collecting dreams for him. I've got them stored in my room. I'm going to take them to him tomorrow, hopefully." Trinket hummed thoughtfully,

"I think he'll appreciate that."

"I think so too." Elliot agreed, "But, I was wondering if I might ask you for another favour."

"Oh?" Trinket asked him curiously.

"Could you keep teaching me swordplay?"

Maybe it was just Elliot's imagination, but he could have sworn that Trinket's smile had grown slightly wider.

Just because his goal of saving Casper was over didn't mean it was *over* just yet. He'd go back to the Kingdom of Dreams the next day. He'd contemplated a lot what he would do when he met Slomoe again. He'd thought about quitting, but realized, he didn't want to quit.

What job could ever be more spectacular than collecting dreams?

Trinket showed Elliot where he kept the equipment and the two of them dressed up in padded gear, carrying up their dulled, blunt blades, then heading to the roof top to spar.

"A firm stance, Elliot Crow." Trinket hit one of his legs, causing him to topple over. The tip of the sword was pointed at his head.

"Come now, Elliot Crow, is that all you've got?"

Elliot got up, parrying his sword, then thrusting it forward before snapping his wrist back, forcing the tip into a small circle then lunging again. His eyes widened as the tip caught the left part of his shoulder. Well, not his actual shoulder, but a bit of bunched up fabric at the side. This was the closest he'd gotten to actually having hit him.

Then, with an upwards thrust, as though surprised by his own accomplishment, the blade slashed into the air nearly hitting Trinket's head. It would have too, had he not ducked. Trinket hadn't been wearing a helmet. He never did during their practices.

Elliot lowered his sword, disbelief painted his face.

A black hat fell to the ground. It bounced once, then rolled around on it's side before coming to a stop.

Let's write a poem for Elliot Crow,
The boy who thought he had died.
It is a tale of magic and dreams,
And trinkets and gears of all things!
Up on a blimp, so disorienting so,
They mistakenly named it the Youfoe.
And onto a train,
Ridding 'round in the rain,
Towards dreams and reflections and mirrors and things.
Surrounded by nonsense, no reason at all,
He knew that he needed to fight.
So defeated the witch,
From a land just like this,
Where a sword gives the worthy their right.

About the Author

A.R. Shanks is a young writer from Edmonton Alberta. *The Murder of Elliot Crow* is her first novel.

She started writing during her junior high school years and was soon completing novel-length works during high school. It was when she was studying in Japan on a two-month exchange that she started writing about Elliot Crow.

After high school, she attended two years of university studying anthropology before dropping out. She worked for a year at Tim Hortons to support herself while trying to complete three different novels. Elliot Crow is the first of what is planned to be a chronicle of different stories all taking pace in the world of Those with Responsibilities.

Made in the USA
Middletown, DE
13 May 2018